THE DEADLY SUNSHADE

PHOEBE ATWOOD TAYLOR

THE
DEADLY
SUNSHADE

An Asey Mayo Cape Cod Mystery

A Foul Play Press Book

THE COUNTRYMAN PRESS
Woodstock, Vermont

THE DEADLY SUNSHADE

ONE.

IF PICKLEPUSS is comin', I," Asey Mayo informed his Cousin Jennie, "am goin'. Give me my coat so I can get out of this kitchen. Never mind sewin' on that button. I'll do it myself."

Ignoring his outstretched hand, Jennie stabbed her needle through the blue flannel of Asey's best blue jacket and shook her head vigorously.

"You sit down an' wait till I get this button fixed right!" she said. "An' don't call Mrs. Belcher by that horrid name! I don't think you've any call to insult her just because she's in the pickle business!"

Asey raised his eyebrows at Jennie's vehemence.

"Why, Jennie," he said, "I picked up that nickname from you! I've heard you call her Picklepuss a thousand times. I've even heard you say that in a green dress you couldn't tell her apart from one of her own pickles! Come on, now, give me my coat. I got to get goin'. I can't waste the mornin' listenin' to Picklepuss gossip, an' I don't want to buy any pickles, either! Give me my coat."

"Soon as I get your ole button on, you can rush off

as fast as you want," Jennie returned. "Because Mrs. Belcher hasn't any intention of sellin' you any pickles, an' she isn't comin' to see you anyway. She's comin' to see me. About the—that is, on business. We got some very important things to talk over."

"Oho!" Asey perched on the corner of the kitchen table and surveyed his cousin quizzically. "Oho. I think I begin to see things. So Picklepuss is the one!"

Jennie said she didn't know what he was talking about, she was sure.

"An' stop lookin' at me with that detectin' look," Jennie continued. "I guess my havin' a mornin' caller isn't goin' to interfere with your housework any."

"So it's Picklepuss," Asey said, "who's the organizin' power behind this half-baked League of—what's the name of that crazy radio news fellow, Lancelot Jones?"

"Rounceval Jones, an' he isn't crazy! He's the best news commentator there is, an' the most patriotic! Gracious, Asey, can't you speak of anybody without bein' insultin' today?"

"I ought to have guessed," Asey said, "that Pickle-puss Belcher was the only woman around with enough dogged zeal to keep on organizin' this crazy League to Uphold America—"

"It's a branch of the Woman's League to Defend America at all Costs with Action!" Jennie interrupted hotly. "An' it isn't crazy! You know perfectly well if we're invaded, Cape Cod'll be the first place they'll invade! It's the first place you come to, isn't it? You cross the Atlantic, an' here you are. The Pilgrims landed here, didn't they? The Vikings landed here, didn't they? The British tried to in 1812, didn't they? Well! An' Syl, he thinks so, too!"

"Your husband," Asey told her, "is a fine man, but I don't think he's been in what you'd call his right frame of mind since Dunkerque an' France. An' I do think, Jennie, that you ought to think twice an' maybe even ponder a little before you let yourself get carried away any further by Picklepuss an' this League. Now, unless you want me to turn up at the Yacht Club in my shirtsleeves, give me my coat. I hear Picklepuss chargin' up the driveway."

"Sometimes," Jennie said, "I don't think you're a bit patriotic!"

"Jennie, I don't see how I can help my country any by havin' to listen to you an' Picklepuss dissect your friends with one hand while you organize 'em into Minutewomen with the other! Now, give me that coat!"

But Jennie, still firmly gripping the blue jacket, was already at the screen door, greeting Mrs. Belcher effusively, and being greeted effusively in return.

With an exclamation of annoyance, Asey started for the dining room door, but the sight of what Mrs. Belcher had tucked under her arm caused him to turn and walk slowly back to perch again on the kitchen table.

"Jennie, I've got eighteen!" Mrs. Belcher said. "Oh,

hello, Asey. Aren't you dressed up! Where are you going?"

"Is that," Asey inquired, "a genuine twenty-two rifle you're carryin'?"

"Yes. Jennie, he really looks quite nice when he takes the trouble to get out of his old dungarees, doesn't he? Quite distinguished."

"Thanks." Asey decided it would be wiser if he refrained from commenting on her green dress and hat. "Tell me, Pick—uh—Pussy, what's the idea of the twenty-two?"

"Asey's on his way to the Sketicket Yacht Club," Jennie informed Mrs. Belcher hastily. "He's just waiting for me to finish sewin' this button on his coat."

"The Yacht Club?" Mrs. Belcher sniffed as she sat down in the rocker. "I should think that Asey might find more to do for his country these days than wear white flannels and go to Yacht Clubs!"

"It's only business, Pussy," Jennie said almost apologetically. "Business for Bill Porter. Here, Asey, here's your coat. Now you can rush right along. Don't let us keep you!"

"Thanks," Asey said. "Er—you always carry a twenty-two, Pussy?"

"He's going to see Commodore Bunting." Jennie brushed some imaginary dust from Asey's shoulder, and gave him a little push toward the door. "There, now you can hurry right along. You mustn't keep the commodore waitin'. Good-by!"

Asey moved away from Jennie's propelling hand.

"Tell me about this twenty-two," he said. "What in time are you luggin' it around for?"

"It's one of the eighteen guns I've collected," Mrs. Belcher told him. "And if you're going to see Bunting, tell him I'll pick up the rest of his guns this afternoon. He's an awfully smart man, isn't he? I never thought so much of him before he took over the club, but I must say he's done a wonderful job on it, with all those new ells and decorations. He's a genius for getting money, I think!"

"Bill Porter thinks so, too," Asey said dryly. "Look, I want to know—"

"That reminds me," Mrs. Belcher interrupted. "Did you hear he was getting married?"

"Bill's been married for years," Asey said. "About that twen—"

"I mean Bunting. He's been a widower so long, no one ever thought he'd get married again, but it's common talk he's going to marry that Mrs. Newell—you know her, Jennie," Mrs. Belcher added parenthetically. "The one who's lived abroad so much. But she came home quick enough when the war started! She's rented half my sister Sarah's house since April. Has a little red bantam car."

"Oh, that one! I know her," Jennie said. "She's always calling for Asey to fix the car. So she's going to marry Bunting, is she?"

"That twenty-two," Asey began. "Why—"

But Mrs. Belcher was already talking.

"At first," she said, "Sarah thought she was going to marry the Bunting boy. He's just got to be a doctor. But now she's going around with the father— Asey Mayo, what are you balancing that custard pie on your finger for? You'll drop it!"

"I'm tryin'," Asey said, "to get your attention. Will you tell me why you're carryin' a twenty-two?"

"Why, I told you! It's one of the guns I've collected for the League. Have you decided when you can start the first class?"

"What first class?" Asey asked.

"Didn't Jennie tell you? We're going to have you show us how to shoot guns. You know, Rounceval Jones says every housewife in America should have a gun and learn how to shoot. When can you start?"

Asey drew a long breath.

"Pussy," he said, "you make good pickles. Aunt Pussy's Perfect Pickles are mighty good pickles. You started from scratch in the pickle business, an' you got a fine, goin' concern. Can't you be content with a successful pickle business? Can't you stick to pickles? Can't you leave national defense to the Army an' Navy?"

"Rounceval says—" Mrs. Belcher stopped abruptly as the toe of Jennie's white shoe, unseen by Asey, planted itself firmly on her instep.

"Yup. Rounceval wants to arm American housewives to the teeth. A gun in every pantry, an' a hand grenade in every work basket. But if you'll take my advice, Pussy, you'll march them eighteen guns back to the folks you wangled 'em from, an' hold yourself down to somethin' more restrained. Roll bandages. Knit. Honest, don't you think things is confused enough without havin' a lot of housewives shootin' left an' right?"

Jennie's foot bore down again on Mrs. Belcher's instep.

"Well," Asey said, "don't you honestly think so? Don't you think the sooner you give up this Rifle Brigade idea, the better—not to mention the safer?"

He anticipated something in the nature of a full broadside from Picklepuss, whose green eyes were glinting angrily.

It came as a distinct shock when she merely nodded her head in agreement.

"Yes, Asey," Jennie said. "Maybe you're right. Good-by, now. Run along. You mustn't be late."

Asey looked from her to Mrs. Belcher.

Then he shrugged.

"You're not foolin' me, either of you," he informed them as he walked to the door, "sittin' there like two bland clams! But let me warn you, if I hear any stray guns blastin' around, I'm goin' to remember I'm a deputy sheriff. I don't remember the exact penalty for bearin' unlicensed weapons an' endangerin' the public with same, but it's somethin' like ten thousand dollars in fines, an' ten years in jail."

"But—" Mrs. Belcher bit off the rest of her sentence as Jennie's foot went into action again.

"Or," Asey opened the screen door, "both. Remember that!"

Putting on his yachting cap, he strode down the orchard path toward the garage.

If Picklepuss was the tight-fisted business woman he thought she was, she would ponder about that fine. And Jennie, who wept for a week when her husband got a parking ticket, would certainly sit up and take notice at the suggestion of ten years in prison.

And if it turned out that they weren't squelched, Asey thought, he'd hunt up his deputy's badge and harry them until they gave up all their silly nonsense.

He paused for a moment by the apple tree and considered returning at once to the house and ostentatiously finding the badge. Then he decided against the move. There was plenty of time for that later, if they chose to ignore his warning. Besides, he had to get on and interview Commodore Bunting.

It was not going to be a pleasant interview, either, Asey decided. From the way that the commodore had been giving him the run-around, it rather looked as if Bill Porter's five thousand dollar check to the Sketicket Yacht Club was going to take a lot of investigating.

Opening the side door of the garage, Asey was just stepping over the threshold as Jennie called to him from the house.

"A-sey! A-sey Ma-yo!"

Automatically, Asey turned his head, and as he did, something whined past his ear and thudded into the lintel of the door.

"Huh!" Asey muttered, and crumpled himself into a squatting position from which he edged forward over the threshold and into the garage. "Huh!"

The report of a rifle that sounded in the distance was so faint that Asey wasn't even sure he'd heard it.

"A-sey Ma-yo!"

Jennie's voice called out again, and then an old-fashioned hand bell started clanging, punctuated by repeated commands for him to come to the phone, someone wanted him.

But Asey, crouched on the cement of the garage floor, waited and looked thoughtfully up at where the bullet had plowed through the lintel, through two cross beams, and out the opposite side of the building.

That bullet, he decided grimly, was nothing that anyone could lightly sum up as spent.

That was a deliberate, and very nearly successful shot.

"A-sey!" Jennie called in exasperation, and set the cow bell pealing. "Asey!"

Walking to the window by the side door, Asey looked out at the blue smear of ocean and at the arm of Clam Island that marked the inlet entrance half a mile away.

Any bullet that could penetrate a good twelve inches

of pine like that came from a high-powered rifle. And the only possible place it could have come from was the long dune on Clam Island.

On the face of it, Asey thought, it looked as if someone had hidden himself over there in the tall beach grass, with his rifle trained on the side door, and his eye fixed to telescopic sights, waiting for him to play the role of target.

Of course, it might have been someone just aimlessly potting, but no sane man would aim toward shore with a weapon like that. No sane man would lug a heavy-barreled rifle out to a sand dune, and then aim anywhere but out to sea. No sane man—

"By golly!" Asey said out loud. "No man would. But I wonder—yessiree, I wonder if one of Picklepuss's Minutewomen has already started practicin'! Huh!"

Swinging open the garage doors, he climbed into his long, sleek Porter roadster and streaked up to the kitchen door.

"Where've you been?" Jennie demanded. "Didn't you hear me callin' an' ringin' for you? It was that Mrs. Newell on the phone. She says she's in dire peril —I s'pose that means she's got somethin' the matter with her car again. She said she was at the Yacht Club, an' she wanted you right away. I told her to hold the line, an' when you didn't come, I told her you'd left for the club anyway. Asey, I think you ought to put your foot down, an' make her call a regular garage man when she's in trouble. I think she just pretends that you're the only person who can fix her car because she knows you won't take any money for it. She's just usin' you, that's all. What're you gettin' out for? You comin' back in here?"

"Uh-huh. Little matter," Asey said as he entered the kitchen, "I want to take up with Pussy. Pussy, have you distributed any of these guns you've collected?"

"I don't see," Mrs. Belcher said, "that it makes any difference to you, if you're not going to trouble yourself to help!"

"Jennie'll tell you that there's a point," Asey spoke rather sharply, "beyond which it isn't awful wise to rile me, Pussy. Did you or didn't you distribute them guns around?"

"Yes, I did, if you must know! And some of the girls are already practicing! Mabelle and Effie started for the dunes the minute they got theirs this morning!"

"Uh-huh. I see. What kind of guns did they have, Pussy?"

"Why, guns!" Mrs. Belcher said. "Just guns. I don't know what kind! A gun is a gun, isn't it?"

"Were they guns like this twenty-two you got here, or were they bigger? Did you have any bigger ones?"

"Oh, yes. One we got from Commodore Bunting was awfully big and heavy."

"Huh!" Asey said. "What'n time did the fool idiot let you women have a rifle like that for, I wonder?

Did he *know* what you wanted guns for? Oho!" he added as Mrs. Belcher's cheeks reddened. "I see. He didn't know. Did he give you any ammunition, Pussy?"

"That's none of your business!"

"As a matter of fact, it is. Huh. I bet you told Bunting some cock an' bull yarn, an' he gave you some of his gun collection, an' some ammunition too. Didn't he? Yes, I thought so. Now, I'll tell you what you're goin' to do, Pussy. You're goin' to collect every last gun, an' bring 'em here to me," Asey glanced up at the clock, "in an hour. Otherwise, you an' your Minutewomen'll find yourselves charged with attempted murder. That clear?"

"Murder?" Jennie gave a little scream. "Asey, what do you mean, murder?"

"Just that. If you hadn't called me when you did, Jennie, an' if I hadn't jerked my head around toward the house, you'd have a corpse on your hands right now. If you don't believe me, you two march down an' take a look at the lintel of the side garage door. Mabelle or Effie's got hold of a .30-06. An' in a playful moment, they aimed it smack at my head!"

"But we didn't hear any shot!" Jennie said.

Asey pointed out that they wouldn't be likely to.

"Not indoors, talkin' a streak, with a west wind, an' the gun half a mile away. Pussy, get those guns before some innocent bystander gets killed!"

"I—I don't believe you *were* shot at!" Mrs. Belcher's voice contained a slight quaver. "And if you were, I'm sure no one meant to shoot you!"

"Go look at the gashes that bullet left," Asey said, "an' then consider how much it'd matter if anyone meant to kill me or not! As far's a dead innocent bystander's concerned, Pussy, it don't largely matter if a jury's verdict is murder or manslaughter. Go get the guns!"

"But how can I get them back in an hour?" Mrs. Belcher asked. "Suppose people aren't home? Suppose they're out?"

Asey sighed.

"How'd you get pickles back, if you found out a lot was bad?"

"I never had any bad pickles!"

"Jennie," Asey said, "grab your grocery pad an' pencil, an' make a list of who she give guns to. Then phone every last woman to bring the guns here. If a woman ain't home, have someone in her family bring it, or go after it yourself. While you take care of that, Pussy can drive over to the beach in her car, an' hotfoot out to the dune an' collar Mabelle an' Effie in person. Now, get goin'!"

He stood over them ominously until Mrs. Belcher had supplied the names of her armed forces, and departed in a thoroughly chastened mood for the beach.

"Now, leave the rest to me, Asey," Jennie said as she picked up the list. "I'll get 'em back before you come home. I'll go right in to the phone, an'—oh, dear, there it is ringin'! Wait. It's probably someone for you."

She bustled off into the dining room, and bustled back almost at once to inform him that it was that Mrs. Newell again.

"She says she's simply in the direst kind of peril, an' she wants to see you right away, an' when are you comin'?"

"Ask her what the trouble is," Asey said.

"I did. I said did she want to talk to you, because you was right here, but she said it's nothin' she can explain over the phone. That's what she always says, Asey! It's just a trick to make you go to her. An' she says it's very dire, an' please hurry."

"I suppose her muffler's worked loose again," Asey said. "Well, tell her I'm on my way. Get after those guns, Jennie, an' if you run into any difficulties, call me at the club."

He was swinging himself in behind the wheel of his roadster when he saw the old sedan of his friend Dr. Cummings tearing along the lane at a pace which, for the doctor, was suicidal.

With a great squealing of brakes, the doctor drew up beside the roadster, and thrust his round face out the window.

"Asey, you've got to put a stop to it!" Cummings spluttered indignantly. "You know what? I've just nearly been killed in cold blood! I've just been shot at!"

"Was it," Asey inquired, "the Minutewomen?"

"Minutewomen? You mean, madwomen! I don't know what the hell they call themselves, but it's this damn fool League of that mealy-mouthed radio news fellow. Somebody Jones. Asey, those addle-pated women have guns, and they're shooting them!"

"Uh-huh," Asey said. "Was it Mabelle an' Effie?"

"It was my own wife!" Cummings said bitterly. "She was potting at tomato-juice cans beyond the back garden, and when I called and asked her what the hell she thought she was doing, she turned around and absent-mindedly pulled the trigger at the same time! I tell you, it's God's grace I'm alive! She missed me by a hair. And what do you think the woman said?"

"What?" Asey asked obediently.

"Said I shouldn't have distracted her! Nearly murders her own husband, mind you, and then says I shouldn't distract her! And she wouldn't give up the gun! Well, you can't argue with a woman armed with a rifle, so I left. Asey, you've got to get those guns away from these madwomen before they slaughter people in winnows!"

"Steps have already been taken," Asey assured him. "I took 'em after I got fired on." He told the doctor briefly about the bullet that had whined past his ear. "So, the guns are now bein' recalled, an' Picklepuss's gone off with her tail between her legs."

"And you're sure my wife's on the list? Sure? Thank God!" Cummings said with relief. "Now I can hustle on to the hospital. I'm forty minutes late." He started his car, and then poked his head out the window once more. "Say, know how Picklepuss got the guns? She said they were going to put on an exhibition of firearms to encourage enlisting. I pumped that much out of my wife. By George, you can't tell what a woman'll do next, can you? Think of 'em, potting at you!"

"I don't mind bein' potted at," Asey said. "What I resent was the beginner's luck that brought 'em so close. I thought at first that some expert was erasin' me. A crack shot couldn't have done any better. Want me to drive on out of your way?"

"I'll turn and go first," Cummings said. "I don't want to chew your fiery dust all the way to the main road. Look, you're going to check up on these guns, aren't you?"

Asey nodded. "I've virtually promised to jail the Minutewomen in a bunch if the girls don't have every last gun rounded up when I get back from the Yacht Club."

"Oh," Cummings said interestedly, "finally going to have it out with Bunting about Bill's money, eh?"

"I hope so," Asey said. "He tried to stall me again when I phoned him early this mornin' an' told him I was comin'. Said he was unusually busy, had previous engagements, important guests, vital dentist's appointments, an' I don't know what all else besides."

"If you ask me," Cummings said, "Brother Bunting's been doing some amateur embezzling!"

"He's certainly used up all the excuses in dodging me," Asey said. "But I told him he could either see Bill's lawyer before noon tomorrow, or he could see me before noon today, an' he caved in at that, an' said he'd see me. So, it kind of behooves me to turn up at the club by noon an' have it out with him. If it wasn't for Bunting, I'd go collect these guns myself. But I think Jennie's able to handle the girls."

"She'd better," Cummings said. "I shall never return to my legal abode till I've got proof that my wife is disarmed. I've got to rush. See you later!"

Asey grinned as he watched Cummings's sedan bounce off down the lane. Then, when the dust from the ruts had settled, he started off himself.

There was a certain amount of inescapable truth, he thought, in the doctor's often repeated sentiments about women doing the unexpected. It was incredible to think of Jennie, and Picklepuss Belcher, and Mrs. Cummings, all women who ordinarily cringed at the sight of any sort of lethal weapon, all jauntily arming themselves with guns. That they should actually start shooting was a fact bordering on the fantastic. But the most incredible and fantastic and uncanny thing of all was the fraction of an inch by which that bullet had missed him. Whatever the girls were aiming at, they would never come any nearer to scoring a bull's-eye.

Bringing the roadster to a stop before he swung from the lane onto the main road, Asey shook his head at the miracle of that miss, and tilted his yachting cap back on his head.

Then, suddenly, his foot jammed down on the accelerator, and the roadster streaked away toward the village.

For the second bullet, the bullet which had just sent his yachting cap spinning through the air, made Asey realize grimly that his first reaction, back in the garage, had been the right one after all.

Somebody was using him for a target.

And it wasn't the Minutewomen. Zealous housewives couldn't miss like that, twice.

Someone, Asey thought as he headed for the railroad crossing where the state police usually lurked, someone was using him for a target, and someone was coming too close for comfort!

TWO.

UNDER the hot midday sun, Sketicket Bay became a smooth sheet of green glass, and the usually bustling Yacht Club turned into a drowsy, listless still life of gray, weathered buildings, tan sand, and gaily striped umbrellas.

From his mahogany desk in the club's trophy room, Commodore Humphrey Bunting considered the peace and calm of the scene outside, and then wearily looked up at the wrathful face of his tall son.

"Which damn widow do you mean, Ben?" he asked. "And look, stop slashing around and pounding the trophy cases. Glass breaks. What widow are you ranting about?"

"Lucia Newell! Who else would I mean?" Ben said angrily. "Dad, can't she stop butting in? Can't she pursue you like a lady? Does she have to mess up everything? You could race with me perfectly well next week if you wanted to. You don't *have* to cart Lucia to that banquet! The whole trouble is, she's got a half nelson on you!"

Humphrey Bunting sighed.

"Ben, I can't race with you. I know it's the last

chance we'll have to race together before you start interning. I'd like nothing better than to race with you, but I'm just too busy here! Why, I've got so much to do today, I don't know where to begin! Mayo's due here any minute, and then I've got those two for lunch—"

"Mayo? Asey Mayo? Dad, are you just getting around to seeing him?"

"I only found those accounts last night," the commodore said. "They got put in the wrong file. I knew if I waited, they'd turn up."

"And so you've been stalling him for the last three weeks? Dad, you mustn't do that sort of thing! You only leave yourself wide open!"

"Mayo'll understand," the commodore said. "So will Bill Porter. The point is, Ben, I'm busy today, I'm busy tomorrow, I'm busy next week. And Lucia hasn't a thing in the world to do with it."

Ben started to kick at a chair leg, and Humphrey Bunting realized belatedly that he should never have made the mistake of bringing Lucia's name back into the conversation.

"So Lucia hasn't anything to do with it?" Ben said. "Not much she hasn't! If Lucia hadn't wheedled you into being commodore, you'd have spent a normal summer, sailing and racing with me. Instead, you haven't set foot on a boat. You've been chained to this damn desk since spring, balancing the club's damn budget, and cadging money like a professional beggar. It's all her fault!"

"But—"

"Oh, it is too, dad, and you know it! She thought you'd look ducky in gold braid, and she kept telling you so until you got to believe it! Let's face facts. Lucia egged you on to take this job, and instead of gold braid and glory, you get budget trouble!"

"That's just it! Budget trouble!" The commodore jumped at the chance to swing the discussion away from Lucia. "If it wasn't for budget trouble, I'd race with you next week. But we're in the red again."

"Again?" Ben stared at his father. "My God, what now? What do you *do* with money? You get it, and everything's fine, and then bang! In the red again. What's the matter now? I suppose Lucia's sold you the idea of throwing out another ell for a couple more powder rooms?"

"We've got to repair the south wharf, Ben. I've been hoping it would last through the summer, but now someone's foot went through—"

"Phooey! That wharf may look punk, but it's perfectly sound. Who went through?"

Humphrey Bunting waited prudently until Ben had passed the largest of the glass cases.

"Dudley French—and *don't* kick that stand! Sit down before you smash something, Ben. I've got troubles enough today without having those cases smashed! French couldn't help himself. The planking was rotten."

Ben snorted.

"I might have known," he said disgustedly as he slung himself into a chair, "if it wasn't Lucia Newell wanting something new and expensive, it'd be her fat pig of a cousin wanting expensive repairs. Those two are the reason for your lopsided budget, dad! You scrime around and get money for one thing, and then they wheedle you and bully you into blowing it for something else entirely. How can you ever balance the damn budget if you keep on letting them carry you away on these expensive whimsies? You're just putty in their hands!"

"The point is—"

"The point," Ben said, "is that you're too amiable, dad! If you'd only speak your mind once in a while, instead of stalling around, hoping that everything'll turn out all right in the end!"

"The point," Humphrey Bunting said quietly, "is not my idiosyncrasies, but the fact that the south wharf needs repairs. And I've got to figure out some way of getting the money to fix it."

"If Dudley French busted the wharf, let him pay for it!" Ben said. "The fat pig's got money. That's why he's here. Personally, I'm tired of cherishing this illusion that we all love Dudley dearly for himself alone. Don't you think it's time that someone, like you, for example, took Dudley aside and explained that we only tolerate him for his bank roll?"

"On the theory," Humphrey returned, "that the news will encourage him to spend money like a drunken sailor? Be sensible, Ben. Dudley pays his way, and if I play my cards right, I'll have him paying for the wharf without his ever knowing it. Lucia will help me."

"Lucia, Lucia, Lucia!" Ben said. "I'm sick of Lucia! I'm sick of that fat oaf French. Every time I come inside this building, there's French shooting his mouth off, yapping about this and complaining about that! And every time I go outside, there's Lucia parading around in another bathing suit, waiting to pounce on you with some simply ducky thoughts for changing the décor of the ladies' room!"

"Ben—"

"Let me finish, dad! The best thing you could do for this club is to stop letting those two run you. Stop being so amiable, and stop stalling, and stop being run by Lucia and Dudley! Dudley and Lucia! Lucia and Dudley! They're getting to haunt me!"

Humphrey Bunting smiled wryly as he walked over to the window. Rather mechanically, he waved to Lucia, who was just starting down the steps to the beach.

If the truth were told, Lucia and Dudley were haunting him, too. The club itself was haunting him.

He hated running things. He was a yachtsman, not an accountant.

Ben was right, he thought. Between Lucia and Dudley and the bills and the accounts, he was having the hell of a summer.

"You know, Ben," he said aloud, "I've often wished this summer that Dudley'd passed up boats and made a hobby of orchids. Something that would take him out of my sight to a distant jungle. You're right, Ben. Your last vacation hasn't been so hot. But we've got to put up with it till—oh."

He turned around to find that Ben had gone, and that the massive frame of Dudley French was looming in the hall beyond.

"I want you!" French said. "I want to talk to you!"

"Hello," Bunting said. "What became of Ben? Did you see him?"

"That insolent son of yours," Dudley said pettishly as he heaved himself up on the mahogany desk top, "has got to get rid of his Jack the Ripper manner if he ever expects to succeed in the medical profession. Sit down, Bunting. I want to talk to you!"

"I wish—" Humphrey began, and then choked back the rest of his sentence.

He mustn't, he told himself sharply, succumb to that sudden urge to tell Dudley French to shut his fat face, get the hell out of his office, and stay out. Not if he ever expected to ease the money for the south-wharf repairs out of Dudley's pocket!

"Sit down!" Dudley waved toward a chair.

"You couldn't come back later, could you?" Humphrey asked. "I'm more or less tied up, right now. I've got a date with Asey Mayo, and I'm expecting him any minute."

"Who? Asey Mayo? What for?"

"Some business for Bill Porter. I expected him earlier, but he phoned that he'd be late. Could your business wait?"

"Why? You're free enough now, aren't you?" Dudley said. "Mayo isn't here now, is he? And you haven't anything to do till he comes."

"But I do. I'm busy. I have guests for lunch, accounts, a dentist's appointment, an incipient strike in the kitchen—"

"They can wait," Dudley said. "What I want to know is this. When and why did you adopt the policy of having your members systematically insulted?"

"Has Ben said—did Ben say anything to you?" Humphrey asked cautiously.

"Ben didn't pause to chat," Dudley said. "He simply shouldered me out of the way and shoved on down the hall."

The commodore drew a long breath of relief.

"Er—who did insult you, then?"

"That's what I want to know, too. Look out the south window. See that girl at the foot of the dune? The girl in blue shorts, drawing pictures?"

"Did she insult you?" Humphrey tried not to smile.

"Next to her," Dudley ignored his question, "is a man in gray flannels, with a cane and a pair of binoculars. See him? Now, that man has just informed me that he has—I'm quoting—'permission from the commodore of this club to roam at large wherever he so chooses.' Is that true?"

"Yes. You see, he is—"

"Furthermore, he claims that he has your leave to snoop at will through his binoculars, and to say anything his heart desires to anyone he meets. Is that true?"

Humphrey laughed.

"Yes. But I think there's been a slight misunderstanding. You see, he's my—"

"In short," Dudley interrupted, "you gave him carte blanche to insult the club members. Just what I thought!"

"He happens to be Ross Ward," Humphrey said, "and he got my permission this morning to roam around, look at things, talk with people, and write an article about the club. The girl in the blue shorts is his illustrator. A Miss Heath. You've heard of Ward. He's the war correspondent. He's just flown home on the Clipper to recuperate from a leg wound he got in France."

"What's he doing here?"

"I told you, writing about the club for one of the Cape Cod articles he's doing for a syndicate. I gave him permission because I thought it would be good publicity, and might even bring us in a member or two. Lots of people read Ward."

Dudley got up from the desk.

"I don't believe you!" he said.

Humphrey looked at him curiously. He was accustomed to Dudley's rudeness, but this forthright rancor was something new.

"Don't believe what, French?" he asked.

"I don't believe he's a reporter. He's some fellow your son planted out there to insult me!"

"Look here," Humphrey said, "tell me just what happened between you and Ross Ward, will you? What did Ward say to you? What—er—what did you say to him? You didn't order him off, or anything like that, did you?"

"Obviously," Dudley said from the doorway, "it amuses you to hear that I have been insulted. It's all you can do to keep a smile from your face! I guessed it was Ben's work. I've heard the things he's said about me!"

"Wait!" Humphrey said. "Don't go off in a huff, Dudley! No one's deliberately insulted you. Ross Ward hasn't been planted here for any other purpose than to write about the club. Ben never saw him till this morning. If you'll just tell me what happened, we'll clear this right up now. Then, at one, you come back and lunch with Ward and Miss Heath and Lucia and me. Lucia used to know Ward. And I thought of asking Asey Mayo—"

Humphrey broke off as Dudley flounced up the hall. Then, grinning broadly, he sat down at his desk.

On the confused, jumbled sort of day this was turning out to be, it was pleasant to find such a bright spot, like this discovery that Dudley French had for once been on the receiving end. Whatever Ross Ward might have said, Humphrey felt very sure that Dudley both provoked and deserved the crack.

Of course, the whole thing would have to be smoothed over, for the sake of the south wharf. Ward would have to be primed, but Ward was a good fellow, and he'd understand about the necessity for the wharf repairs. A little flattery and a little cajoling and a good lunch would bring Dudley out of his mad.

Picking up his binoculars, Humphrey looked out just in time to see Ross Ward, rocking with laughter, throw his arm up in a mock Fascist salute as Dudley marched past him on his way to the south wharf.

Humphrey put down his glasses and grinned again. Ross thought it was funny, so whatever had happened couldn't be very serious. He wished that Asey Mayo would hurry up. As soon as he got through with the business of Bill Porter's check, Humphrey thought, he'd go out and get Ward's version of the story. And privately give him a vote of thanks.

He waved a hand in Ward's direction, and turned back to his desk.

Out at the foot of the dune, Clare Heath sharpened a pencil and spoke to Ross Ward.

"I think Commodore Bunting's watching us from his office. I just saw the sun flash on his spyglass."

"You mean binoculars." Ward put down his own. "I spotted 'em. He's giving us the once over, after listening to Fatty gripe about what a stinker I am. And I'm not sure he didn't wave us a blessing. Infant, just for the record, how did that fracas with Fatty start? It's my impression that I was minding my own business, scanning the skyline, when he upped and ordered us to get the hell out."

Clare squinted at her sketch of the club house.

"You continued to scan," she said absently, "and the third time he told us to get the hell off, you said, 'Fatty, the skyline of quaint West Gusset village stinks enough without adding your waistline to my view.' Or something like that. And he said the town was Sketicket, and you said it still stank. As a matter of fact, I rather like those church spires, and the hills, and the elms. It's a nice skyline."

"It was a terrible waistline," Ward said. "Like bread dough. Made me gag."

"But did you really have to go into such vivid detail about all the other loathsome things it reminded you of?" Clare asked. "I didn't care much for his waistline myself, and I'm not squeamish, but some of your comparisons were pretty nasty. Like that white-bellied anteater."

"You wrong me, child," Ward said. "I never heard

of a white-bellied anteater. I don't know what a white-bellied anteater is."

"Well, you told Fatty he was the spitting image of one!"

"Must have been something I made up on the spur of the moment," Ward said. "It's not a bad description, you know. Not bad at all. If I were about to create a white-bellied anteater, I should bear Fatty well in mind. Yes, I think that sums Fatty up very adequately."

"It would have, if you'd stopped there," Clare said. "I began to feel sorry for Fatty when you really hit your stride."

"Fatty was no damn Lord Chesterfield himself," Ward returned. "In fact, if he hadn't been so rude in the first place, he wouldn't have brought any of this on himself. Aren't you pretty daring, infant, criticizing your boss's extended invective?"

Clare smiled.

"When I joined you Monday, I was so thrilled at the thought of working for the great Ross Ward, I couldn't speak. Yesterday, you had me paralyzed with fear. Today, I'm on to you. And I still think you could have curbed yourself. Your script done?"

"Today's installment of quaint Cape Cod tripe," Ward said, "is ready for the panting masses. How's your quaint old vignette?"

"Not very good. Tell me, Ward, why are you writing this stuff?" Clare put down her pencil and looked at him. "I've wondered for three solid days."

"Infant, when you're my forty," Ward said lightly, "instead of your twenty-three, you'll know that well-paid tripe is not stuff. It's art. What's on the list for this afternoon?"

"Well, I've got to sketch the town pump, and Captain Somebody's house with nineteen chimneys, and a statue of Captain Somebody Else who was swallowed by a whale."

"Now I wonder," Ward said, "why did they make a statue of the captain and not the whale? No sense of proportion, that's what's wrong with people. What've I got to do?"

"Interview Asey Mayo while I sketch him."

"Ah!" Ward said. "Cape Cod's gift to the detective world. Well, you hunt up the Codfish Sherlock and sketch him. I'm taking a holiday."

"What about your interview?"

"I can dash off the Codfish Sherlock with my eyes closed, infant. Know it by heart. The homespun Jack-of-all-trades. Porter's hired man and yacht captain, now a director of Porter Motors. Drives a Porter Sixteen roadster. Tall, lean. Flannel shirt, dungarees, rubber boots, Cape drawl, and a lobster pot in either hand. You go sketch the Lithe Hayseed Sleuth, and I'll renew my youth with Lucia Newell, and thank God that Jack Newell beat me to her. Well, amuse yourself till lunch. The commodore's son seemed on the surly side, but he eyed you intently, and I dare say he'd show you the far dunes with pleasure. So long!"

Clare waved at him as he limped to the club, and turned again to consider her sketch.

After a moment's study, she impulsively crumpled it into a ball and started to work on another.

It was nearly one o'clock when she looked up to find a tall man in white flannels and a blue coat gazing appreciatively at her completed second sketch.

"Very nice," he said. "The waves look wet, an' they match the wind. I don't like to bother you, but have you seen Commodore Bunting wandering out here? I'm huntin' him."

"No, but he ought to be around," Clare said. "He must be. He's supposed to give us some lunch in a few minutes. Did you ask inside the club?"

"They thought he was out here. They said that Mrs. Newell was on the beach, too. I wonder if you've happened to see her?"

Clare nodded.

"She's under that big striped umbrella, way at the end beyond the club, I think. That's where Ross Ward was, anyway, and he told me he was going to see her."

"Ross Ward? Golly, come to think of it, I was supposed to have a date with him this afternoon! I forgot all about that!"

Clare looked from the beautifully cut flannel jacket and the immaculate white flannels to the man's lean, tanned face. Then she noticed the bulletlike Porter Sixteen roadster parked on the club road beyond.

"You couldn't—you wouldn't be Asey Mayo, would you?"

"Uh-huh."

"Really? Oh, let me introduce you to Ward, will you? Right now? He described you to me a while ago," she started to gather up her things, "as the Hayseed Sleuth. In dungarees and rubber boots!"

Asey chuckled.

"Maybe I ought to dress up more often," he said. "I aroused a lot of comment this mornin' because of my clothes. Everyone from my cousin's caller to the state police has had a few words to say on the topic. Let me carry that case. By the way, would you know what's wrong with Mrs. Newell's car?"

"I don't even know Mrs. Newell," Clare said. "But she's an old flame of Ward's—yes, she *is* under that red-striped umbrella at the end, Mr. Mayo. Ward's walking over to her now. Would you mind sort of rushing? I want awfully to spring you on him before she or anyone else has a chance to point you out. Never mind my easel. I'll get that later. Will you hurry, please?"

With the spur of her infectious enthusiasm, Asey obligingly sprinted beside her along the beach toward Mrs. Newell's umbrella.

"Ward!" Clare called out as they approached. "Oh, damn, he's there already, bending over talking with

her! But I don't think she can see us, can she, the way
the umbrella's lying? Ward was just so cocksure about
you and your dungarees and all—oh, Ward! Ward,
look here!"

Slowly, Ward straightened up and turned around
from the striped umbrella.

"Ward," Clare said, "I've got a surprise for you. I
want you to meet Asey Mayo!" She paused. "Oh, Mrs.
Newell's already told you! Somebody told you!"

"No," Ward said.

"Aren't you surprised at the way he looks, Ward?
Ward, what's the matter? What's wrong?"

Ward's lips were twisted into a sardonic smile.

He leaned on his cane and looked at Asey.

"Ah," he said. "The Codfish Sherlock, on the spot.
Well, Mayo, who's killed Mrs. Newell?"

THREE.

CLARE'S shocked cry of disbelief was effectively silenced by Ward's hand, firmly placed over her mouth.

"Keep quiet, infant, and stand back," he said. "I'm not jesting. I'm not kidding. Lucia's been killed."

"Shot?" Asey asked quickly, with a glance toward the dunes.

"Poisoned."

"Poisoned?"

"That's what I said. Take a look, Mayo."

Ward nudged Asey forward, gave Clare a shove back, and then, leaning on his cane, stood like a bulwark between the girl and the figure under the striped umbrella.

The small waves that lapped along the Sketicket shore seemed to bang in Clare's ears, and the putt-putt of a motor boat sounded like a cannonade. A little farther down the beach, a group of children were playing ball with a life guard, zigzagging around him noisily. Above, a flock of sea gulls swooped in wide circles. Suddenly the rows of green and red umbrellas began to spin as she looked at them. The whole beach was spinning. The only stationary things were Ward's twisted smile, and Asey Mayo's blue flannel back, and the slim, curiously mottled ankle of Lucia Newell, at which Clare kept trying not to look.

"Steady, infant," Ward said. "This is no time for an act from you. Well, Mayo, what about it? She's dead, isn't she?"

Asey nodded as he stood up.

"Tell me, Mr. Ward, when did you speak with her last?"

"Earlier this morning," Ward told him. "When I first came to the club. I strolled over here an hour or more ago. Around eleven-thirty or so, I think. But she was asleep. At least, she seemed asleep. So I didn't disturb her. I came back again just now. Did you ever," he added, "slap an old friend on the shoulder, and discover she was dead? It's a thoroughly shattering experience."

It was thoroughly shattering just to listen to, Clare thought. She was grateful when Asey asked her if she would find Commodore Bunting. Without the stimulus of an order, her feet would never have been able to move.

"Ask Humphrey Bunting," Asey continued, "to send his doctor son out here, an' to call Doc Cummings at the hospital, an' tell him to come over right away. 'N'en you better sit yourself down an' take several deep breaths. Want me to go along with you?"

"I'm all right, thanks."

"An' tell Bunting not to raise any fuss about this yet," Asey said, "an' don't you mention it to anyone, will you?"

"I almost couldn't," Clare said.

Ward nodded as she darted toward the west wing of the club house.

"Sound psychology," he said. "When a woman seems about to be emotional or troublesome, or both, send her at once on an errand. Well, Mayo, where do you like to begin?"

"Begin what?"

"Detecting. Sleuthing. Ferreting. Whatever you prefer calling it. What line of action do you usually follow? Do you buzz like a bee from fact to fact, or do you follow a hunch?"

"Right now," Asey said, "I'm goin' to follow the line of least resistance, an' sit down. There's nothin' I can do till Doc Cummings takes a hand."

"And how long," Ward inquired, "d'you think it will take the estimable doc to put in an appearance?"

Asey shrugged.

"Your guess's as good as mine, Mr. Ward."

"You mean that while valuable minutes tick themselves away, you're merely going to sit on the beach and absorb the sun's health-giving rays?"

"You make it sound," Asey said, "like a heinous crime in itself. But till the doc comes, there's nothin' I can do but sit an' brood. This has been a very peculiar mornin', Mr. Ward. Worth a good brood."

"Ah!" Ward said. "What a stirring reaction! What a magnificent example of rapid, decisive brain work! While a murderer betakes himself to other climes, the great Mayo lounges on a beach and broods! Just a man of action, aren't you?"

Asey chuckled. "Why are you so all-powerful sure, Mr. Ward, that Mrs. Newell was poisoned?"

"My good man, look at her! Of course she was!"

"Like," Asey asked, "with what?"

"How should I know? I'm no chemist! But I've had enough training in the addition of obvious facts to know that Lucia's been murdered!"

"Like," Asey persisted, "what obvious facts, Mr. Ward?"

"You super-sleuths!" Ward said as he impatiently ground the tip of his cane into the sand. "You're all alike! You can solve the esoteric, but you simply can't cope with the commonplace! You've heard of that master mind, Barlo Spratt, haven't you? Well, Barlo and I met in the murder of Wilton, the shipping tycoon. And while Barlo fumbled around with microscopes and shreds of oakum he found in Wilton's bath salts, I got two water-front bums arrested and indicted. Barlo disdained the obvious, too. Now, Mayo, you've seen sunstroke cases in the tropics, haven't you?"

"Uh-huh."

"Have you ever," Ward said, "seen anything look more like a case of sunstroke than this?"

"Wa-el," Asey drawled a little, "seemingly, no."

It was not his intention to be maneuvered into commenting on Mrs. Newell's dilated pupils. Not, at least, until Ward mentioned them first.

"Well, my fine codfish ball," Ward said with satisfaction, "observe that the lady wears a broad-brimmed straw hat. Observe that she's further protected from the sun by a large striped umbrella. Observe that the sun, although hot, is by no means tropically hot. Observe the lady's heavy tan. She's been exposed over long periods to hotter suns. She's accustomed to direct sunlight. In short, Comrade Mayo, did you ever hear of anyone having sunstroke under a sunshade?"

"Not as a general rule," Asey said. "But all that observin' is sort of circumstantial evidence, Mr. Ward. Isn't there somethin' specific that convinces you she's been poisoned?"

"Your mental resemblance to Barlo Spratt is phenomenal," Ward said. "You and Barlo both ask the same type of idiotic questions! I told you I was no chemist. I'm no doctor, either. I know nothing about poisons or their clinical symptoms. I do know that Lucia, who was in perfect health a few hours ago, is dead. She hasn't been shot, stabbed or strangled. She couldn't have suffered the sunstroke she seems to have had. Therefore, she has been poisoned. I don't know with what. But I think I do know why."

Asey sat up.

"Do you, now? Why?"

"Mayo," Ward said, "why did you come here to the club? Why are you here?"

"To see Humphrey Bunting on a matter of business for a friend of mine."

"But wasn't it your intention," Ward said, "to see Lucia Newell, too? Wasn't Lucia expecting you? Hadn't she summoned you?"

"You newspaper fellows," Asey said, "kind of dumfound me now an' then. How did you happen to know that?"

"From Lucia herself. She told me earlier, Mayo, that she had something rather important and vital to look into this morning, and it was possible, she said, that she might call in an investigator!"

"Go on," Asey said. "Don't stop. Why did she want a detective?"

"I don't know. She didn't tell me. At the time," Ward said regretfully, "I didn't even catch on that she meant a detective. She didn't mention your name. In fact, I got the impression, I don't know why, that she was speaking about an insurance claim, or some sort of insurance investigator. But now I understand what she meant. She meant you, didn't she?"

"An' how does her callin' me in tie up," Asey inquired, "with her bein' poisoned?"

"Why, it's clearer than the nose on your face, Mayo! Lucia had something of vital importance to tell you, and someone killed her before she had the chance to talk. Don't you get it?"

"It's a nice fancy," Asey said.

"No fancy about it! It's fact! Someone gave her poison that leaves the earmarks of sunstroke, and someone very probably would have got away with it if I hadn't been around. It's—what are you murmuring under your breath?"

"I said, what nice headlines for you," Asey told him. " 'Mysterious Sunstroke Death on Quaint Cape Cod!' 'Famed War Scribe Sees Foul Play. Claims Widow Slain.' 'Quaint—' "

"Are you insinuating that I might be playing this up for my own benefit?" Ward interrupted. "Master Fishcake, let's clear up one point right here and now. I was fond of Lucia. At one time I'd have married her, only she jilted me first. But I still was very fond of Lucia. Understand?"

"I understand."

"There you go!" Ward thumped his cane tip in the sand. "Cocking your eyebrows at me just the way Barlo used to cock his whenever any of the Wilton case witnesses told him anything on their own initiative! Why must you amateurs feel that no information's worth a hoot unless it's been sweated out of someone? Just like the cops thinking no one tells 'em the truth except at the end of a length of rubber hose! Well, I was fond of Lucia!"

"You don't need to protest so," Asey said. "I believe you."

"She jilted me, and I was still fond of her!" Ward

said. "And you can cock your eyebrows and make mountains out of it, if you care to. I liked Lucia! And I don't think even Barlo would be crass enough to insinuate that I'd try to capitalize on her murder!"

"I wonder," Asey said, "if Barlo'd be crass enough to point out that you laid yourself wide open to insinuations when you announced that what seems to be a case of death by sunstroke is really a case of murder by poison? An' then—"

"Ssh!" Ward said suddenly. "Stop babbling! Facts are beginning to simmer in my mind!"

Asey watched thoughtfully as Ward took several steps toward the water's edge, and then turned and leaned on his cane.

"I'm getting it, Mayo!" he said. "Look. Lucia's got on the track of something. Lucia checks up on it this morning. Lucia calls you. But Lucia's dead before you come. If she was poisoned, it must have been after— oh, where's this doctor of yours? Where *is* he? He could fill in those details in a minute. D'you suppose the infant collapsed? D'you suppose she fainted before she found Bunting?"

"I don't think so. A steward's rowin' out to Bunting's boat to get young Ben—see, yonder? I suppose Humphrey didn't want to bellow for him through the megaphone, under the circumstances. Mr. Ward, I hate to disillusion you, but I'm sort of afraid that maybe perhaps your idea of Mrs. Newell bein' killed to keep her from tellin' me somethin' important isn't exactly goin' to pan out. She only wanted me to fix her little red car."

"To fix her car?" Ward stared at him. "Why should she call you to fix her car? I never heard anything more ridiculous! If her car needed fixing, why didn't she call a regular garageman?"

"Wa-el," Asey explained, "it seems that one summer when Mrs. Newell was a young child, she stayed with some relation or other in Wellfleet, an' he had a car I used to tinker with. An' it seems like she's just always remembered me throughout the years as a tinkerin' mechanic you call for when somethin' goes wrong. So, she's been callin' me ever since she come back this spring."

"It sounds practically nostalgic!" Ward said. "And what was the matter with her car this morning?"

"She didn't state the problem," Asey said, "but off-hand, I'd say it was most likely her muffler. It usually is."

"Aha!" Ward waved his cane gleefully. "Then she didn't actually say that something was wrong with the car! What, exactly, *did* she say to you?"

"Wa-el, she didn't speak with me, but she told my cousin Jennie that she was in dire peril—wait, Mr. Ward! Don't go hurlin' your cane into the bay in a fit of excitement! She said she was in dire peril both times she phoned. But that phrase don't mean a thing. It's what she always said when she called for me. Dire peril was the way she summed up everything from muffler trouble to a flat tire or a busted cigarette lighter."

"I call on my Maker!" Ward said. "Such things can't be! A woman phones you twice, says she's in dire peril, and you smugly conclude her muffler's out of order! Why, Comrade Mayo, didn't you talk with her? Why didn't you leap into your car and rush to her without an instant's delay?"

"Wa-el," Asey said, "in my experiences with Mrs. Newell, her dire perils never turned out to be any-thin' worth rushin' to. Furthermore, this's been sort of a peculiar mornin', like I said. I think things is under control now, but even if I'd had any real inklin' that Mrs. Newell was in honest to goodness peril, I couldn't have got here much quicker than I did. I offered to talk with her over the phone, but she wasn't anxious to discuss her perils with me. If she really was in trouble, she should have spoken with me an' made it clear. But she didn't."

"Nonsense!" Ward said. "Lucia *was* in peril. I'm sure of it. Look, Mayo, after she mentioned that she had something to look into that might require an investigator, she drew me to one side and said she had a terrifically exciting story to tell me!"

"What was it?"

"Damn!" Ward said vehemently, "I don't know! I put her off! Sidetracked her. I didn't give her the chance to talk!"

"When a lady," Asey said slyly, "has a terrifically

excitin' story to tell, why in the name of your Maker didn't you rush to listen?"

"Because usually when she's got a terrifically exciting story to tell, it only means she's found another ideal man like Jack Newell! I wasn't in any mood at nine o'clock in the morning to be told what an ideal person Commodore Bunting was—obviously, he was her latest! I sidetracked her. Oh, if only I'd realized then that she meant something else! What are you murmuring about now?"

"Just wonderin'," Asey said with a grin, "if you can really blame me for not comin' to aid her in her dire peril, if you prevented her from tellin' you what the dire peril, if any, was about."

"Oh, don't let's play pot and kettle!" Ward said. "There's no excuse for either of us! I should have listened to her. You should have rushed here. Both of us were dolts, and see what's happened because of us! Mayo, when are you going to get started? How much longer do you intend to sit here, wasting time?"

"I'd say," Asey told him, "that far from bein' time wasted, it's been a very profitable quarter of an hour. Tell me some more, Mr. Ward, about your simmerin' thoughts. They advancin' much?"

"Certainly! I'm not divorcing myself from all thought merely because no doctor's turned up to inform me what type of poison was employed! And don't pretend any longer," Ward waggled his cane tip at Asey, "that she wasn't poisoned! You know she was! You're just hoping you can trap me into mentioning some clinical symptoms I shouldn't know about if I were completely innocent! She was poisoned, cleverly and efficiently. And that leads you to the first great truth in any poison case, namely, that poison is not easy for the layman to come by, and exceedingly tricky for the layman to employ. Right?"

"The common or garden ant an' rat poisons aren't too hard to get," Asey said, "but I'll string along with you on their use. You can't always bank on results, because folks don't react the same way to the same amounts of the same poison. An' it ain't simple to cover up a poisonin'."

"Exactly," Ward said. "Exactly. The average layman couldn't even try, for example, to make a poisoning look like a case of sunstroke. But a doctor could. A doctor has access to poisons. A doctor would know about dosages. Is it superfluous to point out that the Bunting lad is a doctor?"

"It ain't superfluous, but it's askin' a lot of me," Asey said, "to look on little Benny Bunting as a potential murderer."

"Little? That towering fellow is six feet three if he's an inch! And little Benny," Ward said, "was in a towering sulk this morning when I came. He hardly spoke to his father, although you could tell that he adored him. He hardly spoke to Lucia, and you could tell that he hated her guts. Now—Mayo, you're not murmuring any more, are you?"

"I remembered somethin'," Asey said, and thought back to what Picklepuss Belcher had told Jennie about Mrs. Newell. First she had gone out a lot with the Bunting boy, Picklepuss said. Now it was common talk she was going to marry the commodore. "Go on, Ward."

"Well, there's definitely a Freudian angle there," Ward said. "Gives you clear-cut jealousy as a basic motive. Son adores father, is jealous of good-looking widow's attraction to him. And so on. I won't bother to work it all out, but what do you think of that?"

"I'm not up on Freud," Asey said, "but I been told there's nothin' like a good jilt to promote jealousy. Then I s'pose if you found yourself passed over for a commodore with a lot of gold braid, that might rankle some, too. How's your access to poison, Mr. Ward, or is that the kind of crass question Barlo'd ask?"

Ward gritted his teeth audibly.

"At least," he said, "Barlo never tried to be witty! Mayo, I can recognize an eclipse without being the cause of it. By the same token, I can recognize a poisoning without being the cause of that, either. You automatically exclude young Bunting as a possible poisoner because you knew little Benny as a child. Doubtless you dandled little Benny on your knees. But face the facts, Mayo, face the facts!"

"Supposin' for the sake of the argument," Asey said, "that Mrs. Newell had somethin' vitally important to tell me, an' was killed before she had the chance to talk. What in time could be the vitally important things she'd be knowin'? What about? Who about? Why would they matter to Ben Bunting? Ben's just a youngster out of medical school, an' you make him out a kind of archvillain who'd poison a woman because of the vitally important things she knew."

Ward stomped in a wide circle around Asey.

"It's so clear, man alive, it's so clear! And you're so stupid! Look, Mayo. Ben Bunting wanted Lucia out of the way. He's jealous of her because she's taking his father away from him. Now, Lucia finds out that Ben intends to kill her. Very likely he's tried before. Something happens this morning that convinces Lucia she's in dire peril. So she telephones you. She's in dire peril of her life, you vast nincompoop, because young Bunting's plotting to kill her! Can't you get that through your thick head?"

Asey leaned back and grinned.

"You know," he said, "many's the mornin' I've wondered if folks like you really existed in flesh an' blood."

"If you're being subtle," Ward said, "you're entirely successful. I haven't the faintest idea of what you're driving at."

"I'm thinkin'," Asey said, "how much you sound like the continued stories my cousin Jennie listens to on the radio in the mornin's. All the soap chip an' shortenin' operas. The people in 'em all live under a magnifyin' glass, sort of. Nobody ever sneezes that they aren't goin' to die at least of pneumonia before the week's out. There's never a knock on the door that it's not the cruel warden come to take some innocent soul back to prison for life. If a landlord drops in, it's only to dispossess you. If a neighbor asks you to come for a drive, you're as good as kidnaped right then an' there. Now, I do think that Mrs. Newell's been poisoned, but—"

"It's nice," Ward interrupted, "to realize you've progressed that far. That's pretty damn keen of you, Mayo!"

"But until we find out what kind of poison, an' how it was given, an' when, an' how much, an' a lot of assorted items like that," Asey went on, "you're hardly in any position to point your finger at anyone an' say he's probably a murderer. You can't rationalize around in any soap opera fashion, like you was someone out of a drama called 'The Dire Peril of Lucia Newell, or Young Benny Bunting's Revenge.'"

"Mayo," Ward said, "that's good! Sometimes I catch a faint glimpse of humor in you! So you can't take my simmering thoughts?"

Asey shook his head.

"Not when I could present you with jealousy for a motive, credit you with intelligence enough to get poison an' use it on Mrs. Newell yourself, an' make just as good a yarn of you as you've made of Benny Bunting."

Ward picked up a shell and skipped it into the incoming waves.

"Suppose I can prove it, Mayo?"

"Like," Asey said, "how?"

"I'll bet you a hundred to one I can prove it," Ward said. "I don't often bet, but every now and then I have a sharp twinge in my bad leg which leads me to take a brief flier. I'll wager you a hundred bucks to one that when young Dr. Bunting finally gets here and looks at Lucia, he'll say it's sunstroke. Not poison. Sunstroke. Because sunstroke is the verdict as he planned it. Done?"

"I've got a brand new Porter roadster standin' out in the road," Asey said. "I'll throw it in with my dollar that Ben says poison."

Ten minutes later, Ben Bunting straightened up, turned away from the umbrella, looked Asey straight in the face and said, "Sunstroke."

FOUR.

"Ah," Ward said. "Sunstroke! Hear that, Mayo? Sunstroke!"

"I heard," Asey said.

"Sunstroke! It almost," Ward said, "seems incredible. I'm afraid this will be rather a blow to your father, Bunting."

"It'll be a blow to all her friends," Ben returned.

"But I thought," Ward said, "that your father was going to marry Lucia."

"He never discussed it with me," Ben said. "Asey, shall I take her into the club now, or wait till some more of the crowd's gone, or call the ambulance, or what?"

"I think we'll leave things as they are," Asey said, "until Doc Cummings finally gets here."

"Who?" Ben swung around quickly and looked at Asey.

"Cummings."

"Why Cummings? What do you want him for? Have you called him?"

"He's the medical examiner," Asey said.

"But this is sunstroke! You don't have to call in a

medical examiner for a case of sunstroke! You can't call this a violent death!"

"Maybe not," Asey said, "but it comes under the headin' of sudden death, don't you think? Suppose you go back to the club an' check up, an' make sure your father located the doc. If we have to wait any considerable length of time, we'll take her inside."

"But—oh, well! All right!"

Ben stalked off toward the club.

"What a naïve young man!" Ward said. "What a startlingly naïve and innocent young man! Did you notice his Adam's apple buckjump when you mentioned the medical examiner? That was his only departure from the role of young Dr. Kildare giving a clear-cut, young American verdict. To think he could have lulled himself with the notion that his verdict would be final! Ah, me, ah, me! I'm not a man to gloat, Mayo, but what price soap operas now?"

Asey detached a key from his chain and held it out with a dollar bill.

"You'll find her a nice car to handle," he said, "particularly in a hurry. Bring her back in about five hundred miles, an' I'll throw in a free tune-up job."

Ward took the dollar and waved the key away.

"I'm a fair man, Mayo," he said. "We'll make it the best two out of three falls for the car, shall we? So long!"

"Not leavin'?"

"Yes," Ward said, "I feel it's time someone made a

gesture of action. I'll leave the details to you and the
estimable doc. Solving Lucia's death going to be much
more absorbing than writing quaint tripe on the West
Gusset town pump. You take the high road, Mayo,
and I'll take the low road, and by tomorrow or the
next day, I'll be touring the quaint Cape highways
and byways in my Porter Sixteen, while thousands
cheer."

Asey grinned.

"Let me know before you make any arrests, won't
you?"

"Oh, I'm not going to do what you like to think
of as detective work," Ward said airily. "Nothing so
esoteric. I'm just going to plod on, following the obvious. While you and old Doc Thingummy sit and
brood, and measure out how many cubic centimeters
of what stuff caused Lucia's death, I shall merely bore
from within, in my own soap opera fashion. I'm even
going to bore by proxy."

"Like how?" Asey asked.

"I'm going to remove Clare from her job of limning
quaint vignettes, and set her to work on young Dr.
Bunting, of the sunstroke diagnosis Buntings. Having
noted what Clare's starry eyes do to the males at our
Inn, I'd say she could ferret out much of interest. Yell
for me in the bar when the doc's named the poison."

Asey watched him limp along the beach, between
the symmetrical rows of red and green umbrellas
whose occupants had by now all departed.

There was probably nothing which pleased Mr. Ward more, Asey thought, than to be considered a problem child. And very possibly Mr. Ward might turn out to be just that.

But Mr. Ward was far from being a fool. He was a deft thinker and a deft worker. His gratuitous disclosure of his relationship as Mrs. Newell's loyal ex-suitor, coupled with his focusing of suspicion on Ben Bunting was as masterly a bit of machination as Asey had encountered in a long while.

And for all of Asey's efforts to find out, he still didn't know whether Ward had spotted those dilated pupils, or whether he had arrived at his verdict of poison simply by the process of elimination, as he claimed.

But no matter how you looked at the situation, there was little excuse for Ben Bunting's not spotting them.

That angle was one which Asey didn't pretend to understand, and one which he mentally pigeonholed for later discussion with Dr. Cummings. The doc would know how much of that sunstroke verdict might be ascribed to Ben's youth, and inexperience, and nervousness, and how much was pure, unadulterated lying.

Asey pulled out his pipe and chewed at the stem.

He wondered how much of Ward's tale of Mrs. Newell's calling in an investigator and having some exciting story to relate might be Ward's own colorful, post-mortem romancing, and how much might be true. If Mrs. Newell had really been in dire peril, why in time hadn't she said so with emphasis, and explained in full? She could have, easily enough. With all the telephone booths Asey had noticed earlier in the club house, while he was hunting Humphrey, Mrs. Newell certainly could have found one where she wouldn't have been overheard.

And Asey wondered why Mrs. Newell should have chosen to draw Ward aside as a possible confidant instead of one of the two Buntings.

"Apparently," he said aloud to himself, "she simply wanted to see me right here at the club. An' she preferred talkin' to Ward instead of Humphrey Bunting or Ben. Huh!"

He filled his pipe only to discover that the pockets of his flannel coat contained no matches, so he reached out and drew Mrs. Newell's capacious knitting bag toward him.

Rather gingerly, he fished out a half-finished skiing mitten whose intricate patterns seemed to call for yarn of every color in the rainbow. Asey neatly wound up the dangling balls, and proceeded on to the bag's next stratum, which consisted of dog-eared sheets of knitting instructions, and three digest magazines.

Underneath them was the usual feminine clutter of cold cream, suntan oil, lipstick, powder, comb, and coin purse.

Then came a torn cashmere sweater, to which was pinned a crumpled note.

" 'Hope you can mend this,' " Asey read. " 'Delighted if you could. Picking you up at eight tonight. Humphrey.' "

The note was dated Thursday the eleventh, which, Asey calculated, was Thursday, May eleventh, and proved only that Mrs. Newell was inclined to procrastinate.

Hidden in the bottom seam of the bag, he finally found a single kitchen match, which spluttered out almost before it was struck.

Asey shrugged, and chewed at his pipe stem.

He was still chewing at it an hour later, when Dr. Cummings beckoned him from the hall to a room in the club's west wing.

"What's the story?" Asey asked.

"Sit down." Cummings plumped his stocky form into a chair. "And for heaven's sakes, take that thwarted look off your face! I never saw you look so thwarted!"

Asey said that was exactly the way he felt.

"Come, come, find some balm in Gilead!" Cummings said. "Think what you'd be having on your hands if she'd been killed by a stray bullet from the Defenders of Democracy. By the way, I'm happy to report that the girls have returned to the pursuits of peace. I saw Picklepuss and some of her cohorts eating hot dogs and ice cream cones outside Johnson's in

Orleans as I came along here. Man, why are you so glum?"

"I'll tell you all about it," Asey said, "after you've spoken your piece. What killed her, doc?"

"Well," Cummings leaned back comfortably and lighted a cigar, "no one shot poisoned arrows at her, if that relieves you any. And she wasn't injected with anything, and no one held her while poison was poured down her throat. No marks of any kind on her. No signs of violence. Whatever was administered must have been in liquid form, and she took it willingly and drank it down. We're now in the market for some expert chemical analysis."

"I thought you always bragged," Asey said, "that you'd run across everythin' from leprosy to quadruplets durin' your forty years on the Cape. Mean to tell me you're stumped at last?"

The doctor instantly rose to his own defense, as Asey fully expected he would.

"Who says I'm stumped? *I* know what it was! But I'm not issuing any statements till I have proof! Of course I know, but d'you think I'm going to stick my neck out for the papers and the cops to jump on?"

"Doc," Asey said patiently, "I'm not a paper or a cop, an' I'm not goin' to jump on you. All I want is to be confronted with just one little fact! What killed her?"

"D'you remember Hattie Dyer?" Cummings asked reminiscently. "She was one of those Neck Dyers.

Lived out on Pochet Neck. Her father used to drive the meat wagon, and she used to sing in the Methodist choir. Remember Hattie?"

"No," Asey said, "an' I don't want to! At this point, I don't care two figs for all the Dyers in the world! I want to know what killed Mrs. Newell!"

"I'm trying to tell you!" Cummings said. "Years ago, I gave Hattie Dyer a prescription for her stomach trouble. She was supposed to take five drops. But she never stopped to look at the label beyond the five, or else she thought five drops was too little to do her any good, and so she made her first dose five teaspoons. Didn't I *ever* tell you about this before?"

Asey shook his head and instantly regretted that he hadn't nodded, for the doctor plunged with relish into a monologue on Hattie Dyer's stomach trouble and its ramifications.

"Look, doc," Asey at last managed to get a word in edgeways, "Hattie's innards are engrossin', but save 'em for another day! Tell me about Mrs. Newell!"

"I *am* telling you! But you've got to get the picture of Hattie first! She took five teaspoons, see? And when her family called me, I diagnosed sunstroke. She'd been out in the garden, weeding under the hot sun without any hat on. And then I spotted her eyes, and then I spotted this bottle on her bedside table, and then I got to the root of things. Not, of course, that there was much I could do about it then. Well, this is the same sort of thing, see? Only not belladonna."

Asey drew a long breath.

"Doc, what killed her?"

"Why, if it was slipped into something she drank, it was probably atropine. Not belladonna. Five grains of atropine would have about the same effect as Hattie's five teaspoonfuls of belladonna, and a five grain atropine tablet would be a lot more convenient for slipping purposes."

"There were times," Asey said, "when I thought we'd never get here. So she was given atropine in somethin' she drank. When?"

"How do I know when? She was all right when she phoned your house, and she was apparently all right when she went to the beach. It follows that while she was on the beach, someone gave her a drink, and in it was atropine. But I can't tell you what time she drank it. And mind you, until it's proved, I refuse to say what killed her. We'll know tomorrow."

"We'll know this afternoon," Asey said. "Bill Porter's pilot brought Betsey here yesterday, an' he can fly up to Boston. Then Boston can phone you back. By the way, you better call Dudley French an' tell him you're takin' care of Mrs. Newell's body for the time bein'. He's some relation of hers."

"French? Fat fellow? Oh, I know him," Cummings said. "Touchy sort. I lanced a boil for him once. All right, I'll phone him and break the news. Now, Asey, what do you want to do about the police angle? Personally, I don't see any necessity for cluttering this place up with Hanson's cops till we hear from Boston. They'll just be underfoot and in the way. You've been here so long, you must have picked up some ideas you'd like to work on in comparative peace, haven't you?"

Asey smiled.

"You might call this place a hotbed of ideas an' a desert of facts," he said. "Doc, how much of a chance did someone take with this atropine?"

"Ross Ward told you that she appeared to be asleep, didn't he? Well," Cummings said, "I'd say that she drank, fell into a coma, and that was that. No one took much of a chance on the results. No matter how she reacted, the results were pretty certain."

"How come?" Asey asked.

"Well, it looks as though she fell at once into a coma. You see what happened. People thought she was asleep, and left her alone, and when someone finally tried to waken her, she was dead. Now, the atropine might also possibly have set her raving. It could have made her stark, staring mad. But it's still doubtful if anyone could have saved her, even if they got her to a doctor. Probably, if she had started raving, people would have called Ben Bunting, and God knows what he might have diagnosed! Asey, what do you think about Ben and all his idiotic talk about sunstroke? There's absolutely no excuse for that, you know!"

"None at all? I figured that his bein' young an' inexperienced might account for it."

"The average youngster," Cummings said, "would be far more inclined to reverse the situation and call sunstroke a case of poisoning. Kids sheer away from a simple diagnosis. Seems too easy. Now, I don't claim that Ben should have said atropine right off the bat. I still won't say it for publication, myself. But he never should have said sunstroke. I don't understand that at all. I know Ben. He's helped me out once or twice this summer. He's no fool. He knows better!"

"Think he's just lyin'?"

"I don't know what else you'd call it. By the way," Cummings added, "I heard my wife say that his father and Mrs. Newell were going around a lot together, and she said there'd been several scenes in public when they met Ben. I don't know the whys or wherefores, and I don't offer that as any sort of evidence. I just bring the point up in passing."

"It's been brought up before," Asey said. "Huh. Let me think. Suppose, doc, that you don't phone French for a while. Suppose we let Hanson wait. An' Benny, too. Then, if we find out later that Ben's got somethin' up his sleeve, we'll dangle that sunstroke verdict over his head, an' make polite threats about blightin' his future career. But now that I got somethin' to work from, suppose I reconnoiter around a bit, an' see what I can see?"

"Why not?" Cummings returned. "The place was so deserted when we carried her in, I don't think a soul noticed us except Ward and that girl. If any questions should be asked, we can always answer with perfect truth that Mrs. Newell had an ill turn. That's what I told a waiter who asked. You might as well dig around in peace and find out what you can. And, after all, who knows? It may not be atropine at all!"

"As if," Asey said, "you'd ever mentioned the word unless you was positive! Look, doc, you think that whoever gave her the stuff figured that however she might react, by the time anyone found out for sure, it'd be too late to do anything about it. That so?"

Cummings nodded.

"Of course, if she'd taken a similar dose by accident, and instantly phoned a doctor and told him what she'd taken, that would be different. But here, even if Mrs. Newell could have managed to tell someone she felt sick, there'd have been just so much hubbub and to-do even before anyone thought to call a doctor. Probably people would give her soda mints, or aspirin. Or dangle a cold key down her back. All those silly things people do. And then there'd have been more time lost before a doctor—even Ben—got to her."

"So," Asey said, "the margin of error isn't a lot greater than tryin' to polish someone off with a single well-placed bullet?"

"Less. And the nice thing about a well-placed bullet," Cummings said, "is that you know what you've got when you find it. It's all open and aboveboard. I don't like the type of person who slinks around, slipping drugs and poisons into things. It shows a nasty, underhanded mind. Will you be good enough to remember that?"

"I never poisoned anyone!"

"You know what I mean! No one has managed to do away with you yet, Asey, and I know you claim to have nine lives like a cat. But remember that a cat has only one liver. I warn you, don't take any nourishment from strangers for a while. If you have to eat, boil yourself a nice egg. If you're thirsty, milk a nice cow. Atropine is nothing you can dodge like a bullet. You can succumb to atropine in a rum punch as easily as Mrs. Newell did."

"Why in time," Asey demanded, "didn't you *tell* me it was a rum punch?"

Cummings stared at him in disbelief.

"Didn't you know? Where was your nose? I thought you guessed that right away! I thought you'd even grasped some notion of who gave her the rum punch in the first place!"

"So far as I'm concerned," Asey said, "Mrs. Newell leapt up an' quaffed a rum punch presented her by a masked stranger that rolled up the beach in a swirlin' cloud of pink mist. Huh! So the drink was a rum punch!"

"What did you think I meant by a drink, anyway?" Cummings inquired curiously. "I told you atropine was slipped into her drink. I didn't say it was slipped into her chocolate malted milk, or into her Coca-Cola! For heaven's sakes, you weren't going to attempt the impossible chore of tracking down a drink of water, were you?"

"I was plannin'," Asey said, "to devote a week or two to investigatin' all drinks, but I must say that a rum punch shaves the job down to somethin' halfway reasonable. There's a drink somebody made. There's somethin' you can put your finger on!"

"Somebody ordered it, had it made, and carried it out to her," Cummings said, "which ought to give you unlimited opportunities to lay hand on the person involved. Her umbrella was set apart from the rest, up there at the end of the beach. I'm sure someone must have noticed who strolled up there with a drink. My wife would know in a minute, if she'd happened to be on the beach. Any of the Minutewomen, or a reasonable Yacht Club facsimile of 'em, would probably be able to tell you not only who went over to Mrs. Newell's umbrella this morning, but also yesterday morning, or a week ago Friday. You know how women are on a beach when—"

"What's the matter?" Asey asked, as the doctor laughed and pointed to the window.

"Funny thing," Cummings said. "Ever notice how sometimes your thoughts and your speech get tangled up with what you see? When I spoke of the Minute-women, I'd have sworn that a second later I saw a woman with a gun out there on that dune. But there's the woman now, going in the back door with that laundry basket. Someone from the kitchen. Well, you go reconnoiter about the rum punch, and I'll phone about the plane. Suppose I can't get it?"

"Call Anderson. Or Triplett. There's plenty of planes around," Asey said. "Just commandeer one in the name of necessity an' the medical profession. But I'm sure you can get Porter's."

"Okay. I'll commandeer—oh, wait, Asey! I forgot about the door. Will you get Bunting and get the key to this room from him? I don't want to leave the place unlocked. And, say, Asey."

"Uh-huh."

"Where's Bunting been keeping himself? If he was as interested in Lucia Newell as people say, wouldn't you think he'd have at least dropped around to mourn, or inquire, or something? I think it's queer that he hasn't turned up."

"Seems so," Asey said. "Look, doc, I'll wait here while you phone about the plane. When you come back, we'll discuss the matter of Commodore Bunting."

In less than five minutes, the doctor returned.

"All set," he said. "Seems he was running up to Boston anyway later on. He'll drop by here and I'll

explain what I want him to do. Asey, I don't see Bunting around outside anywhere. Where is he?"

"You've touched," Asey said, "on one of the items
thwartin' me when I first came in here. I don't know
where he is."

"You mean he's gone away, or lost, or hidden, or in
seclusion, or what?"

Asey shrugged.

"But he's here, isn't he?" the doctor persisted. "At
the club?"

"I don't know. He wasn't here when I first came,
around one o'clock. After I found the body, I sent
that girl Clare, Ward's illustrator, inside to get him.
But it seems she hunted high and low, and couldn't
locate him, so she finally phoned you herself. After
you came, I had another hunt. But no one's seen him,
or knows where he is."

"You mean to say that Bunting's not explained to
you about that check of Bill Porter's yet?"

"I tell you, I haven't set eye on the man," Asey said.
"An' I'm sure he's not showed up, because I told the
boy at the door to bring him to me at once when he
came, an' I left a note on his office desk, too, sayin'
the same thing."

"Hm!" Cummings said. "Hm! You want to know
what *I* think? I think this case is as clear as the nose
on your face! Why, man alive, it's obvious!"

Asey surveyed him quizzically.

"Them words," he said, "are beginnin' to sound like an old, old refrain. What's so obvious?"

"Why, Humphrey Bunting wangled that five thousand dollar check from Bill Porter, presumably to pay up some club mortgage or other, didn't he? And then he sent Bill another identical begging letter, pleading for money to pay up the same mortgage, after Bill had already sent him a check, didn't he?"

"Uh-huh," Asey said, "an' Bill found out that at least two other men had sent him large checks for the same mortgage. But—"

"Well, there you are!" Cummings said. "When Bunting got those checks, he never paid up the mortgage with 'em. He just frittered the money away. And this Mrs. Newell's at the bottom of it all."

"How?"

"Bunting spent the money on her!" Cummings said with a note of triumph in his voice. "Don't you see? Bunting was always a great hand for spending money. It's common talk that he's run through two trust funds. He's used up the Bunting money. So, he's been embezzling from the club so that he could have money to spend on Lucia Newell—did you notice the bracelets on her wrists and the rings on her fingers?"

"I noticed," Asey said, "that she wore a lot of sparklin' jewelry, but I didn't think it was real. I remember once bein' informed kind of severelike by Betsey Porter that the best people didn't wear diamonds to the beach."

"Possibly not, but those are real! That's the story, Asey! Bunting's stolen money and frittered it away on diamonds for Mrs. Newell. Now that you're forcing him to a showdown on Bill's check, he realizes that the game's about up. He realizes also that Lucia Newell's the one who's egged him on. So he kills her. Then he flees."

"Doc," Asey said, "do you ever listen to them continued stories on the radio in the mornin's?"

"What's that got to do with this?" Cummings asked suspiciously.

"Do you?"

"Listen to that tripe? Certainly not! They're all tripe, all those stories. Excepting 'Just Plain Doc.' He's a pretty smart fellow for a country doctor, and by George, he runs into some interesting cases! 'Pete and Martha's Folks' isn't too bad. But except for those, and a couple of others, all those stories are tripe, and I wouldn't listen to 'em—what're you screaming with laughter about, anyway?"

"You," Asey said, "an' Ward. Every sneeze pneumonia, an' every tough crust a divorce. If what you think is true, doc, why do you suppose Bunting left all this valuable an' sparklin' jewelry behind? Whyn't he take it with him to defray expenses, I wonder?"

"Why," Cummings said seriously, "that would make the motive robbery, and he killed her for revenge. You see, that explains the atropine, Asey. Bunting had only to steal it from Ben's bag. And, of course, that explains why Ben said it was sunstroke. Ben guessed, and he's trying to shield his father. It's just the sort of crazy gesture a kid like that would make. I wondered at first if he might not be shielding someone, but I couldn't think who. I—are you leaving, Asey? Well, see if you can't find a key to this door, will you?"

"You'll find one," Asey told him gently as he swung open the door, "right here, on the outside of the door, doc. Right here in the lock. Here's your key. An' let it be a lesson to you. Oh," he added, as the doctor stepped out into the hall beside him, "you leavin', too?"

"Got to phone my office," Cummings said. "Let *what* be a lesson to me?"

"The key."

Cummings snorted.

"What're you talking about, Asey?"

"Look for things where they are," Asey said. "Don't look for 'em where they ain't. You—"

"You look out, yourself!" Cummings gripped his arm suddenly and pulled Asey back against the wall of the corridor. "Duck, you idiot, can't you see her aiming at you? Look out!"

FIVE.

WHO'S aimin'—"

"Look out, Asey! Can't you see her there on the terrace, aiming that gun at you? *That* way! Out there! Look for things where they are, you idiot, not where they aren't—oh, look out!"

Asey's protest that he didn't know whether the doctor meant him to look outside or to take care was cut short by a bullet that ripped into the white painted molding above his head.

"There!" Cummings said tartly. "Let *that* be a lesson to you!"

"It's gettin' monotonous," Asey said a little wearily. "Plain monotonous! I'm tired of—doc, where you think you're rushin' to? Don't go tearin' out like that! You'll get hurt—oh, wait, will you!"

But Dr. Cummings, running along the hall with an amazing lightness of foot for a man of his girth, disappeared out through the open French door that led to the side terrace.

He reappeared almost at once, tugging after him a woman whose right wrist he held in a viselike grip.

It was Picklepuss Belcher.

And under her left arm, hugged tightly against her green dress, was the little twenty-two she had carried into Asey's kitchen that morning.

"All right!" Cummings said crisply. "Here he is! Now, explain to him why you're trying to kill him, you addle-pated fool!"

"Don't you call me names, you! I never—"

"You," Cummings said, "are an addle-pated fool. That's not a name. That's a description. Why did you try to kill him?"

"I didn't! I wasn't trying to kill him! It just went off!"

Cummings's derisive snort almost achieved the proportions of a factory whistle.

"Well, it did!" Mrs. Belcher said. "I dropped it in the sand, and I wanted to see if I'd hurt it any, so I held it up—"

"You aimed it at him," Cummings said. "I saw you with my own eyes. You deliberately aimed that gun straight at him!"

"I never did! I never even saw him! I never even knew he was in this part of the club! I just raised the gun up to see if it was all right, and it went off. It was an accident. And if it was anyone's fault, it was all Asey's anyway!"

"Pussy," Asey said, "just what—"

"Because if you'd had enough gumption and patriotic spirit to show me and the other girls how guns work," Mrs. Belcher informed him, "it wouldn't have happened. Now, you tell those people," she pointed to a little group of club employees clustered at the end of the hall, "that it was only an accident, and to go away! I can't bear being stared at. It brings on one of my nervous spells!"

Asey motioned to the steward hovering on the edge of the group.

"You can all go," he said. "This was just an accident. An' I wish you'd try to find out what become of the commodore."

As they straggled down the hall, Clare Heath appeared by the French door.

"Ward wants to know if you got killed," she said, "because if you did, he says he'll insert a few kindly words in his 'Old Sea Dogs of Quaint Cape Cod' stint that he's writing for tomorrow."

"Tell Ward," Asey said, "that this particular dog ain't dead yet. But if he wants to include a few acid words about the Female Branch of the League to Uphold Democracy an' Action—"

"The League to Defend America at all Costs with Action!" Mrs. Belcher promptly corrected him.

"Well, if Ward wants to do a job on that," Asey said, "tell him I'll help think up adjectives."

"The—what was that again?" Clare asked.

"Never mind. Tell him nothin' happened," Asey said. "Just a little accident. Now, Picklepuss!"

"Don't call me that!"

"Very well, Pussy. What are you doin' with that

gun? Haven't you collected those guns an' returned 'em like you swore on bended knees you would? Didn't you give me your bounden word you'd return 'em an' stop all this nonsense? Did I explain fifty million times that no matter how patriotic you wanted to be, steamin' around with weapons you didn't know how to handle was dangerous business, as well as illegal, unlawful, an' against the laws of this state?"

"We have licenses now," Mrs. Belcher informed him with a touch of pride.

"My God!" Cummings said. "Where'd you ever get licenses? Who gave 'em to you?"

"My brother-in-law," Mrs. Belcher said, "is chief of police and town clerk in Sketicket, if you'll recall. And just as soon as he heard why we wanted to bear arms, he gave me licenses right away for everybody. So there!"

"What," Asey demanded in his quarter-deck tones, "did you tell him you wanted gun licenses for?"

"To protect you," Mrs. Belcher said simply.

"Ha ha!" Dr. Cummings practically capsized into a wicker barrel chair. "Ha ha! Hear that, Asey? To *protect* you! Oh, I think it's the funniest thing I ever heard in my life. They get gun licenses to protect you, and the next minute they take aim and let you have it! Oh, I never—"

"Shush, doc. Pussy," Asey said, "maybe we better review this situation briefly. When I left my house, Jennie'd already started recallin' those weapons, an' you'd set out for the beach to get the two women who was on the Clam Island dunes, an'—"

"Yes, and I found Mabelle and Effie, too! And they'd never shot that big gun off at all! They couldn't make it work, no matter what they pulled at, or how hard they tried. So there! It wasn't any of our League girls that shot at you by the garage! It was someone else! So there!"

"Hey, Asey, hear that?" Cummings asked anxiously. "If they didn't shoot that gun off, then who shot at you? What do you make of that?"

"That's just what we asked ourselves, what to make of it," Mrs. Belcher said. "We asked ourselves, who did it, and what for? And we thought it all over, and decided we'd protect you, Asey."

"Uh-huh. That's what you said before. Er—protect me from what?"

"From sabotage," Mrs. Belcher said.

"Oh, come!" Asey said. "I'm no powder plant, Pussy!"

"We know," Mrs. Belcher said coyly. "We know. We guessed!"

"You guessed what?"

"Well, after we decided that someone must really be trying to kill you," Mrs. Belcher said, "we girls just sat down and thought it all over, and put two and two together. Isn't," she lowered her voice, "isn't the Porter Motor Car Company making *tanks?*"

"They are not."

"Well, airplanes, then? Or airplane engines? Or Army cars?"

Asey shook his head.

"They did in the last war!" Mrs. Belcher said. "Jennie told us so! She said it was awfully exciting, with spies trying to steal plans from you, and you outwitting them, and all. And if Porter built tanks and things in the last war, I bet they're doing it again, no matter what you say!"

"They're not, Pussy. You want to remember that the Porter Company bears about the same relation in size to the big manufacturers that your pickle factory bears to Heinz. We cater to the carriage trade, but we're awful small."

"Jennie said you'd say that! But she told us all about your mail from Washington." Mrs. Belcher's voice fell to a whisper. "And all those funny packages!"

"Jennie," Asey said, "has been takin' you for a ride!"

"No, she hasn't! She said she hadn't thought much about 'em at the time, but you had lots of mail from Washington. Official mail. And Jennie's husband said so, too. He said he brought dozens of official letters home from the Post Office to you!"

"All the official mail I got from Washington lately," Asey said, "was a bunch of seeds my congressman sent me too late to plant. An' a mess of bulletins about controllin' gypsy moth. An' some excerpts from the *Con-*

gressional Record that you probably got sent too. All about war an' conscription an' the armed forces. That's the sum total of my official mail, an' don't go gettin' any crazy ideas in your head to the contrariwise!"

"I know, I know," Mrs. Belcher said almost soothingly. "I understand. I expected you'd say something like that. We all decided you'd have to, of course. You can't speak right out about being a government agent! But we know!"

"See here, Pussy," Asey said, "you can't stand there an' dream up any such fantastic notion! You can't cococt such—such a—doc," he appealed to Cummings, "help me out! I ain't got words!"

"By George," Cummings said. "Aren't I dumb! I never guessed!"

"In another second," Asey said desperately, "I'm goin' to start tearin' my hair out in bunches! Doc, don't you get carried away! Porter's not involved with any government contracts or secrets! Neither am I! Pussy, you can go an' search my house, go through my desk an' my private papers, an' you won't find any more government instructions to me than the moth bulletins I told you about!"

Mrs. Belcher nodded. "That's all we did find," she said.

"You mean, you already been through my things?"

"We wanted to make sure," Mrs. Belcher said. "It was the only way we girls could think of."

Asey put his hands behind his back and leaned his shoulders against the wall.

"You want to be awful glad," he said, "that I'm a restrained sort of person. Well, Pussy, an' did you find anythin'?"

"No. That's why we're so sure," Mrs. Belcher returned. "There wasn't one single suspicious thing around. Anyway, Asey, so then we girls got together and thought it all out, and we decided that you were right about the guns, and it was too ambitious for us to learn how to be a rifle corps, even though Rounceval Jones thought it would be such a fine thing. But then Rounceval also said that the most valuable service any woman could render her country was to protect important things. And we decided that you were important to the country, so," she concluded proudly, "we're going to protect you!"

"An' you start in protectin'," Asey said, "by poppin' at me with a twenty-two! Pussy, I'm grateful to you ladies for feelin' I'm worth keepin'. I think maybe perhaps you ladies most probably mean awful well. An'— gimme that twenty-two, Pussy! I can't keep up bein' restrained any longer. Give it to me. Now, you go round up the rest of the Minutewomen, an' get the guns from 'em, license or no license! Knit, I tell you! Roll bandages! Take refugee children! But stop this nonsense of guns, an' rifle corps, an' protectin' me!"

"Who's going to protect you from him if we don't?" Mrs. Belcher inquired. "If we don't protect you, Asey

Mayo, I'd like to know what's to keep him from shooting at you again!"

"Keep *who* from shootin' at me?" Asey returned.

"That foreigner."

"Any particular foreigner?"

"The one that Mabelle and Effie saw over on Clam
Island dune! He was the only other person out there
that they saw, so he must have been the one that shot
at you by the garage. He was a dark, sinister, foreign-
looking man, so there!"

"Did he," Asey asked with irony, "have a long
black beard?"

"They didn't say so, and I'm sure they'd have noticed if he had," Mrs. Belcher said seriously. "He had
beady little eyes, and he carried a funny little striped
bag—like a beach bag. And a beach umbrella. The
kind that comes apart into a couple of sections so
you can carry it easily. We think he must have had the
gun hidden in the umbrella. And he wore a blue sort
of blouse that flopped out over his pants. I think Mabelle said they were sort of dark red. And he had on a
pair of those sandal things with rope soles. Mabelle
and Effie are so mad," Mrs. Belcher added, "that they
didn't know then about your being shot at, because
then they really could have taken a *good* look at him.
But they said they'd know him again in a minute."

"By George!" Cummings said. "I think you women
have done a good job! Looks as though maybe they
might have something there, Asey!"

"It looks," Asey said, "as though some innocent tourist went out to have an innocent swim!"

"That's just what Mabelle and Effie said!" Mrs. Belcher announced. "He was so innocent, and so touristy, they guessed he was a fake! Those Fifth Columns, they always look like innocent tourists. It's part of the game. But Mabelle and Effie suspected him even before they knew about his shooting Asey. They're out after him now."

"Doc," Asey said, "hoist yourself up an' let me sit down in that chair. I need it. Are the girls packin' their guns, Pussy?"

Mrs. Belcher nodded. "Just by the merest chance, they happened to notice which way he went when he left the public beach. So, after we talked things over at your house, Mabelle and Effie took their guns and went out to hunt for him. You see, we're all divided up into squads, Asey. I'm going to be your personal bodyguard, and there's going to be a corps of sub-bodyguards that you'll never see. But they'll be there!"

"No, Pussy!" Asey said unhappily. "Not really! You haven't cooked up a bodyguard!"

"Yes, we have. I thought you'd be surprised. And they'll be there, night and day, rain or shine, to watch over you. And we won't be a speck of trouble. What I mean is, the girls won't jump and scream if they see a snake, or it thunders. I explained to them that they mustn't. So, you give me back that gun, Asey. I'm going to protect you. Maybe," she added as an afterthought, "if there are any bullets in it, you'd better take them out. But I'm going to take that gun, and I'm going to protect you!"

Asey sighed. Then, in a flash of inspiration, he remembered something Ward had said earlier, when Clare had looked as if she were going to faint. Something about it being splendid psychology, when women were about to be troublesome, to send them on an errand.

"Pussy," Asey said briskly, "would you really want to help me out? Would you really do something very important an' vital for me?"

Mrs. Belcher's green eyes glinted.

"What?" she asked eagerly.

"Go," Asey said as impressively as he could, "go to your sister Sarah's. Take your squad with you. Find out from Sarah just what—you better write all this down, Pussy. Find out just what Mrs. Newell did yesterday. Who she saw. Who phoned her. If she saw any strangers. Who she talked with. Where she went last night. Find out every blessed thing you can about her. Particularly if she saw any strangers."

At the very least, he thought, he would find out whether or not Ward had been around.

"Strangers," Mrs. Belcher said. "Humph! You know, I wondered in my heart if she wasn't a Fifth Column! She lived abroad so much always."

Asey glanced sideways at Cummings as Pussy wrote energetically on the back of an envelope she had taken from her pocketbook. What he anticipated from the doctor was a quick wink of understanding. What he found, to his surprise, was the doctor nodding in complete agreement with Picklepuss.

Asey swallowed.

"Uh—all the details you can find out about Mrs. Newell, Pussy, an' mind you prove everything! I can't accept any report that says she went to the Post Office an' brought back three letters. You got to check up an' get witnesses an' make sure that every detail's absolutely correct. No hearsay evidence. I'll be in a pile of hot water if every fact ain't corroborated. Got it all straight? Okay. Bring your report in writin' to my house at nine o'clock tonight."

Mrs. Belcher saluted smartly, picked up her empty twenty-two, and marched away.

Cummings looked after her thoughtfully.

"I'll take back some of my cracks," he said. "They've got you a good lead on that garage shooting, and they'll be demons for finding things out. That's a very interesting angle on Mrs. Newell. Hm. I wonder if she was trying to influence Bunting? He was in the Navy once, wasn't he? And why didn't you tell me you were doing government work?"

"I'm not!" Asey said. "Either on my own hook, or Bill Porter's! I haven't got a thing to do with the government or the war or war plans or defense plans or anything else! An' I don't want to hear any more nonsense about it! I don't want any more distractions.

Has it slipped your mind that there was a poisonin' here?"

"No," Cummings said. "I suppose I ought to get things ready for that pilot. And I should phone my office. Really, this is turning out to be a very interesting affair, Asey. I like a case where you can speculate. You'll be careful, won't you?"

As he turned away, the white-coated steward appeared in the hall.

"Mr. Mayo, there's a man just come who says he's from the state police, but he's not in uniform. He'd like to see you."

"Tell him to come here, will you?"

Cummings walked slowly back to where Asey stood.

"A state cop not in uniform," he said. "What is it, code? What's up, Asey? Who is he really?"

"He's a state cop who isn't in uniform, because he happens to be on vacation!" Asey said. "He was chattin' with Bates an' Sorensky at the railroad crossin' when I stopped off to see 'em!"

"What about?"

"Oh, I got shot at again after you left my house this mornin'!" Asey said. "If you hear a gun, it's someone shootin' at me. Took my best yachtin' cap off, that trip!"

"So you knew all the time that it wasn't the women? What did you do?"

"Asked the cops to help me look into it!" Asey said. "At my age an' time of life, I'm not goin' to stroll off single-handed after some fellow in the distance who can come that close with a rifle!"

"Do you think it was this foreigner the women saw?"

"I think," Asey said, "it's some crank. Like that crackpot a couple years ago that made a business of stickin' nails into my tires."

"So you don't think it's the foreigner?" Cummings sounded bitterly disappointed. "Hm. *I* do. But on the other hand, I wonder. Asey, Bunting has a great collection of guns. He lent some to Picklepuss, my wife said. He's an expert shot. Suppose he was trying to keep you from coming to find out about that check!"

"Ward thinks," Asey said, "that Mrs. Newell was killed before I got a chance to hear what she had to say, and now you decide I'm shot at to keep me from —hey!"

"What's the matter?"

"Funny how things work out when you turn 'em around! Look, what *was* I supposed to be killed before I could do? It wouldn't be Bunting an' that check. 'Cause even if I got killed, Bill Porter would still keep on askin'. But, if someone killed me with a well-aimed shot, I wouldn't get to see Mrs. Newell. An' if she was poisoned, there wouldn't be anythin' she could tell me. Huh. That's the only bit of rationalizin' that appeals to me this far. Now, I'm goin'—"

"Here's your cop," Cummings said.

"Oh. Hello, Mike. Find anything after I left?"

"Not a thing, Asey. Not a trace of the guy. The only person anywhere near your place was a tourist coming up from the beach. He hadn't seen anyone, either, he said."

"Did he have on a blue blouse and red pants?" Cummings demanded. And as the cap nodded, "Asey, hear that?"

"I hear," Asey said. "But before I'm the target of any more shots or any more theorizin', I'm goin' to find out about the case in hand. Thanks for coming over, Mike. Did Bates say he expected Lieutenant Hanson to come by this afternoon? Well, will you ask Bates to tell him to find either me or Doc Cummings? He can track us down through the doc's office, or the club here. So long!"

Asey strode up the hall.

Ross Ward, he noticed, was sitting at a table out on the terrace, tapping away at a portable typewriter, while Clare Heath read to him from a paper.

Turning to the right, Asey halted outside a lounge room where two sunburned men, one with an ear trumpet, listened intently to Rounceval Jones mournfully enumerating the sinkings of more English merchant ships. To the question of a third man who called in from the terrace, one of the pair announced that everyone else had gone to Molly's damn relief bazaar, and that they were leaving practically at once. Then he switched the radio to another commentator, who also discussed the torpedoed ships and threw in a few bombings for good measure.

Neither of the two men paid any attention to Asey in the doorway. He doubted if they even knew he was there.

The instant the news broadcast was over, the man with the ear trumpet banged his chair arm with his fist.

"Now," he said belligerently, "you take sea power! Sea power—"

"Sea power nothing!" said the other. "You take air power!"

Asey sighed and turned away.

The pair would provide a field day for Gallup pollers or public opinion surveyers, but they were clearly in no mood to be gently quizzed about Mrs. Newell's rum punch and the person who gave it to her.

He walked on toward the bar at the far end of the wing.

Just as he was about to step inside, a man stamped into the pine-paneled room through the opposite screen door.

"Leo!" Dudley French crossed over and spoke to the bartender. "Leo, where's Mrs. Newell? Have you seen her? Has she been in here? Where'd she go?"

"She hasn't been here, Mr. French. I think I heard someone say she'd had an ill turn, or fainted, or something—"

"Ill turn? Nonsense! Nobody told me anything like

that. They just haven't seen her, and she must be here. Her car is. She's supposed to be telling fortunes at the relief bazaar, and Molly wants her—see here, Leo, what are you doing with that?" He pointed accusingly to something in the man's hand. "What are you—well, of all the damned nerve! Put that bill back where it belongs, in the till! I saw you take that out! What's the big idea, taking money out and putting it into your pocket like that? What's the idea?"

"It's my bill, Mr. French!"

"Yours? What do you mean, yours? What would you be doing with a hundred dollar bill? You never had a hundred dollar bill in your life! Of all the brazen nerve, to swipe that with me right here, watching you! Put that bill back!"

"But—"

"Listen, Leo, I've been keeping my eye on you! You shortchanged me once too often. I've been watching you. I told the commodore so when he said your accounts were haywire. Put that bill back!"

"But it's mine, Mr. French!"

"I suppose," French inquired acidly, "you're going to tell me it's a tip?"

"Yes, sir. That's just what it is. It's a tip."

Asey, out in the corridor, raised his eyebrows.

A hundred dollar tip would have been a rarity at the Sketicket Yacht Club even in the good old days of its youth, when its yachts anchored outside were steam yachts and not a handful of catboats, and when Sketicket natives referred to the place as Billionaires' Beach. A hundred dollar tip at the Sketicket Yacht Club now, Asey thought, was a gesture you might sum up as an unnatural phenomenon. Under the circumstances, you might even classify it as a suspiciously unnatural phenomenon.

Dudley hooted his derision.

"A tip! A tip that size in this dump? That's likely! I'll take this up with the commodore, Leo. My God, what a place! If rotten wharves aren't giving way under your feet, then rascally bartenders are thieving in broad daylight! You'll hear plenty about your tip, my man, very soon!"

Dudley banged out, slamming the screen door behind him.

"Fat Stuff!" Leo muttered angrily. "Think you own the club! Fat Stuff!"

He thumbed his nose toward the screen door, and then snapped on a portable radio on a shelf behind him.

Asey winced as still another commentator, with a sub-machine-gun delivery, rasped into still another discussion of sea power versus air power.

Before the merchant vessels could be torpedoed all over again, Asey strolled in.

At once the radio was snapped off, and Leo turned briskly toward him.

"Yes, sir?"

"Tell me," Asey pulled out his watch, "what time is it?"

"Five past three, sir."

"And what time is this bazaar thing that everyone's going to?"

"From two till six, sir. At Mrs. Coppinger's."

"Thanks." Asey started for the screen door, and then diffidently turned back. "Say, Mr. Ward just told me you might be able to give me a hundred dollar bill for some small bills—could you?"

"Yes, sir. I can do it. I still have his bill. Right here." Leo displayed the hundred dollar bill with pride.

Asey pulled out his wallet.

"Why—let's see. Ten, twenty, thirty—why didn't Ward want anyone to know that he took that rum punch out to Mrs. Newell?"

"Oh, he didn't. He didn't take it out, sir." Leo tumbled headlong into Asey's trap. "He just ordered it. Dr. Bunting, he was the one who carried it out to her."

Asey's fingers never faltered in the process of bill counting, and his face, as he looked up, was a picture of bland unconcern.

"Seventy, an' three tens makes a hundred. There you are, an' I'll take the hundred. What's the matter, you choke on something?"

Leo was gulping violently.

"Swallow your gum, maybe?" Asey said.

"Gee, yes!" Leo leapt at the suggestion. "That's it. Gee, I guess I swallowed it all right. Gee, I guess that's it. I guess I better go do something about it quick." He picked up the bills Asey laid down. "You want anything else before I go, sir?"

"Closin' up?"

"No, sir, but it's my half day. Gee, I guess I better do something about that gum I swallowed, quick! I'll call Henry if you want anything, sir. Henry ought to of been here at three. Gee, I guess I better hurry. Good-by."

"Come back here, Leo!" Asey said.

"Gee, that gum—"

"You didn't have any gum. What you have hundred dollar bills around for?"

"It's mine!"

"Uh-huh. I know. Why did Ward give it to you?"

"He didn't!"

"You already said it was his bill. Why'd he give it to you, Leo? Why did Ward give you a hundred dollar tip? Was it to bribe you to tell me that Ben Bunting took that rum punch out to Mrs. Newell?"

"No, sir! He didn't even know that Dr. Bunting took it out. He thought I did."

"I see," Asey said. "Then he gave you the hundred to keep your mouth shut about his orderin' that drink in the first place, huh?"

Leo wet his lips nervously and looked with longing toward the door.

"I got an awful pain, like," he said. "I guess—that is, I guess—"

He paused as Asey drew out his wallet and thumbed over the bills inside. A wistful sparkle came to his eyes.

"What do you guess, Leo?" Asey said.

"Well," Leo, without taking his eyes from the wallet, edged a little nearer, "well, I'll tell you how it was. If you really want to know, that is."

"Wa-el," Asey said, "I don't know as it's so important to me—hey, feller! Give me back them good bills I gave you! What d'you mean, givin' me that hundred?"

"Is it a phoney?" Leo demanded.

"Look at it!" Asey said. "Look at that picture of Franklin! Look at this picture of Independence Hall! Look at 'em!"

Both the pictures and the bill itself were perfectly all right as far as Asey could tell, but he continued to point his finger accusingly at it, and Leo's eyes narrowed.

"So it's a phoney, is it? Well, that louse! That dirty louse! So he was bribing me with a phoney, was he?"

"I guess," Asey said, "you better take this back, Leo, an' give me back my good bills."

"Those smart guys," Leo said out of the corner of his mouth, "they burn me up! I thought it was the hell of a lot of dough just to keep my mouth shut about that drink! Here's your bills. Give me that hundred, and I'll go tell that guy Ward a few things!"

"Think that's a wise move?" Asey asked.

"What do you mean? He give me a phoney bill, didn't he? Well, he can take it back and give me a hundred bucks in real money!"

"Suppose," Asey suggested, "he says it isn't a phoney?"

"Sure it is! Look at the pictures, like you said! It's phoney!"

"Wait a sec," Asey said. "Did anyone else see him give it to you?"

"There wasn't anyone else around. But he did!"

"Uh-huh, but can you prove he did?" Asey said. "Suppose he claims he never gave it to you in the first place? Aren't you kind of on the spot with that bill, then?"

Leo's face grew red with anger.

"I'll fix that guy!" he said. "I'll do just what he didn't want me to do! When the commodore gets back, I'll tell him this guy Ward's cutting in on him! I'll tell him about the drink, and the poetry, and all the rest! I'll tell him everything! I'll see that louse gets kicked out of here on the seat of his pants! I'll fix that smart guy!"

"You haven't really got anythin' on Ward, have you?" Asey asked.

"Haven't I?"

"Honest? Say," Asey said confidentially, "maybe we could make a deal, huh? I'd like to get something on Ward, myself. Suppose you give me back that century note, an' I'll give you back the small bills—but maybe you don't want to tell me."

"What I want is my money!" Leo held out the hundred dollar bill. "That's what I want! You give me the hundred in little bills, and I'll tell you the whole thing."

A few minutes later, Asey was in possession of some highly interesting facts.

Shortly after Ward arrived at the club that morning, he had come into the bar and ordered a rum punch to be taken to Mrs. Newell at exactly eleven-thirty. It was to have been accompanied by a piece of poetry, but that part had been abandoned when Leo proved incapable of memorizing it.

"All about old flames never dying, and stuff like that. But I couldn't remember it. So Ward said, 'Hell, man,'" Leo achieved a very passable imitation of Ward's sardonic tone, "'tell her it's an old Spanish custom that's being revived!'"

So, shortly before eleven-thirty, Leo put on a silver tray the rum punch he had compounded with such care, and set out to locate Mrs. Newell.

He got as far as the west hall when Ben Bunting appeared in a towering fury and ordered Leo summarily to go to the locker room and fetch his kitbag, at once.

"He was mad as hell, and in an awful rush, and he wouldn't listen to me when I tried to say I was busy,"

Leo explained. "I kept telling him I'd get the bag later, just as soon as I took the drink out to Mrs. Newell. And he said for me to fetch the bag, and he'd take the drink out to her—he said she'd just gone out to the beach, and he knew where she was. So I said okay. You don't," he concluded, "argue with the boss's son, see? So I gave him the tray, and I went and got his bag."

"What did he want with his bag?" Asey asked.

"Aw, I don't know. I don't know where he thought he was going, but he sure was in the hell of a hurry to get there. Between you and me," Leo winked, "I think he'd been having a fight with his old man. You know, it was Ben fell for Newell first, see? Then she ditched him for the commodore. Well, I got the bag, and he took out the drink, and then Ward come in here an hour or so ago, and give me that phoney to keep it all dark. The louse!"

"Did he say why he wanted to keep it a secret?"

"Oh, he had a lot of guff about how he used to know Newell pretty well, and how he'd just discovered she and the commodore was like that," Leo held up two fingers, "so he wanted to soft-pedal the drink and the poetry and all. And a lot of hot air about a guy not wanting to bust in on romance, and all. That's —well, it's about time, Henry." Leo frowned at the blond man who hurried in. "You call this three o'clock? Get to work on those dirty ash trays! So that's the story, sir."

"Know where Mrs. Newell is now?" Asey asked.

"I thought someone said she was sick, but Mr. French couldn't find her, so I guess she's gone over to the bazaar with everybody else. She's always on the move, she is."

Asey presented him with another bill.

"This twenty," he said, "is a retainin' fee. Let me know if you get any more offers about anythin'. Thanks, Leo."

Asey strolled out through the screen door to the front terrace of the club.

Snatches of tonnage figures of sunken convoy ships came to him from a portable radio carried by one of the sunburned pair from the lounge, who were now getting into an open roadster. The one with the ear trumpet said peevishly that Molly Coppinger had absolutely no respect for world crises, and the other shouted his agreement into the trumpet, and added that Molly would probably be running a damned bazaar if the world was invaded by Martians in rocket ships.

Their departure cleared the parking space of cars, except for a coupé with New York license plates and a Press card on the windshield, which was undoubtedly Ward's. The little red Austin was by the tennis court, and Dr. Cummings's sedan was parked beside Asey's Porter on the beach road.

Apparently, Asey thought, no one was doing any

guilty lingering to see what had become of Mrs. Newell.

He sat down next to a dried-up evergreen tree in a wooden tub on the top step of the terrace, and considered the situation.

Ross Ward had ordered the rum punch as a sentimental gesture, but Ward had nothing to do with the actual making of the drink.

Leo had made it, but you could hardly credit Leo either with brains enough or with the desire to insert any atrophine in it.

Ben Bunting, in a temper, had taken the drink out, but up to the time he met Leo in the corridor, Ben's mind had evidently been occupied only with a kitbag, and not with rum punches.

There were several ways of viewing Ward's effort to bribe Leo. Ward was either very, very bright, or very, very dumb, or else he was as naïve as Ben had been in his sunstroke diagnosis.

Then there were other problems. There was the problem of Humphrey Bunting, who had so curiously removed himself from the whole mess. And there was the problem of that little red Austin. Asey had investigated the little car while Dr. Cummings had been busy with Mrs. Newell. There wasn't a thing the matter with that car. Nothing loose or broken or missing that Mrs. Newell could have called him about.

Asey leaned against the wooden tub, and suddenly found himself looking into it, hard.

On the dry earth at the top was a brown cloth knitting bag.

Asey sat up.

It was Mrs. Newell's knitting bag, with strands of colored wool creeping out.

SIX.

LESS than half an hour before, that knitting bag was on a chair in the room whose door Dr. Cummings had firmly locked with the key there'd been so much to-do about.

What, Asey wondered, was the bag now doing in the tub?

Who put it there?

And why?

Asey got up quickly.

The bag certainly hadn't flown through a locked door and made a three point landing in that wooden tub all of its own accord. Someone put it there, and someone must have had a reason for the act. And certainly no one would ever come near the bag if he continued to sit there beside it, or if he gave any indication of knowing of its presence in the tub.

Asey went in through the French doors, and hurried along the west corridor to the little lounge where he had first seen the two sunburned men.

Almost before he could settle himself at the window, a beachwagon bounded over the oyster shell road from the boathouse, and ground to a stop in front of the club.

Ben Bunting leapt out from behind the wheel and took the terrace steps three at a time to the main entrance.

Almost immediately he emerged, laden with a kit-bag and a duffel bag and an assortment of coats and jackets and miscellaneous paper-wrapped bundles. Stopping by the wooden tub, he dumped everything down on the bricks, redistributed the clothes and the bundles, shifted the leather bag to his right hand and the canvas bag to his left.

And if Asey had not been watching the tub like a hawk, he never would have noticed that the brown knitting bag somehow disappeared during the course of the elaborate shiftings.

By the time that Asey got to the French doors, the beachwagon was bounding off in a cloud of dust along the shore lane.

Asey set out for his own roadster on a dead run.

The strip beyond the shore lane was a mess of pot-holes where the Town of Sketicket's annual construction binge had petered out, and he could easily catch up and discover just exactly what young Benny Bunting thought he was doing.

He was thankful, as he backed the roadster around, for the dust and for the beachwagon's curtained back. Both would prevent Ben from spotting the new Porter Bullet's chromium plate. Asey approved of the car, and he knew that he could overtake anything on wheels. But for trailing purposes, that glaring chromium finish had all the stealth and secrecy of a circus calliope.

He followed the beachwagon past the potholes and then just kept the car in sight along the main tarred road. A scant mile beyond Sketicket Center, Ben swerved off suddenly on an old rutted side road that led down the Cape.

Asey frowned.

With all the twists and turns in that lane, anyone but a blind child would catch on to the fact that he was being followed.

Slowing down, he watched Ben's choice of roads at the first fork, and then plunged his roadster into what the average person would have considered an impassable thicket. To Asey, it was simply a stretch of the old coach road.

He drove on, ignoring the branches and brambles that scratched at the chromium, and a stubborn scrub pine that smashed one of his headlights. He had no time to bother with such minor mishaps. What he wanted to do was to get to High Toss Hill in time to see where Benny Bunting was going next, and why.

He almost crowed when he reached the hill and found the beachwagon stopping, below and to his right, by the shore of a fresh water pond.

"Now, little one," Asey murmured as he parked

the Bullet in a clump of scrub oaks, "we'll see what you got on your mind!"

Very cautiously, keeping Ben in sight, he started down the hill.

This particular business was screwball, he thought as he edged around a patch of poison ivy. Ben's actions were silly, no matter how you chose to consider them. And when you figured that he was acting this way all because of Mrs. Newell's knitting bag, it smacked of insanity.

Clearly, Ben had known that the bag was in the evergreen tub, so the chances were that Ben had put it there himself. That meant that Ben must have entered that room where Mrs. Newell was with a pass key, just to steal the bag. Or else Ben had watched his chance and slipped in while Cummings was phoning his office, during the time that Asey himself was talking with Leo in the bar.

But the long and short of it was that Ben had gone to a considerable amount of trouble and taken a considerable amount of risk, all in order to bring that knitting bag here.

Knowing the contents, Asey couldn't imagine why he should feel impelled to do any such thing.

He covered the last lap of his downhill journey on his hands and knees, crawling through a maze of blackberry vines and low-bush blueberry bushes, and coming to a stop not twenty feet from where Ben

Bunting sat on the beachwagon's running board, investigating the contents of the knitting bag.

Asey had a score of ant bites and a cramp in his right leg before Ben finally stuffed Mrs. Newell's belongings back into her bag and carried it over to the sandy shore of the pond.

He stood there indecisively for several minutes, and twice he made a gesture as if he were about to hurl the bag out into the depths beyond the lily pads.

Then he put the bag down and hunted hurriedly through the pockets of his checked tweed jacket.

Then he pawed all through the brown knitting bag again.

Asey grinned.

Apparently, he thought, he was not the only person who was inclined to forget matches.

Ben walked over to the beachwagon and pushed his thumb down on the dashboard cigarette lighter. While it failed under repeated stabbings to produce even a slight glow, it did nevertheless succeed in evoking a heated and lurid flood of sea talk from Ben.

"Tch, tch!" Asey murmured, clicking his tongue. "Bury the bag, feller, an' be quick, before I turn into a livin' ant hill!"

Almost as if he had heard and were obeying, Ben started to dig a hole in the sand with a shovel he took from the back of the beachwagon.

In no time at all, the brown knitting bag was peacefully reposing under a good three feet of sand.

Then, with a final vicious stamp on the burial spot, Ben tossed the shovel back into the beachwagon.

"Damn!" he said in a loud voice. "Where *is* it?"

Asey, who was on the verge of rising up out of the ant hills, suddenly changed his mind.

Perhaps, instead of grabbing Ben at once and trying to force explanations from him, it might be wiser to remain in the background until Ben actually found the thing he was seeking. Because, to judge from the boy's tone of voice and the determined look on his face, Ben certainly intended to continue his search to the bitter end.

Asey speculated rapidly about the object Ben was after.

It couldn't of necessity be large in size, but it must loom important in Ben's mind to cause him to rush away to this lonely spot before opening the bag. And the thing couldn't be heavy, or Ben wouldn't have been fooled into thinking it was in the bag in the first place.

Mentally, Asey ran through a list of small light objects, and came to the conclusion that Ben was hunting for a note or a letter. It had to be something like that, for Mrs. Newell wouldn't have carried anything of great face value around in that sloppy brown bag that didn't even have a catch of any kind. A letter, Asey decided, seemed the best bet.

And well worth following up, too. A letter of such apparent importance to Ben might well cast some light on that sunstroke verdict, or maybe even on Humphrey Bunting's disappearance. In fact, almost anything that might turn up concerning the Bunting family ought to prove useful.

As Ben jumped suddenly into the beachwagon and kicked down on the starter, Asey began to wonder if he could ever manage to hustle back up the hill to his roadster before Ben drove out of sight.

He wiggled his cramped right leg and tentatively stretched it. The instant that beachwagon started moving, he was going to have to make an almighty dash, cramp or no cramp. There wouldn't even be time to take a quick scratch at the ant bites.

The noise of the racing motor effectively drowned out the sound of a footstep and of twigs that crackled behind him, but even as he struggled to raise his cramped body, Asey sensed the presence of someone waiting there in the background.

He even had a sense that a blow was falling, and made a superhuman effort to get to his feet.

And he would have succeeded, too, if his heel hadn't caught in a blackberry vine just as the blow fell.

It knocked him flat and dazed him, and his head spun like a top, and the pine trees and the pond and the moving beachwagon jumbled themselves into a kaleidoscope of green and blue and tan.

Then twigs crackled behind him, and then a woman screamed.

Asey's first coherent reaction, that Picklepuss and

her Minutewomen might again have inserted themselves into the picture, was dispelled when he recognized Clare Heath's voice.

"Ward!"

It was her voice, all right, with that same horrified note it had contained earlier when Mrs. Newell's body had been found.

"Ward, you never should have done that! What did you hit him with, your cane?"

Asey lay still while more bushes crackled.

"Ward, d'you hear me? You shouldn't have done this!"

"I didn't, infant," Ward said. "It was two other guys."

"Who?"

"Not having the eye of an eagle," Ward said, "I can't tell you with my accustomed accuracy. What I saw was largely a matter of moving bushes, without sex or form. Come on."

"Who could it have been?" Clare demanded.

"C," Ward said promptly.

"Who?"

"Well, A or Asey, is following B, or Ben—how well that works out, doesn't it? And A is, in turn, followed by an unknown, or C. C biffed him. C has now been scared off by us, and I doubt if he returns. Come on, will you?"

"Ward, wait! Why?"

"Why come on? Because I've no desire, my sweet,

to be the first to greet Comrade Mayo when he comes
to. He'd never believe it wasn't me that biffed him, not
in a hundred years. You don't, yourself. Do you, now?
You think I sneaked down this way and bashed him
with my cane. Don't you?"

"Well," Clare said hesitantly, "no. But I didn't see
anyone else. I thought we were the only ones following him. Where was this other person? Where did
he come from?"

"If we can trail Asey," Ward said, "so can someone
else. C did. C has now departed. And I am now departing. Come on."

"But, Ward, we were following Asey—was this person behind us?"

"For all we know, there was a virtual procession.
Come on!"

"Where did C go?" Clare demanded.

"My dear child, I don't know! Possibly he turned
into a robin redbreast and flew away, chirruping. I'd
like to do the same. If Mayo reacts to this the way
Barlo Spratt would, he'll thrust me into irons at once.
You're no use as a witness because you weren't with
me. And, as they say, vice versa. Come along before he
puts you into irons, too."

"Ward, we can't leave the man here like this! I can
see now that he's breathing, but—"

"Breathing," Ward said, "like a sturdy Percheron or
dray horse. The Codfish Sherlock has a head like a
steel trap. It says so in the papers. And a mere biff

never injured a steel trap. Barely raised a lump, as you'll see if you look. And now, I'm getting the hell out of here."

"But, Ward, how can you go? The coupé's stuck, and—"

"The coupé's more than stuck, infant. The coupé's busted. My God, I'd heard he drove that Porter like a fiend, and I'll concede that he does. I'll never follow him again unless I'm in a large Army tank, perferably driven by De Palma. Come on. Start walking. You'll get used to it before we reach West Gusset."

"I can't go," Clare said. "I can't, Ward! It would simply prey on me to leave him this way. I'm going to wait and make sure he's all right."

"Dear child," Ward spoke in the tones of one goaded beyond endurance, "this inert lad is one of the best little ferreters in the business. He's already marked me down on his list for some fancy ferreting. Now it may be that your past is like the driven snow, and you've nothing to hide. But I've no desire to have my obsolete foibles hauled forth for dissection by the Codfish Sherlock. The man's really uncanny, Clare. He picks flaws and weak spots by instinct. And his timing's incredible. He just happens on things. See what he's happened on today! I'm now departing to send that damned barman on an extended cruise of South America. Good-by. I've warned you."

"Whatever did you bribe him for, anyway?" Clare asked. "I think you were terribly silly!"

Ward sighed.

"It turns out I was, but I didn't think so at the time. Be charitable, child, we all err as we age. I only hope to God that Mayo didn't get around to pumping that weak-jawed idiot!" Ward's cane tip thumped the ground. "I wish I'd taken the chance and hung around! I wish I'd never let myself be distracted by this wild-goose chase! I wish—"

"I wish," Clare said, "you'd done what I suggested, and told Asey all about that drink in the first place, instead of bribing Leo, and all!"

"To have been that guileless," Ward said, "would have taxed me more than Mayo. Only the very young can say innocent things innocently. I'm now going to see Leo, and—"

"Please, Ward, don't go! Stay, and tell him the whole story!"

"It would have such a peachy sound," Ward said, "wouldn't it? 'Dear Asey, in a fit of temporary madness, I bribed the barman not to tell you that I ordered a rum punch sent out to Lucia on the beach this morning. It was purely a sentimental gesture, and truly, if anyone put poison in that drink, it must have been someone else!' Mayo'd believe every word, wouldn't he?"

"Well, if it's the truth, it's the truth," Clare said, "and you can't help how silly it sounds. I wish you'd stay!"

"Nuh-uh. But—look, infant, maybe it would be best

if you did. There's no reason for Mayo to suspect or pump you. You stay and look after him. Tell him I've gone for help. That'll give me time to settle Leo. You owe me something, after the way you let me down with Ben Bunting. Honestly, didn't you get anywhere with him? Didn't you find out a thing?"

"I don't think he even saw me or heard me, or knew I was there talking to him. He was too busy brooding."

"Something in the way you say that," Ward said, "leads me to believe that you don't often lick the dust. Where was your pride?"

"I am not," Clare returned, "through with him yet! You wait and see! And if you want to sneak away, really, you'd better go. I think Asey just moved—"

The bushes crackled as Ward turned and hurried off.

As soon as the sound of his footsteps had died away, Asey rolled over on his back and then sat up, tailor fashion, with his knees crossed.

"So you were faking!" Clare said. "I thought so a long while ago. You wiggled."

"I was scratchin'," Asey said. "For genuine comfort, don't ever choose a hill of red ants to eavesdrop in."

"Why did you?"

"I didn't choose the place," Asey said. "It was forced on me."

"I mean, why did you eavesdrop? Did you hear everything?"

"Uh-huh," Asey said, "an' all very enlightenin' it was. Ward done very well."

"Asey, d'you mean to say you think he knew you were faking, all the time?"

"Whether he did or didn't, he sure got his points across," Asey said. "Is his car really broken down?"

"We followed you," Clare said, as though that explained everything.

"Coach road too much for his car, huh?"

"I don't know if it was what you laughingly call a road," Clare said, "or the speed we burst through it. Anyway, the coupé's jammed between two pine trees with all the underpinning falling out like a gored bull." She hesitated. "Er—we *really* didn't have anything to do with your being knocked out, you know. That was someone else. We were following you, but so was someone else."

"C," Asey said. "I know. C, as for Clare."

"But I never hit you! Neither did Ward! He didn't have time after we separated coming down the hill. I was nearer you than he was. Hadn't I better rush after him and howl at him to go back with us? Er— you are taking us back with you, aren't you?"

Asey grinned.

"It'll give me pleasure to drive you, but I think a nice four-mile walk'll be good for Ward. Whet his vocabulary somethin' spectacular, I bet."

"But his leg! He's getting over that wound he got

in France. He really shouldn't walk that far," Clare said. "And besides, he doesn't know the way!"

"His yesterday's article on Cape Cod," Asey reminded her, "had a real ornate map of this section alongside it, an' a description of all the quaint ole highways an' byways. I think he'll most likely manage, providin' he takes the trouble to read his own stuff."

"It is terrible, isn't it?" Clare said.

"Wa-el," Asey said, "I s'pose in all charity you could say it'd make good advertisin' copy for a tea shoppe, or some quaint ole inn. How come he's writin' such stuff, anyhow? I can't seem to hitch up these junky Cape articles of his with the sort of person he is."

"Neither can I," Clare said. "Those articles simply drip. They reek. He says himself that the stuff stinks, and he does nothing but make fun of the Cape. But he gets paid fabulous sums, and I suppose that's all he cares about. Asey, what made you follow Ben Bunting like that? We were so startled to see you dashing down the terrace steps after him!"

Asey got to his feet.

"It kind of startled me, too. Did you happen to notice which way he turned when he left?"

"Over there to the right, I think," Clare said. "What did he come here for?"

"Didn't you see the performance?" Asey asked.

"No, he was just getting into the beachwagon when we came over the top of the hill. We lost loads of time finding your car after ours got stuck, and loads more finding which way you'd gone after we finally found your roadster. What was this all about?"

"A knittin' bag," Asey said, "which I s'pose I might as well stop an' dig up right now, though I hadn't intended to. If Ben turned right, he's goin' back to Sketicket Center. Huh. Now I wonder if maybe his next logical stop wouldn't be where Mrs. Newell stayed. I think it would."

And there, Asey thought, Ben would run into the obstacle of Picklepuss and the rest of her cohorts. He couldn't do any hunting with those women around, which meant that Ben would have to cool his heels until they departed.

"You mean that Sludgeberry place where she lived?" Clare asked unexpectedly.

"Thackaberry. Sadie Thackaberry's. How in time did you happen to know she lived there?"

"Oh," Clare said, "Ward phoned there five times yesterday, trying to get hold of Mrs. Newell. The woman who answered is deaf, and screams at the top of her lungs when she talks on the phone. You could hear her in the next room. Ward got so mad. He called her everything from Sludgeberry to Checkerberry—can't I help you wipe those ants and things off your collar?"

Asey took off his jacket and held it out to her.

"I think it needs more than a little wipin'," he said. "You might give it a beatin' while I dig up that knittin' bag."

"That's what it sounded like before," Clare said. "Did you really say you were going to dig up a knitting bag?"

"Uh-huh," Asey said. "Mrs. Newell's bag, that Ben swiped from the club, an' brought here an' then buried when he couldn't find what he thought was in it."

"But what did he *bury* it for?"

"Wa-el," Asey said, "largely because he was fresh out of matches, an' I think the prospect of puttin' the bag back where he got it was a problem he didn't feel up to solvin'. So Ward was huntin' Mrs. Newell yesterday, was he?"

He had deliberately refrained from pursuing the topic when Clare brought it up, and he tried hard to make his question casual.

But Clare paused in her task of brushing off his jacket and informed him coldly that he wasn't being fair.

"You make it sound as though Ward tracked her with bloodhounds, and as a matter of fact, he didn't even know she was on Cape Cod till he found her name in the phone book."

Asey, as he started to dig the sand off the bag's grave, suggested dryly that that was a customary procedure.

"You know how it is," he said. "You take a name, an' pick up a phone book, an' hunt around till you find the name. An' there you are. It happens every day."

"Look, Asey," Clare said, "Ward was just sitting down reading the phone book, and he happened to find her name, and her address at this Thackaberry Homestead, and so he telephoned her! He seemed terribly pleased to find her name. If you want to know, he said, 'By God, good old Lucia! I'd lost track of good old Lucia!'"

"I s'pose," Asey scooped away at the sand, "a feller like Ward, he just often sits an' reads through phone books, huh? Makes a pretty picture. I like to think of him, sittin' an' readin' phone books from Maine to California."

Clare giggled.

"You do make things sound so foolish! But that's just what he was doing. Just sitting and aimlessly reading the Cape phone book. I don't think it meant anything more than that he'd exhausted all the old magazines at our boarding house. His comments on the *Old Farmer's Almanac* were pretty choice and precious."

"He's a funny fellow, isn't he?" Asey decided to try another tack.

"He's amusing," Clare said, "and he really knows lots about the Cape. He's dug out all sorts of fascinating tidbits of information."

"I wonder why he doesn't use 'em in his articles," Asey said, "instead of that junk?"

"I'll never understand!" Clare said. "When I think of all the odd places he's scanned through his binoculars in the last few days, and all the questions he's asked, and all the nooks and crannies he's driven around! And then he just bangs out that drippy tripe!"

Asey glanced at her quickly.

"You know," he said thoughtfully, as he scooped out a handful of sand, "ever since I met Ward, I kept askin' myself what he was really doin' here. Of course, I suppose he makes a heap of money for these Cape articles, but it don't seem to me that's all he's here for. He could make more money doin' somethin' else, a man of his reputation."

Clare walked right into it.

"Isn't it funny?" she said. "His hiring me is awfully funny, too, I think. Of course it's a stroke of luck for me, but I still can't understand why he didn't hire a regular illustrator. Someone with real experience in this sort of work. I've never done anything like this before, you know. I usually get fashion jobs."

"That so?" Asey said. "There, I think I've reached this bag at last! So you don't do scenery as a general thing?"

Clare shook her head. "But Ward told the agency that he wanted something different, and he told me when he interviewed me that at least I wasn't a world-weary hag, and I ought to have a fresh slant even on something as perennially trite and stereotyped as Cape Cod. I must say," she added, "he's certainly not troubling himself to write any fresh angles. What do you think he's really here for?"

Asey shrugged.

"Wa-el," he said, "last Sunday's tabloids said there was a dope ring operatin' in New England. Maybe he's on the trail of that."

"I'm sure he isn't," Clare said. "He mentioned that story and said the man who wrote it had practically earned a living writing dope ring scares, and white-slave stories, and things like that."

"Well," Asey said, "what do you think he's up to?"

"I don't know, Asey. But he's up to something. I think he's hunting something important. Nothing that has anything to do with Mrs. Newell at all, either. Because he honestly didn't know she was here till yesterday afternoon. But I keep getting this funny feeling—I don't know how to explain it. It's—well, when you start in on an Oppenheim book, and an inconspicuous man in tweeds and a Homburg hat enters a first-class railway carriage and nervously pulls down the shades, you just instinctively know he's fleeing with a bunch of secret treaties, and that very shortly things are going to start popping. You get this sense of—of—"

"Impendin' action?" Asey suggested as Clare groped for words.

"I think that's it. That's more or less what I've been feeling since I joined him. A sense of impending action. On the surface, he's simply writing articles and I'm illustrating 'em. But I keep feeling that something's going on underneath. On the other hand, Asey, it may just be Ward himself. He can't even order a cup of coffee without making it sound like the first act of a melodrama."

Asey grinned.

"Like the continued stories you hear on the radio in the mornin's," he said.

"There! Now you've put your finger on it! Did you ever listen to the adventures of Nicolette Murphy?"

"She the nurse?" Asey thrust his arm deep down into the hole he had scooped away in the sand, and tugged at the knitting bag. "You know, this process is kind of like diggin' clams without the benefit of a clam hoe. Is Nicolette the nurse with the broken heart?"

"No, Nicolette's the artist who's married to a Georgian prince who's conspiring to destroy the entire United States Navy," Clare said. "If my Aunt Kate doesn't hear her daily dollop of Nicolette, she counts that day lost—can't I help you grub around?"

"I got it loosened up now, I think. Ben was feelin' so violent, he packed the sand down pretty hard with that shovel of his," Asey said. "Yup, I recall Nicolette, now. She was my Cousin Jennie's favorite some time this spring. Really loves the coxswain of the cap'n's gig of the U.S.S. *Albuquerque*, don't she? There! There it is!"

Clare surveyed with obvious disappointment the

well-sanded brown knitting bag which Asey held up for her inspection.

"I must say," she remarked, "that there's very little Nicolette Murphy glamour about that! And to think that Ben Bunting rushed off here, and you rushed after him, and we rushed after you, all for that! And you said what Ben was after wasn't in it, anyway! Really, the whole episode hasn't *advanced* anything, has it?"

"Wa-el," Asey said, "in one sense, no. S'pose we hike back to the car."

But at least, he privately amended, his suspicions about Ross Ward had advanced. He felt sure that if Ward were engaged in bona fide work, Ward would have hired a regular illustrator. Not an inexperienced child, however charming and competent she might be. Ward wouldn't be writing that trash if he were really being paid any enormous sums. Ward was using his articles on the Cape as a blind. And if you looked on the situation at its face value, disregarding Clare's natural tendency to swing all the evidence in Ward's favor, it certainly looked as if Lucia Newell entered somewhere into Ward's machinations. That little item of finding her name while reading aimlessly through the phone book, Asey thought, was only one of many little items he found hard to swallow.

"You know," Clare said suddenly, "you'll probably scream with laughter, but I have a—oh, dear, is that all poison ivy?"

"We'll cut around it," Asey said. "You have a what that I'll scream with laughter at?"

"Well, I guess it's a theory," Clare said. "I've been thinking about Mrs. Newell and all. I told Ward, and he simply howled. But I still think it was that fat man."

"What fat man?"

"The nasty one that ordered Ward and me off the beach. Awfully snoopy, bossy sort. And fat as a pig. You must know who he is. He has sort of waterglass eyes."

"I can't place him," Asey said. "The only fat man I remember at the club had an ear trumpet an' a red face, an' was in his sixties. But—oh, I do know who you mean. You mean Dudley French."

"Well," Clare said, "I think he's responsible for Mrs. Newell. I think he killed her."

Asey stopped short and looked at her.

"Why on earth do you pick on him?"

"His eyes," Clare said simply. "I never trust people with those waterglass eyes. You know. That pale gray-blue kind. He probably was in love with Mrs. Newell, and she turned him down."

"I hate to break the news to you, Nicolette," Asey said, "but as a matter of fact, Dudley French is Mrs. Newell's cousin."

"I knew you'd make fun of me, too," Clare said. "Just the same, I think he killed her. He *looks* like a villain. He's the only person around who does, too.

And he was so snoopy and nasty. He's just the sort of person who'd kill someone. Was Mrs. Newell very rich? Maybe it'll turn out that she was going to leave him money, if she was a relation."

Asey chuckled.

"Your Nicolettin' would work out better," he said, "if French wasn't the rich one, an' Mrs. Newell the poor one. Poor in comparison, that is. She wasn't what you'd call an object of charity, but this war put a considerable crimp in her finances. She was tellin' me about it a few weeks ago. Her house in France got bombed to bits, along with most of the stuff she owned. An' what money she had in banks abroad was pretty well froze for keeps. No, I agree with you that if you could pick by looks alone, French'd make a nice villain in the Charles Laughton manner. But I don't think there's a chance he is. Better circle that clump of poison ivy."

"I still think," Clare said as she skirted the ivy, "that I'm right. Maybe, if he's so rich and she was short of cash, she tried to borrow money from him. Maybe she was being a poor relation, and he got tired of helping her. I mean, you always read about rich men being killed for their money, but I keep wondering why it shouldn't be the other way around. Like the rich one killing the poor one who's trying to get his money away."

"It's a refreshin' idea," Asey said. "Man bites dog."

"How did French make his money?" Clare asked.

"Whew, I'm pooped! He certainly doesn't look like a businessman."

"He got his money left him," Asey said. "Want to wait a sec an' catch your breath?"

"Yes. For a small hill, this is tough climbing. All this stuff underfoot. Do you ever feel you're being watched, Asey?" she asked unexpectedly.

"I have," Asey said. "Why? Do you feel you're bein' watched now?"

"Ever since you dug up that bag," Clare said, "I've felt as if someone was staring at me. Asey, this person that Ward called C. What happened to him? Who was he? I can't see how he could follow you very well without following us, because we were more or less right behind you. And if he followed us, how did he get to you before we did? And where's he gone? Where'd he go? Who is he? And why did he hit you?"

"Wa-el," Asey said, "I thought your first impulse was Ward, himself."

"Oh, it wasn't! I mean, *I* did think he hit you at first, but I'm sure now that he didn't. I didn't stop to consider, at first, that there could be someone else. Asey, who is this person? Why did he *hit* you?"

"You know," Asey said, "you raise an interestin' point that I hadn't considered. Why did he *hit* me? Why didn't he keep on with his shootin'? He was gettin' real warm."

"Keep on? You mean you've been shot at? Why?"

"Wa-el," Asey said, "you can't ever tell why people

shoot at you. May be that they want to kill you, may be that someone promised 'em a box of cigars for nickin' your ear. Huh. Now I wonder, if it was that feller that potted at me this mornin', why would he give up his long-range tactics? He was doin' all right, an' this is an ideal place for pottin'. Ssh a sec, an' let me think. It might be that he wouldn't want to let Ben hear the sound of a shot. But Ben didn't know I was there, an' a shot in the distance wouldn't have moved him much. Even if Ben'd troubled to look around, the feller could have been over the hills an' far away long before Ben found me among the ants. You know what I think?"

"In all honesty," Clare said, "I don't even understand what you're talking about."

"I think," Asey said, "that he didn't have his pop-gun with him. That's why he was closin' in. It's the only explanation, considerin' what an elegant setup he had for his rifle. Now, let's see. I didn't hear the feller till he was quite near me, because Ben was racin' the beachwagon's engine. I wonder if that engine didn't drown out the sound of you an' Ward for him. My twistin' kind of spoiled his blow, an' before he could biff me again, he realized you an' Ward was in the vicinity."

"But he must have known we were there," Clare said. "How could he possibly have followed us, and not known we were there?"

"That's just it. I don't think he followed you. I

think he was here all the time. That's why he didn't
have his gun. He wasn't expectin' me. He couldn't
have expected me. I didn't know I was goin' to be here
myself, till I arrived."

"But why would anyone be *here?* Here, in this godforsaken—Asey, look over there, quick! Someone
moved! Look!"

Asey took her arm and turned her around.

"I'm gettin' you jittery," he said. "You—"

"I'm not jittery! I saw someone move! In those
bushes, over there to the left of the pond. Come on!
Let's see who—"

"No," Asey said firmly. "No tag!"

"Why not? Don't you want to find out who this
person *is?*"

"Sure I do! But this neck of the woods ain't a good
place for impulsive pursuin'. With all these miles of
rut roads that look alike, an' all the underbrush for a
screen, we could play tag till doomsday, an' never get
anywhere."

"Asey, you know there's someone lurking around!
And you want to find out who! There are two of us!
We could ambush him!"

"Uh-huh," Asey said, "providin' he didn't ambush
us first. If this was some other terrain, an' if I had a
gun, I might chance a game of tag. But our best
course, youngster, is to go along back to the village an'
tell the cops to take a look. I know too much about

this area to think I could win any tag games here by myself, or with you."

"But—"

Asey started to propel her up the hill toward the car.

"Believe me," Asey said, "this is a place where I know best!"

"Oh, I suppose you do, but it's so exasperating! And how do you happen to know this region so well? Ward wondered when we were following you."

Asey grinned.

"This region," he said, "was a great source of anguish an' confusion to the cops durin' prohibition days. The rum trucks used to use these roads gettin' to an' from the shore. Some of those drivers could pull a truck through here without lights in a howlin' storm, switchin' from road to road like they was on a four lane turnpike. Once in a while I used to help chase the boys when they got too fresh. It was sort of fun, tearin' around after 'em, an' I sort of got to know the lay of the land."

"What sinister fun!" Clare said. "But you don't always tear, do you? Ward said so, but I didn't believe him."

"Except on back roads I know," Asey said, "I don't drive so awful fast. On main roads, I been known to poke along in a very dignified fashion."

"Like when I passed you yesterday," Clare said. "Did you hear me yell about snails?"

"You passed me yesterday? When?"

"Oh, in the afternoon around four or so. On that narrow strip by the beach in Orleans. You were crawling like a snail and simply hogging the whole road, and I was hurrying back with a sketch Ward wanted. I was simply frothing before I got by."

"I was fishin' all yesterday afternoon," Asey said. "Must have been another Porter. Get in, youngster, an' let's start back—"

"I'd swear it was this car," Clare said. "I— Look! Look, quick! There he is!"

Asey swung around just in time to see the figure of a man dart over the ridge beyond the pond.

"There!" Clare said. "There *is* someone, and now he thinks we're leaving, so he is, too! Asey, couldn't you possibly circle around some way, if you know this region so well? You don't have to come to blows with him, but you certainly oughtn't to lose the chance of finding out who he is! Can't you sneak around somehow and take a look at him?"

"Yes," Asey said slowly, "I think I could. I could head off to the left, an' watch as he crossed the far lane. Only—"

"Oh, go on, and stop worrying about me! That's what's bothering you, isn't it? Well, don't think about me! I'm perfectly all right. Hurry up and at least see who this man is! You'd go if you were alone, wouldn't you?"

"Wa-el, yes," Asey admitted. "Now that he seems

to be retreatin', I think that maybe perhaps I might. But you—"

"Never mind about me! Look, I'll sit right here in the car with my hand on the horn," Clare said, "and if anyone comes this way, I'll blow it. No one wants *me*, Asey! No one cares about me! No one knows me! I don't know a soul on the Cape! I'm perfectly safe! Now, you hurry after him!"

"Well," Asey said hesitatingly, "I guess maybe I will take just a look. Fish around in that glove compartment, will you, an' see if there's a pair of binoculars?"

"Here!" Clare held them out. "Now, hurry up before he goes!"

"Will you promise me that you won't stir out of the car? You'll just sit there with your hand on the horn?"

"Yes, yes! Get on!"

Asey started away, and then turned back.

"Better still," he said, "start the car. Here's the keys. Starter button's the red one. Keep her runnin'. If you catch sight of anyone, blow the horn, an' start movin'. Okay?"

"Yes, yes, yes! Will you hurry!"

When Asey returned less than five minutes later, Mrs. Newell's brown knitting bag was on the seat of the roadster.

So was his blue jacket. So was Clare's small, blue-checked gingham purse.

And the engine was running.

But there was no sign of Clare.

SEVEN.

FIFTEEN minutes later, Asey sat down dejectedly on the narrow running board of his roadster.

His throat was dry from constant calling out, his shoes and ankles were scratched from the acres of prickly vines he had trampled through. Both knees of his once white flannels were torn, and his left arm was bleeding from cuts in half a dozen places where he had yanked aside overhanging brambles.

There was no sign of the girl. No trace of her. No clew as to where she might have gone, or how she might have gone. There was nothing to indicate whether she had slipped away of her own accord, or whether she had been snatched away.

If she had blown off in a puff of wind, Asey decided, she couldn't have vanished more completely.

There was always the chance that she might have slipped away by herself, of course. She had been more than anxious for him to leave. She might have been urging him to go just to create for herself the opportunity of sliding out of the picture.

And if this had happened at any other spot, Asey

thought, you might feel justified in shrugging and saying that she just wanted to run out on you.

But not here.

Not in this place, where natives who had lived all their lives three miles away in Sketicket often got lost during the blueberrying season. Not in this maze of lanes, this mess of underbrush and scrub oaks and scrub pines. In following him here with Ward, the girl had arrived by a tortuous and circuitous route. Asey doubted if she even knew in what direction the village lay. She could always locate herself by the sun, but from Asey's experience with summer visitors and tourists, he knew that an ability to point to the west rarely aided anyone much in locating things. People always forgot how the Cape hooked around.

Asey reached over and picked up the little checked purse.

Despite its minute size, it contained a lipstick, a handkerchief, half a package of cigarettes, a flap of paper matches, six one-dollar bills tightly bunched together, and forty-two cents in change.

Nothing spectacular, Asey thought as he stuffed the contents back and snapped the purse shut. On the other hand, it was nothing for the girl to leave behind had she actually planned to rush off alone.

He shook his head.

It was still possible that she had done just that. As the doctor always maintained, you couldn't tell what a woman might do next. But when you added this left-behind purse to her ignorance of the region, such a possibility looked very slim indeed.

But if the girl had seen someone, why hadn't she blown the horn, or started to drive off, as he'd told her to?

There was enough of a clearing near the car for her to have seen anyone approaching. With the car's two side mirrors and the rear-view mirror, she could practically have stared straight ahead and still have been able to see in all directions. She never could have been taken by surprise!

From that point on, Asey thought wearily, all speculations went haywire.

Certainly Clare wouldn't have gone away like a willing lamb with the first stranger who showed his nose. But if she'd been taken away by force, why wasn't there some trace of a struggle? Why hadn't the girl sounded the horn, or made some noise, or let out a few good screams? To cart an able-bodied girl like Clare away against her will would have been no cinch of a job.

And where had she been taken to? And who took her? And how had it all been managed?

And if she had just marched off willingly with someone, who was it? And where had they gone?

Asey sighed.

There was only one conclusion he could reach concerning the whole strange business, and that reflected very little credit on himself and on his thought processes.

"You're a fool, Mayo!" he told himself bitterly. "A dummed old fool!"

For, no matter whether the girl had gone away willingly or unwillingly, the fact remained that he had been taken in by just about the oldest trick in the world.

Just because it took only one man to biff him over the head, he had proceeded on the dumb assumption that only one person was lurking about.

There had been two, and maybe more.

And one had been deliberately planted over on the ridge.

"So you'd see the feller, you numbwit!" Asey murmured, "an' go trailin' after him. Leavin' the coast clear for anyone to do what they wanted with Clare."

It was an almighty wonder, he thought, that someone hadn't brought out a baby for him to hold.

He got up, slung his binocular strap over his shoulder, and strode to the tallest of the surrounding pines.

His shirt was torn and his hands covered with pine pitch by the time he achieved the top, where he balanced precariously and slowly scanned the surrounding landscape.

He was presenting a grand target for anyone who might be watching him from under cover, but he was too annoyed with himself to care.

But he could see only what he had seen before,

acres of underbrush and scrub without any sign of
Clare or anyone else.

Then, just as he braced his foot to climb down, he
spotted a gray-clad figure emerging from the bushes
onto one of the roads near by.

It was Ross Ward.

Asey watched through the glasses as Ward paused
and swabbed at his face, and looked rather apprehen-
sively behind him as if he expected someone to jump
out of the bushes and follow him.

Then he limped on towards the hill where Asey
waited.

He stopped, as the lane he was on suddenly crossed
off on another, and stood pensively eyeing the fork.

In a moment, he walked off to the right.

Then he slowly retraced his steps and picked the
other road.

Then, after a few yards, he sat down, took what
seemed to be a map out of his pocket, and studied it.

Then he squinted up at the sun, rolled the map
into a ball and threw it as far as he could send it.

Finally he walked on in a tentative fashion, as if he
really didn't care a hoot which road he took, but was
pretty equally bored with all of them.

If Ward was not good and lost, Asey thought, he
was putting on a very good pantomime of a man who
was.

It flashed through his mind suddenly that if Ward
had appeared by the roadster, it was entirely possible

that Clare would neither have blown the horn nor called out. Probably, if Ward had beckoned to her, she would have followed him without hesitation.

Asey's eyes narrowed, and he considered the situation as Ward limped up the near slope of the hill toward him.

After several fruitless circlings, Ward caught sight of the roadster and stopped short.

"Thank God!" he said feelingly, and marched over to it.

He punched at the horn half a dozen times, and then sat down on the leather seat and lighted a cigarette.

By the time Asey returned to the car, Ward had both shoes off and was draped across the seat as if it were a sofa.

Ward surveyed him from head to foot, and then he shuddered.

"Go away!" he said. "Mother told me never to talk with tramps."

"So?" Asey said.

"If you don't mind my saying so," Ward continued, "you don't look as much of a Hayseed as a Sewer Sleuth. Aren't you a mess!"

"Uh-huh. Have you," Asey asked, "seen Clare?"

Ward sat up.

"Isn't she with you? I left her with you."

"She was."

"Where is she now?" Ward demanded.

Asey shook his head. "I don't know. Haven't you seen any sight of her?"

"No! Is she lost? How'd you lose her? What happened?"

"Wa-el," Asey said, "move over an' let me sit down, an' I'll tell you."

Ward moaned gently at the conclusion of his story.

"Observe, gentlemen," he said, "that my left hand is absolutely empty. Watch my left hand, gentlemen. Watch it!"

"I know," Asey said. "Don't rub it in."

"They must have coined money off you in the pea-and-shell games at county fairs," Ward said. "Oh, my! I don't know if you discourage me or if you renew my faith in human nature. At least you prove that the brightest of us fall. Only you shouldn't have. Who's got her, Mayo?"

"Are you sure," Asey said, "that you haven't?"

"Me? I? Be reasonable, man!" Ward said. "There's only one of me. I couldn't have enticed you away and taken her, too! And look at my poor tired feet! No man with feet in this condition could go in for active villainy. Asey, who's got her?"

"Honest, I don't know!" Asey said. "I can't understand any of this. You sure she don't know anybody on the Cape?"

"Only some callow youths at our Inn, who made sheep eyes at her. But they'd never be here—er—you don't suppose she rushed off to powder her chin, or anything like that, do you? In which case," Ward said, "it's possible that your antics and screaming about for her might have caused her some acute embarrassment. Yes, I know it's a crazy suggestion, but it might conceivably account for her leaving her purse and not raising any din. By God, Asey, that's queer, her not uttering a sound!"

Asey nodded.

"I think," he said, "you can even go so far's to call it queer-plus. Here's the girl in the car here. She's on the lookout, she's on the alert, she knows there's someone about, she's got her hand right on this horn. She can't miss seein' anyone. You'd think she'd have beat a tattoo on this horn, no matter who loomed in sight. Even if it was one of those crazy fool coincidences that happens once in a billion years, an' the person that loomed turned out to be her Aunt Kate, you'd still think she'd have made a lot of noise about it, just out of sheer surprise! You'd—"

"Wait!" Ward said excitedly. "I've got it! I know what happened!"

"What?"

"It *was* a woman!"

"You mean," Asey said, "on the theory that Clare wouldn't raise the racket at the sight of a strange woman that she might have raised at the sight of a strange man?"

"I'm sure it was a woman. I know it was a woman. That's the answer, Asey. Clare saw a woman."

"What makes you so sure?" Asey asked curiously.

"Because," Ward said, "I saw a woman, myself. In fact, I saw two women. In fact, I frightened 'em, and they chased me. They chased me, furthermore, brandishing guns. That's how I happened to get lost."

"Women with guns?" Asey winced. "Ward, tell me you're makin' this up as you go along! Not women with guns!"

"That's right. They chased me. It was about fifteen minutes after I left you and Clare by the pond. There were two women with guns—"

"Oh," Asey said, "those nuts! Those—those women! I was so sure I had the whole caboodle of 'em bottled up for the day. I was so sure I had 'em all out of the way! Huh! Now I wonder, could it be the two that set out to track down the feller they saw on the dunes! What did they look like, Ward? Were they natives?"

"What do you mean, were they natives?" Ward said. "How in the name of God can you tell natives from non-natives? D'you expect 'em to be wearing sarongs, and a couple of hibiscus flowers over one ear?"

"Were they local women? You can tell 'em," Asey said, "most always. They wear more clothes than tourists, an' they're usually sunburned instead of tanned black. What did this pair look like?"

"My dear man, they might have been local girls, or they might have been a couple of schoolteachers from Kokomo, or the daughters of a retired bishop! I don't know! I was simply tramping along toward the village, minding my own business and whistling as I tramped, and I turned a corner, and here were these two females!"

"What happened? Did you hold any conversation with 'em?" Asey asked.

"They looked at me," Ward said, "let out blood-thirsty yells, and aimed rifles at me. Whereupon I prudently turned and fled. They yelled some more and raced after me, and sometime during the ensuing chase I became thoroughly lost. That's how I happened to wander the hell back here, you see. It had been easy enough to tell my way when I started from the pond, but once I lost that road, I was done for. My highways and byways map wasn't any good. I didn't know what lane I was on, or where it went."

Asey looked at him quizzically.

"So you figured that you must have scared these women, an' that's why you got chased with all that vigor?"

"I assumed as much," Ward said. "Of course, one never knows. It might all have been due to my devastating charm. I mean, they may have been chasing me for myself alone, so to speak."

Asey chuckled.

"What I'm aimin' at, Ward, is why did you cut an' run?"

"Insinuating," Ward said, "that in the face of two armed dervishes, I should have stood my ground, bowed from the waist, and inquired politely as to the state of their health? Pooh!"

"Why did you let yourself be chased?"

"It's my invariable custom," Ward said, "to avoid the other sex when they're armed. Hell hath no fury like an armed woman. My mother told me that in my cradle. I didn't *let* myself be chased, Asey! I was merely actively evading two women with guns. That they had the effrontery to follow me was no part of my plan! I could hardly help it if they chose to turn my strategic retreat into a rout!"

"You seem to take all of this," Asey said, "as a matter of course. Didn't you think it was sort of unusual, bein' pursued by women with guns?"

"After what I've seen since Poland," Ward said, "it takes more than a couple of armed women to upset me beyond the mere effort of running away. I don't seem to question things as I once did. In Belgium, for example, I was chased by a gentleman of the Luftwaffe who pepped up the proceedings with machine-gun bullets. I didn't pause to shout up at him and ask him why or wherefore. I didn't quietly ponder the situation any more than I did this. I simply departed with all possible haste. Do I make my point?"

"As an old point-maker," Asey said, "you got few equals. Now, I wonder—"

"These women are the answer to Clare," Ward said. "They've wafted her away. Asey, you know something about these women, don't you?"

"Uh-huh. But I can't figure out why in time they'd wander here an' entice Clare away! On the other hand, they've mixed themselves up with so much today, you couldn't be sure that they aren't mixed up in this."

"Who *are* they?" Ward asked. "What goes on? Weren't there some women wandering around the Yacht Club, too? I sent Clare inside to ask you if I hadn't heard a shot, but I couldn't make head nor tail of what she said you told her. What *is* all this?"

"Wa-el," Asey said, "it's the Female Division of the League to Defend America at all Costs with Action."

"The *what?* Oh, wait, I know! It's Rounceval Jones's brainchild, isn't it? The Militant Housewifery, or something. But what are these misbeguided home-makers up to, Asey?"

Briefly, Asey summed up their activity to date.

"Oh, hell, then they're the answer all right!" Ward said. "The girls probably decided that Clare was a beautiful spy of some foreign power, all set to lure you from the path of duty with her wicked, wanton wiles. It's just exactly the sort of thing they'd think of. Let's track 'em down, Asey, and get Clare back before they tie her up in a cellar in the Oppenheim manner!"

Asey considered.

"I was plannin'," he said, "to go back to the village an' phone for a batch of state cops to do some professional scourin'. But if these women really pulled this in a frenzy of enthusiasm an' patriotism, we'd probably do better to get the girl back from 'em ourselves. Huh. I suppose that the fellow I tried to spot with the binoculars—"

"By the way," Ward interrupted, "you didn't say whether or not you caught a glimpse of him. Did you?"

"Uh-huh. One of those awful enlightenin' glimpses," Asey said, "of a head with a cap on it, disappearin' around a bend in a lane. I never could have caught up with him, even if I'd had the car. Huh. I suppose he might just have been departin', like I thought at first, an' the girls just happened to come on my car an' Clare at that particular time while I was away. But it's kind of strainin' coincidence, Ward, just the same."

"From what you've told me of the Minutewomen with your own lips," Ward said, "I don't think they'd balk at straining coincidence! I think they'd strangle coincidence with their bare hands, if they happened to get the chance! Come on, Asey, let's get after the girls!"

"Think you could ever lead me back to where you saw 'em?"

"I don't see why not," Ward said. "The road I was on led directly from the pond. We might as well have a try. Tell me," he added as Asey started the car, "about this region. These roads around here and this region seem familiar to me. I seem to remember being here before. Wasn't Alex Moriarty's old dance joint somewhere in this vicinity? The Casa—what was the name? Casa Something."

"Casa Valencia," Asey said. "How'd you know about that joint?"

Ward laughed.

"I did a series of rum-row articles in the good old days," he said. "My, my, it's like a breath of lavendered old lace just to think about it. Must be all of sixteen or seventeen years ago. Wasn't it over that way, to the left?"

"To the right," Asey pointed. "Mile or more over the hill. Know who owns the place now? The head push of the Minutewomen. Picklepuss Belcher."

Ward looked puzzled.

"But I thought you said these women were all honest burghers. Or burgheresses," he said. "You didn't say they ran joints!"

"It's not a joint now. It's a pickle factory."

"Ah," Ward said. "From fleshpot to stinkpot, or Yankee ingenuity. I wonder what would impel a woman to convert the Casa Valencia into a pickle factory? Somehow it's an angle that would never enter my head."

"Wa-el," Asey said, "Picklepuss's husband died, leavin' her no resources but a good recipe for pickles. This road, or the other? This one? Okay. So Picklepuss bought the place cheap, an' planted a few Dorothy Perkinses over the front door, an' turned it into the home of Aunt Pussy's Perfect Pickles. Ward, what are you really on the Cape for?"

"Those damn articles," Ward said. "Turn ahead."

Asey glanced at him sharply as he swung the roadster off on another lane.

"No other reason, huh?"

"Slow down, or I'll get lost," Ward said. "I got fed up, Asey. Eleven months of war was enough. So when my leg got plugged, I romped home. Broke, I might add. I'm doing tripe to keep body and soul together. And d'you know, I find it's very relaxing to write about sea captains swallowed by whales for a change."

He laughed suddenly, and slapped his knee with his fist.

"What's so funny?" Asey asked.

"I keep thinking of the Casa Valencia, and interviewing Alex Moriarty," Ward said. "I expected a thug, and Alex had six bodyguards in cummerbunds, and his college degree framed on his office wall next to an autographed picture of the district attorney. 'To Alex from his Pal and Well-wisher.' Did they ever nab Alex?"

"Income tax," Asey said. "Alex was real hurt. He issued a statement sayin' he'd always tried to treat the government fair an' square an' with every courtesy. Which turn here?"

Ward looked around as Asey slowed down.

"D'you want to know the bitter truth, Sherlock? I never saw this particular fork before in all my life.

I never saw that stone. Go back to the last turn. That's where I got balled up. Did they get all of Alex's gang, too?"

Asey nodded. "On one count or another. Barradio, Lopez, an' all the rest. It was those convictions got Merriam Lysander Bogert made governor for a couple of terms. He cleaned up this glorious Commonwealth, the posters said."

"I wonder what you said," Ward remarked. "Did you think Alex ran that whole show?"

"Wa-el," Asey returned, "I'm not a one to contradict that great crusader, Merriam Lysander Bogert. But I never thought Merriam got quite to the root of things. I knew too much about—here we are. Now, think hard which lane you was on."

"The one with more pines," Ward said without hesitation. "I remember the pines. Creep along, Asey. The women were on this one, farther along. Where the hell do all these roads go, anyway? They look traveled."

"They go to the shore. There's camps there that duck hunters use, an' odds an' ends of cottages built on tax claim land. You know, Ward, you've brought up one of my favorite arguments with Doc Cummings."

"About these roads?"

"About Alex an' his gang. The doc got a lot of practical experience with gunshot wounds, patchin' the boys up. He knew a lot of 'em. An' he always claims that Alex was the brains. I never thought so, myself. I knew Alex, an' his strong-arm boys with the wavy hair an' the painted fingernails, an' I knew a lot of the truck drivers an' the fellows that ran the pickup boats into the harbor. But I never felt that outfit could run so slick an' easy with just Alex behind it, for all his college degrees. The doc claims that any bunch of thugs can run slick an' easy if they only co-operate, an' that they just co-operated. But Alex wasn't quick-thinkin' enough—you sure we're on the right road now, Ward?"

"Positive. Over there's where I sat down to soothe my feet. Asey, I don't want to seem to tear you away from the engrossing topic of Alex and the good old days, but what about Lucia? Why did you rush after Ben Bunting?"

Asey grinned.

"I s'pose you thought you had another leg on this car when you seen me tear after him, huh?"

"I hoped so. I like this vehicle. What about Ben? And did you and Dr. Cummings manage to get any-where?"

"We speculated," Asey told him, "an' that's about all. Ward, I ought to get back an' see him, an' find out what the news from Boston is, an' find out where Ben went, an' what become of Humphrey. I think I'll fol-low my original plans an' let the state cops tackle this business of Clare. I don't see them two women, or any trace of 'em, an' if they did take her, they might be clear to Provincetown by now. It's gettin' on for five o'clock, an' I think we better turn back to town an' get a hunt organized while it's still light."

"Maybe you're right," Ward said. "All this 's distracting you from the main issue, and frankly, I think Clare's sufficiently levelheaded to take care of herself, no matter what may have happened to her. I don't mean that I'm not worried about her. I am. But as I used to cable 'em back at the office, I do not feel that the situation has progressed to a point of utter despair. By the way, mind if I turn on your radio?"

"This button," Asey said. "Here. The news ought to be on, if that's what you're after."

They listened, as the roadster coasted down a little hillside, to the breathless voice of the Boston announcer.

"These bombs, it was claimed, utterly destroyed the already crippled cruiser. The total of shipping destroyed for the day was forty-seven thousand six hundred and twenty-nine tons, making a claimed total for the week past of seven hundred thirty-three thousand, eight hundred and seventy-seven tons. Claimed losses included a number of armed merchant vessels, several destroyers, also a number of trawlers, mine sweepers and small craft. It is reliably reported from usually well-informed persons close to official circles that the losses suffered were—"

Ward leaned over and switched the radio off.

"Or do you want it on?" he inquired. "I can finish

it for you, anyway. Something about conflicting claims making it very difficult to gauge accurately either the damages claimed or the losses sustained, or the extent of either. Or both. You know, some time after this is all over and done with and safely tucked away in the last chapter of a history book, I'm going abroad to find those well-informed persons, and when I do, I intend to destroy them personally—Asey, look!"

He pointed excitedly toward the rise ahead.

A woman had appeared out of the bushes at the right of the road, was crossing the ruts, and as Asey looked, she disappeared into the bushes at the left.

Close at her heels was another woman.

Both of them carried rifles.

"Clare's got away!" Ward said. "They're chasing her! Hustle, Asey!"

The roadster shot up the rise as if it had been fired from a gun.

Asey leapt out, Ward leapt after him, and the two crashed through the bushes after the women.

"Where are they?" Ward panted as he limped along. "I can hear 'em somewhere ahead, but I can't see 'em! Where'd they go?"

Asey paused just long enough to cock an ear.

"This way," he said, and started off again. "Left. You needn't try to run—golly, hear that!"

Ward, with an expression of bewilderment on his face, stopped short and listened to the bloodcurdling yell that issued from the bushes somewhere to his left.

Before the last eerie echo died away, another and even more hideous yell rent the air.

It was followed by several short, yipping screeches, and then by a series of crescendo screams, which suddenly ceased with marked abruptness.

"Quaint Cape Cod!" Ward muttered, and limped off in the direction Asey had taken.

By the time he reached a clearing some sixty yards beyond, Asey was sitting on a tree stump, holding two rifles firmly on his knees.

In front of him stood two red-faced women who were having mild hysterics on each other's shoulders.

And, glaring furiously at both Asey and the women, there was also an irate man.

Ward's eyes opened wide, and then he leaned on his cane and hooted.

"Fatty!" he said. "If it isn't Fatty himself! By God, you do look like a white-bellied anteater in that white linen suit! I say, girls," he addressed the women, "do either of you happen to have a spare pin on your person?"

After favoring him with a resentful stare, the two women returned to their intermittent sobbing.

"I only wanted one to stick into Fatty," Ward said. "Wanted to see if he'd really burst."

"You!" Dudley French said violently. "You—you—you—"

"Stinker?" Ward suggested as he sat down beside Asey. "Skunk? Scoundrel? Scallywag? Come, come, what's the matter? Cat got your tongue? You were so fluent this morning, it seems a pity you've run dry. Get your breath, Fatty. I'll wait. Did the girls snatch her, Asey? Where is she?"

"I ain't," Asey said, "tried to find out yet. I was waitin' for 'em to calm down. Er—are you two Mabel an' Effie?"

"I'm Mabelle," the taller one said. "Mabelle, not Mabel. She's Effie. Are—are you Asey Mayo?"

"My God!" Ward said. "Don't you girls recognize your local hero? Of course he's Asey Mayo! Who'd you think he was, the Lone Ranger?"

"I never saw him all dressed up in white pants before," Mabelle said. "Did you, Effie?"

Effie said plantively that she never even saw him out of his car before.

"He's always driving somewhere when he goes past my house," she added. "I always think of him bein' in a car."

"He's only temporarily unhorsed," Ward said. "His car's in the offing—girls, let's get down to business. Where's Clare, have you tied her to a tree?"

"What you say?" Mabelle demanded.

Ward repeated his statement. "Clare. Where is she? You know, the young thing in blue shorts. What did you do with her?"

Effie edged a little nearer to Mabelle, and both of them surveyed Ward with suspicion.

"The infant!" Ward said impatiently. "Where is

she? We want Clare! Oh, my God, Asey, don't they understand English?"

"Not yours much, I don't think," Asey said. "Tell me, why was you two ladies chasin' Mr. French?"

"We weren't!" Mabelle said.

"Oh. Why was you chasin' Mr. Ward, here?"

"We weren't chasing him either!"

"Now go 'long with you, girls!" Ward said. "You did so! Here, take my handkerchief to wipe your face, Mabelle. It's cleaner than yours. Sit down, girls. Relax. Here's a comb. Now, tidy up, and pull yourselves together, and let's see if we can't whisk away the dross and the chaff and stuff, and gnaw on the basic essentials. Here, I've found some peppermints in my pocket. Have one. Nothing more refreshing than a nice peppermint, and lousy with vitamins, too, I've no doubt. The girl we refer to—"

"I want to know the meaning of this outrageous scene!" Dudley French said. "I want—"

"Oh, hush, Cap'n Bligh," Ward said. "Let the girls get pulled together before you start being pettish. Who were you chasing, girls?"

"We were after the man with the blue blouse and the red pants! We weren't chasing you," Effie said with a sniff, "or him, either!"

"You mean," Ward said, "you were just chasing Fatty and me to keep your hand in? Just training, as you might say?"

"We're chasing him till we find him!" Mabelle said. "We're chasing everyone till we find him!"

"We got him twice!" Effie said plantively. "And we're going to find him again! We'd have got him the last time if Mabelle hadn't slipped!"

"Who says I slipped? You slipped! You did!"

They both talked energetically at once until Asey finally took a hand.

"Wait, you two! You mean, you actually seen that feller from the dune, around here in the woods?"

They assured him that they had seen the man, had chased him, and twice been on the verge of actually capturing him.

"I demand to know the meaning of this outra—"

"Yes, French," Asey said. "I know. But just you wait till I get this part straightened out. You women mean that just by chance, when you picked up the chase again after Blue Blouse got away, you happened to land on Ward, an' later on French. I see. Now, have you set eyes on a girl dressed in blue shorts? Slight, kind of pretty girl?"

Both Mabelle and Effie denied having caught even a glimpse of any girl at all.

"I see," Asey said. "Now, you two haven't had a bite to eat today, have you? Whyn't you go on back an' eat, an' call it a day? I'm goin' to call the cops to come over here for some searchin', an' they'll pick up Blue Blouse. I think, myself, that you done a pretty good job for amateur chasers, an'—"

"I demand," French said, "to know the meaning of this outrageous scene! Who are these women, Mayo? What are they doing here? What are you doing here? Why have I been pursued with weapons? Set upon, ambushed, virtually assaulted? What is that fellow," he pointed to Ward, "doing here?"

"Wa-el, now," Asey said, "when you come right down to it, what are you doin' here, French?"

"Who has a better right? This is my own land! My own cottage is on the shore beyond! I was returning to get a package for Molly Coppinger's bazaar when I saw these women trespassing on my property, and I naturally investigated, only to be pursued and tackled—"

"Girls," Ward said briskly, "did you tackle Fatty? Honestly? Girls, take a trip to Boston and buy yourselves some hats on me! Buy yourselves the best lunch in town. Do a matinee. Have a time—you don't need to look at Asey! I mean it!"

"All of you," Dudley pointed his finger at them, "are trespassing on my land! I demand—"

"You're certainly down on trespassers, aren't you?" Ward interrupted. "Turn the other cheek, Fatty. Forgive our trespasses—you know, I think the workout the girls gave you has done you a world of good. You've definitely lost a few ounces around the waistline. Or have you got on a girdle? Frankly, I think you ought to hire the girls to chase you three times a day for a month. The chances of your surviving after fifty would be enormously improved!"

Before Dudley French had a chance to open his mouth and spit out the words he had obviously been treasuring on his tonguetip, Asey spoke to him.

"French, have you seen or heard from Doc Cummings?"

"Cummings? Why?" Dudley retorted. "Why in God's name should I see that old fool? I wouldn't trust him with a sick dog!"

"I suggest," Asey said, "that you get in touch with him quite soon. Now, girls, where'd you leave your car? You think you can find it without any trouble?"

"Well," Effie said hesitantly, "I parked it by a pine tree with branches that stuck out like this—" She thrust her hands out at forty-degree angles.

"Uh-huh. I see," Asey said. "Like that. Huh. Maybe I better help you find it. Come on, an'—"

"I want an apology!" French said. "I demand an apology! I demand some rational explanation of this outrageous scene! Don't think you can get away with any such nonsense, Mayo, you and this fake hack! You and these women are tres—"

"I think," Asey said, "that the girls are too hot an' too tired to go into a lot of explanations just for the sake of your pride, French. They just mistook you for someone else, an' you know that's all there is to it."

"I have been attacked!" French said. "I have—"

"I don't think," Asey said, "that you been injured

much. An' I know you're mistaken about us all trespassin' on your land. This wood lot here happens to belong to my cousin, Syl Mayo. You can see his markin's blazed on that stump yonder. If anyone's trespassin', French, you are."

"Do you," French demanded hotly, "expect me to overlook this outrage as if it didn't matter? To brush off this attack on me? To toss the whole outrageous scene aside as if it were a joke?"

"Uh-huh," Asey said. "I expect you to see the wisdom of makin' a funny story out of this before I do, with Ward's help. When you return to the village, French, get in touch with Doc Cummings at once, please. I'll see you myself, later, after I got some odds an' ends cleared up."

"Say, Fatty," Ward said, "maybe you might have caught sight of Clare. You know, the girl in shorts who was with me this morning when you opened fire out on the dune. Have you seen her?"

Dudley smiled.

"No," he said very deliberately.

"You have!" Ward said. "You lie like a fat pig in a slough! Where did you see her?"

"I feel under no obligation," Dudley said, "to give you any information concerning anyone, after the insulting treatment I have—"

"Where," Asey's voice broke in like the crack of a whip, "did you see the girl?"

"I refuse to be ques—"

"French," Asey said, "stop this pettish fussin' around! Unless you want to be on the pursued end of a man-size chase, tell me where you saw that girl!"

"In a car," French said sullenly. "With a young fellow."

"What kind of a car?" Ward demanded. "What did he look like? What was the license number? What road were they on? Where? How long ago?"

"Half an hour ago," Dudley said. "On my own road. Headed toward the village. Like all trespassing tourists, they held the middle of the road while I had to go into the ditch to cut around them!"

"What kind of a car?" Asey said. "What did the fellow look like?"

"My dear Mayo," Dudley said, "I don't know! I was too busily engaged in the process of keeping my own car from turning over in the ditch to pay any attention to the color of the fellow's eyes or the name on his hubcaps! It was a small, open roadster. More than that, I'm sure I can't be of any assistance!"

Turning on his heel, Dudley departed with pompous dignity from the clearing.

"The pompous ass!" Ward said. "If I were half his size, I'd turn him over my knee—well, let's go, Asey! Let's go, girls!"

Fifteen minutes later, after Mabelle and Effie had been speeded on their way, Asey stowed the two con-fiscated rifles in the rumble seat of his roadster, and set off for town.

"What now?" Ward asked. "Where do we go from here?"

"I'm goin' to stop at the drugstore on Main Street an' call Lieutenant Hanson," Asey said. "I'm goin' to ask him to send some of his state cops over to the woods."

"After Clare, you mean?" Ward said. "Asey, do you think she's still there? Don't you believe what Fat Stuff said about her going off with someone in a car?"

"I believe him," Asey said. "I can't think of any reason why he'd lie. He don't even know about Mrs. Newell yet. What I was thinkin' about, Ward, was this fellow in the blue blouse an' red pants. I think maybe he better be tracked down. You see, like I told you earlier, I had kind of a peculiar mornin', what with people pottin' at me from afar—"

"You never told me you'd been potted at!" Ward interrupted.

"Didn't I?" Asey asked wearily. "Somehow it seems to me that I been broadcastin' the fact all day long. I told my Cousin Jennie, an' Picklepuss, an' the cops by the crossin', an' the doc, an' Clare, an'—"

"You never told me!"

"Okay, then." Asey condensed the story of the two rifle shots into half a dozen succinct sentences. "So maybe," he concluded, "the girls was on the right track in tryin' to chase this blue-bloused lad they seen over on the dune. I think Hanson better look into him officiallike."

"I'd think so," Ward said as they drew up to the curb, "considering he turned up by your house after the second shot, and now again! Well, well, so you were shot at as well as biffed. My, my and a couple of la la's. People were just as anxious to keep you from seeing Lucia today as they were to get her out of the picture, weren't they?"

"Seems so," Asey said. "The biff I got back there by the pond was an error, though, I think. I'll be right back."

A faint smile played around Ward's lips as he watched Asey stride into the drugstore, and he drummed thoughtfully against the side of the car door with his knuckles.

"I spoke with Hanson," Asey said when he returned a few minutes later. "He's over at the Yacht Club, an' I had to wait till they located him. He's goin' to send three men over to the woods. Wa-el, now I want to drive along to where Mrs. Newell lived, an' see if Ben Bunting's been there, an' then I want to locate him, an' his father, too. Then—"

"Asey," Ward said, "is there any place near where I can hire a car?"

"Guess they'd rent you one at the garage around the corner," Asey said. "What do you aim to do, hunt Clare yourself?"

Ward nodded.

"I feel uneasy about her," he said. "I'd like to go and drive around those lanes some more. Suppose you could draw me a map of the more traveled roads so I wouldn't get too lost?"

"Give me your pencil an' a piece of paper," Asey said, "an' I'll have a try."

Ward surveyed the results critically.

"Frankly, Mayo," he said, "you're no artist. This might be almost anything from the lesser tributaries of the Amazon to the veinous system of the common frog. But it's certainly better than the town map I had. I'll take a look around, and then I'll hunt you up. Now, where's this garage?"

"I'll take you there."

When Asey left the garage ten minutes later, Ward was still torn between his Hobsonian choice of a comparatively recent model beachwagon with dangerously bad tires, and a stripped-down, antiquated sedan with excellent rubber but no body or brakes to speak of.

At the town four corners, Asey paused and reflected.

He wanted first of all to check up on Ben Bunting, to see if, as he anticipated, the boy had gone to the Thackaberry house and attempted to find among Mrs. Newell's belongings whatever it was that he had been seeking in the knitting bag.

And he wanted to find out if Picklepuss Belcher and her cohorts were still at Thackaberry's, and still occupied with their chore of finding out about Mrs. Newell.

But what Asey did not want was to run the risk of being seen and sidetracked by the Minutewomen.

They had, he thought, provided just about enough in the line of distraction for one day.

So Asey decided to eschew the Sketicket Center Road, which ran directly past the Thackaberry house, in favor of the East Sketicket fork, which didn't. From the East Sketicket hill, he could get a sufficiently good view of the Thackaberry house with his binoculars to see whether or not the place was crammed with Minutewomen. If it was, Asey intended to phone from a safe distance and inquire if Ben had been there. On the other hand, if he could see no trace of the Minutewomen, he would drop off and investigate in person.

Another stretch of potholes and petered-out road construction forced him to slow down, halfway up the East Sketicket hill, and a car full of tourists streaking down the incline compelled him to pull off the road entirely to avoid a head-on collision.

Muttering uncomplimentary things about the tourist trade, Asey waited while two other out-of-state cars sped by, and then he grimly sat back and waited some more while four others raced blithely past.

Then his eye fell on something in the valley below that made him chuckle and reach out for his binoculars.

Partly hidden in a clump of trees in a lane below was a beachwagon.

Ben Bunting's old rattletrap beachwagon with its flapping side curtains.

And seated on the ground beyond was Ben himself. Asey focused the binoculars.

Through the trees and the foliage he could just make out the driveway of the Thackaberry house, and it seemed to be teeming with cars.

It had all worked out as he'd hoped it might. Pickle-puss and her Minutewomen were still there, and they had prevented Ben from continuing his search. The boy must have sat there, waiting and watching and glowering, all the living afternoon long.

Grinning, Asey turned his roadster around, headed back to the village and the four corners, and swung off on the Sketicket shore road.

With Ben as good as on ice for a while, he could devote himself to the problem of Commodore Humphrey Bunting.

He had found out, while he was phoning in the drugstore, what house the Buntings were renting that summer, and now he intended to go there and see if the Bunting servants or anyone in the neighborhood knew where Humphrey was.

Just a brisk look through the contents of Humphrey's closet, Asey thought, ought to disclose whether or not the man had made any preparations for going away on any long, long journey in a hurry.

And it rather looked as if he might have done just that, for Hanson had reported that Humphrey hadn't turned up at the club, hadn't telephoned the place, and no one Hanson had talked with had any notion of where the man might be.

Asey had to weave his way carefully among the number of cars parked on either side of the road outside the big Coppinger estate, where the relief bazaar was obviously in full swing with banners and flags fluttering in the breeze and a band blaring somewhere in the distance.

He braked quickly and sighed a little as a green sedan suddenly backed without warning from its parking space ahead, and he waited while the car, for no apparent reason, was edged along into another space twenty feet beyond.

With his elbows resting on the wheel and his chin cupped in his hands, Asey continued to wait until the sedan, after innumerable backings, was finally placed to the driver's exact liking.

Then, as Asey wondered casually what the woman looked like and what she thought she'd gained by all that fiddling around, Humphrey Bunting emerged from the driver's seat.

"Well, well," Asey murmured. "Well, well!"

He watched while Humphrey reached inside the sedan, and he whistled softly as Humphrey drew out a heavy-barreled rifle.

A .30-06, Asey thought, if ever he saw one!

With great care, Humphrey unlocked the sedan's trunk, put the gun inside, and slammed down the trunk cover.

Then he buttoned up his blue, brass-buttoned coat, adjusted his collar, fingered his tie, and put on his heavily braided yachting cap.

He didn't see Asey until the latter was at his elbow.

"Why, Mayo!" he said genially. "How are you? Going to take a look at Molly's shindig? Looks from here as if she had quite a turnout. I'll never understand how she can pull 'em in!"

"Amazin'," Asey said. "Er—you remember that date we had?"

"My dear fellow," Humphrey said, "I'm sorry about that! I meant to phone you as soon as I'd seen Molly and done some handshaking around. I presume you thought it was queer of me not to wait for you?"

"Queer wasn't quite the word I thought of," Asey returned. "It was more like suspicious—huh. I wonder!"

He broke off and looked at Humphrey for a moment.

"What's the matter?" Humphrey asked. "Does my face look funny?"

He sounded strangely self-conscious.

"No," Asey said. "I wonder, now. You ain't been to the Yacht Club. Have you seen Ben?"

"Not since this noon. Mayo, I—"

"I wonder," Asey said, "if it's possible that you don't know! Bunting, where have you been?"

"I owe you an apology," Humphrey said earnestly. "No question about it, I owe you an apology, and I owe Ross Ward an apology, and I owe Lucia one, and everyone else. It was rude of me. I shouldn't have done it, and I knew I shouldn't have done it, but I just couldn't help myself. I had to."

"Had," Asey said, "to what?"

"Rush off. Get away from it all. If you want to know the truth, I rebelled, Mayo!"

"So?"

"I had a set-to with Ben," Humphrey continued. "I had another with Dudley French. And when I thought of all the things I had ahead of me, the more I felt I just couldn't stick any of 'em, including you. I just rebelled. Flagler says there's no doubt the tooth was at the bottom of it."

"Tooth?" Asey said. "What tooth?"

"This tooth I just had out!" Humphrey said. "It's been bothering me all summer, and I've always been so damn busy I never could see my way clear to taking time off to have it out. Well, today I just said the hell with everything, and Flagler took it out, and he fixed up those other cavities, and I just feel like a new man, I tell you! Flagler says that tooth's been pumping poison into my blood stream since he doesn't know when. He says he thinks that tooth's done more harm than I'll ever guess—say, *does* my face look awfully funny?"

"Let me get this straight," Asey said. "You mean to say that you rushed off from the club an' went to the dentist's, an' had a tooth out? Am I to understand that you been at the dentist's all this time?"

Humphrey nodded.

"Flagler had other appointments, and so he had to keep sandwiching me in when he got the chance. He wasn't a bit keen on doing the whole works today, but I told him to go ahead while I was right there and in the mood. Flagler said my face looked all right, but if it looks so funny that you keep staring at me like that, I won't bother going into this bazaar business at all. It's really quite a hole. See?" Humphrey opened his mouth and held down his lower lip with his forefinger. "The 'olar. The 'ack 'olar."

"Uh-huh. That's considerable of an exc'vation," Asey said. "You—"

He stopped short.

Humphrey, after taking his finger out of his mouth, was wiping it with a large white handkerchief he had yanked out of his coat pocket.

But along with the white handkerchief had come another that fell, unnoticed by Humphrey, to the ground.

Asey looked down at it.

It was a small, feminine, blue-checked thing, and the checks were the same size and the same color as those on that little purse of Clare's that still sat on the seat of his roadster.

Asey bent over and picked the handkerchief up and looked thoughtfully at the initials in the corner.

C. H. stood for Clare Heath.

EIGHT .

WHERE'D that come from?" Humphrey asked curiously. "My pocket?"

"Uh-huh. Know who it belongs to?"

"Probably it's Lucia Newell's," Humphrey said. "She's a great one for sticking things into coat pockets. I had to call a halt on carting her compacts around. The powder smell's bad enough to begin with, and the stuff's the very devil to get off anything dark."

"The initials are C. H.," Asey said.

"C. H.? Well, it isn't Lucia's, then," Humphrey said. "Must be someone else's. I wore this coat to a bridge party last night, and I collected more female truck. Look what I brought to light while I was waiting in Flagler's office."

From his other pocket he pulled out two lipsticks, a pink enameled cigarette lighter, a small jeweled pin in the shape of an elephant, and a wispy black lace handkerchief.

"Damn truck!" he said. "Ben's always kidding me because of the stuff I pick up. But when a woman holds something out and asks you to keep it for her, there isn't much you can do but take it—Mayo, is my face swelling, or is it all right?"

Asey assured him that his face was fine.

"But you keep staring at me so! Look, is it noticeable? I'm not going to parade around and handshake in that fool bazaar if I'm all puffed up. Tell me the truth."

"You're okay. Bunting, I wonder if—"

"Look, Mayo," Humphrey said hurriedly, "if I'm really all right, I want to go in and say hello to Molly and a few people, and then suppose you come back to the club with me, and we'll settle this business of Porter's check. Come on in with me. It'll only take a few minutes!"

"No," Asey said, "I'm not in a bazaar mood right now. S'pose you just settle a few things with me, an' then you can go an' bazaar to your heart's content, if you want to. I—"

"Don't mind about your flannels!" Humphrey interrupted. "That's what's bothering you, isn't it? Well, just don't think about 'em! If I can go in with my face all swelled up, you needn't be sensitive about a few—er—grass stains. But if you'd rather wait out here for me, why don't you? I won't be two minutes! You wouldn't mind waiting a few minutes, would you? Then we'll go on to the club and settle things."

"Bunting," Asey said firmly, "get into your car, an' sit down! Stop this babblin'! I got things I want to settle with you right now, an' they're goin' to be settled right now, without any more dillydallyin' or shillyshallyin'!"

"Why, of course, old man!" Humphrey sounded a little hurt. "If that's the way you feel about it! Of course! Here, you get in first. Have a cigar? Have a cigarette?"

Asey sighed. Trying to be harsh and firm with the commodore, he thought, was like trying to punch a sponge-rubber mattress. It just gave a little, and then bulged out in another direction.

"No cigars, thanks," he said as he climbed into the front seat of the green sedan. "No cigarettes. No crossword puzzles, either. Now, let's see. You don't know anythin' about that handkerchief. You spent the day at the dentist's. Huh! Now, tell me about this rifle I seen you put into your car trunk a few minutes ago."

"Oh," Humphrey said. "That! That's my .30-06, Mayo, and it's the most amazing thing!"

Asey agreed that it was an amazing and a deadly weapon.

"But what I want to know is what you're doin' with one today, Bunting!"

"That's the amazing part," Humphrey said. "That's what I meant when I said it was amazing. You see, these women—well, it was really that Mrs. Belcher. The pickle one. She bullied me into lending her some of my guns for some sort of patriotic exhibition she and the rest of the local women were putting on. I didn't want to let her have 'em, God knows, but you know how it is. You simply have to string along with the local people. You have to soft-soap 'em, and cater to 'em, and do what they want of you, or you run into trouble."

"Uh-huh," Asey said dryly.

"If I don't buy tickets for church suppers," Humphrey went on, "or chances for bedspreads, or if I don't pat their little ones on the head, the next thing I know there's no appropriation for dredging the channel. I tell you, you have to watch your step with the natives every minute!"

"Uh-huh. You sure do," Asey said.

"Oh, I don't mean you, of course!" Humphrey said quickly. "I never think of you as being a native! Never! I never do. I never have!"

"Uh-huh. So, bearin' in mind that Picklepuss Belcher's related to half the town selectmen," Asey said, "you went an' lent her guns for her patriotic exhibition, this .30-06 among 'em. Did you lend her the ammunition, too?"

"She asked for it," Humphrey said. "I didn't want to let her have any, but she bullied me, and when a woman—"

"I know. When a woman asks you, what can you do?" Asey said. "I understand. You just turned to putty in the hands of Picklepuss. Now, where'd you get the gun you put in the car trunk? From one of the women?"

"That's the second time today that I've been compared with putty!" Humphrey said. "I'm not, Mayo! But I have to think of the club, and the channel, and the taxes. In a job like mine, you can't always follow your natural inclinations, as I tried to tell Ben this morning. I have to think first of the club!"

"I'm thinkin' of the gun," Asey reminded him. "Where'd you get it? What you doin' with it?"

"Well, it's like this," Humphrey said, and embarked on rather an elaborate explanation.

Coming out of the dentist's office, he had seen a woman marching along Main Street, carrying the rifle which he recognized as his. The woman was the wife of the tax collector, but Humphrey was puzzled enough by the fact of her carrying his gun to stop her and ask if it wasn't one of those which Mrs. Belcher had borrowed from him.

"She said she thought it might be," Humphrey said, "but she didn't seem to know a thing about the exhibition—don't you think that's odd? I thought it was, and I decided that maybe I'd better take the gun back. I mean, in the first place I didn't want that expensive gun dragged around God knows where, and in the next place, it would reflect on me if it caused any damage or trouble, or anyone got hurt or scared. She didn't want to give it to me, but I simply insisted."

He told Asey in detail what he said, what the woman said, what he told her, and what she told him back.

"And I don't understand even now," he concluded,

"if they'd had this patriotic exhibition, or not. Don't you think it's amazing that she wouldn't *know?* Anyway, I insisted on taking the gun away from her."

"I'm glad," Asey said, "to know that you can insist once in a while! If you'd been more insistent with Picklepuss an' refused to let her take the guns, you—"

He broke off as Humphrey leaned forward and turned on the car radio.

"You don't mind if I listen to the news, do you, Mayo?" he asked apologetically. "I haven't heard the news for nearly an hour. Sea power's certainly proving itself, don't you think? I wonder what station—ah. Here it is!"

He sat back and listened interestedly while an announcer said that a résumé of the day's claimed shipping losses, the reported plane losses and the bombing recapitulations would follow a piece of news that was important for every Thinking American.

The piece of news was a disclosure of a phenomenal sale of three-piece living room suites, at prices that no Thinking American would dare to miss.

"Prices," the announcer said in a ringing voice, "which will rock the foundations of the furniture industry. So come at once! Don't delay! Now, folks, the claimed total tonnage reportedly destroyed in raids today, as passed by the censor—"

Asey snapped off the radio.

"Wait!" Humphrey said. "I want to hear how much they say they sunk—oh, I see. You spotted him."

"Spotted who?" Asey asked in exasperation. "What are you talkin' about now! Who?"

"Flagler. Ahoy, doc!" Humphrey called out. "Ahoy!"

Dr. Flagler, who had been walking toward the entrance to the Coppinger place, turned and walked back to the green sedan.

Leaning an arm over the door, he beamed his wide smile in Asey's direction, and asked how the commodore was feeling now.

"Novocaine's wearing off, eh?"

"I think so," Humphrey said, "but those little white pills did the trick. I'm sure it's wearing off, but I don't feel it, if you know what I mean."

"Good!" Flagler said. "Good! I tell you, Asey, you're sitting beside a pretty brave man! He was in my office from around noon till twenty minutes ago, and I hurt him plenty, but never a murmur out of him! I wish I had more patients like him. Either of you seen my wife running around here?"

"No," Humphrey said, "but we'll go in with you and help you locate her. Come on, Mayo. This affair's almost over, and we better just drop in and take a look around before everyone goes. I promised Molly, and I know Lucia's expec—"

"Go along, doc," Asey said. "I still got some business to talk over with the commodore. Don't bother waitin' for us!"

Humphrey frowned as Dr. Flagler beamed again and walked off.

"Look, Mayo," he said, "I know this check of Porter's seems terribly important to you and all that, but really, I have to think of the club! There are any number of people I ought to see and say a few words to in there, and they'll think it's awfully funny if I don't! I really can't stay out here with you, you know, and chat much longer!"

Asey looked at him thoughtfully.

"I wonder," he said, "if you'll ever realize how lucky it is for you that I've known Flagler for a number of years, an' whatever I think of his professional handiwork, I believe he's a very truthful man. Sit down, Bunting. Try to light."

"Light?"

"Uh-huh. A local expression," Asey said. "I mean that I want you to stop this mental leapin' about. Of course, it may be that the novocaine or the little white pills've got somethin' to do with it. I don't know. I *do* know, though, that by dumb luck you've been alibied out of some mighty suspicious circumstances. Now, while you're here, you might as well explain about Bill Porter's check. He gave you that money to help with a mortgage. Right?"

Humphrey looked a little confused, but he nodded.

"And we certainly needed that money, too!" he said. "We were in such desperate straits, Mayo, that I sat down and wrote thirty men the most forceful begging letters I knew how to write! And I'm proud to say that the response was so great, we not only took care of the mortgage, but we even had a lot left over for other things besides."

"I wonder did it occur to you," Asey said, "that this money was given you to clear up the mortgage problem, an' if there was any left over, you'd ought to have returned it?"

Humphrey made an exclamation of shocked surprise.

"Returned it! After what I went through to *get* it? Mayo, you just don't realize how hard it is to *get* money for the club! It's like pulling teeth—no, it's a lot harder than pulling teeth! Flagler could pull every tooth in my head, and it wouldn't begin to exhaust me as much as one day's conniving to get money for that club! Why, the response to those mortgage letters was the first real response I got! Up till that response, I was at my wit's end!"

"Oho!" Asey said. "I think I begin to get this. The response to the mortgage beggin' letters was so successful, you kept right *on* askin' for mortgage money. That it?"

"I found out a great truth from those letters," Humphrey said. "I found out there were a number of people always willing to give money for a mortgage who'd rot before they'd send me a check for a new ell, or some new furnishings. Now, Mayo, I'll admit I lost it, and that's why I stalled you when you first asked me about it, but I've found that folder now, and it's got in it all the receipts and a full accounting of Bill Porter's money. I can account for every penny."

"Did Bill," Asey inquired, "pay for the new ell?"

"And the little lounge, too!" Humphrey said with pride. "I flatter myself, I stretched that check as far as anyone could. I even managed to have the east gutters repaired. You see my point, now, Mayo. No one wants to fix up gutters. I could have written Porter a hundred letters urgently pointing out the need for new east gutters, but he wouldn't have bothered. Wouldn't have sent me a nickel. Wouldn't have felt it mattered. But when you put a mortgage payment up to people, they feel that matters. A mortgage counts. Take the south wharf. That's desperately in need of repairs right now. Desperately. But who wants to repair an old wharf?"

"If you're fishin'," Asey said, "I tell you right now that I don't, an' I doubt if Bill will."

"See?" Humphrey said. "See? It's just as important to save that wharf as to make a mortgage payment, but people won't look at things that way. I thought up a good scheme today, though, over at Flagler's. Got the idea from a picture some grateful patient sent him to hang in his office. Had a little metal tag on the frame, telling all about it. I decided to have little bronze plates screwed up, saying who fixed what, and all that sort of thing. I think it would appeal to some people, don't you? People like Dudley French, say? Don't you think that's a good idea?"

"It's genius," Asey said. "An' I hope for your sake that it works out. But I think, Bunting, that you ought to be warned that no matter how good your intentions are for helpin' the club an' makin' a go of it, someone's goin' to jump down your neck if you keep on askin' money for the same thing, an' then keep usin' it for somethin' else. There's goin' to be some crude fellow who's goin' to pop up an' accuse you of willfully misappropriatin' funds, you know. Somebody might even use the nasty word embezzle."

"Oh, they couldn't!" Humphrey said. "I can account for every penny! Bill Porter'll understand. He's a good fellow. Tell him all about it. Tell him I'll put up a plate saying he fixed the lounge and paid for the new ell, and all."

"I'm sure," Asey said, "Bill'll enjoy clamberin' up a conductor pipe to see his name engraved for posterity on the east gutters."

"If he'd like his name there," Humphrey said seriously, "I'll see that a plate's put up. Glad to. Well, it's a load off my mind to have all this straightened out. I told Ben you'd understand. Now, I guess I'll run along and find Lucia. I promised her I'd help her—"

"I think, before you go, you better hear what I have to tell you," Asey said, and without further preamble told him that Lucia had been killed.

It was almost fascinating to watch the color drain out of Humphrey's face under his heavy tan. As if, Asey thought, the man was under a spotlight that was changing color. He seemed to slump, too, and the blue coat that had fitted so well across his broad shoulders seemed suddenly to sag and hang loose.

"Where's Ben? Ben—" Humphrey cleared his throat. "How was she killed?"

"Atropine, Dr. Cummings thinks. Your son Ben thinks it's sunstroke."

"Ben—" Humphrey cleared his throat again. "Cummings only thinks so, you say. Then he's not sure?"

"He's as sure as he can be, an' as sure as I'd want him to be, an' sure enough for me," Asey said. "I'm sorry about all this. Now you see why I wanted to know so much from you."

Asey had a suspicion that, although Humphrey nodded and was looking squarely at him, Humphrey hadn't heard a word he'd said.

His suspicion was strengthened after he said good-by, when Humphrey blinked and seemed surprised to find himself all alone in the front seat of the green sedan.

"Oh. Oh, you going, Mayo?"

"Uh-huh. Mind if I keep that handkerchief?"

"Handkerchief?" Humphrey said. "What handkerchief?"

"The blue-checked one that dropped out of your pocket," Asey told him.

"Oh, that. Yes, if you want it. What do you want it for? It isn't Lucia's."

"It belongs to Clare Heath," Asey said.

"Who?"

"Clare Heath. The girl that came with Ross Ward."

"Oh. Oh, yes. Of course. Ward," Humphrey said heavily. "Yes, yes, of course. I dare say she dropped it this morning at the club, and I picked it up—I say, now I think of it, so she did! She was looking at the trophies in my office, and she dropped the handkerchief, and I picked it up. That's how I got it. Not at the bridge last night. Yes, take it along and give it to her if you happen to run into her, Mayo. I suppose I'll see you later?"

"Most likely," Asey said. "Good-by."

"At the club, probably?"

"I shouldn't wonder. So long."

"Wait!"

Humphrey put out his hand as Asey turned to walk back to his roadster.

"Wait, Mayo. I—I must seem stupid to you, but I can't quite comprehend this yet. My mind seems all furry. All confused. I can't talk about it. Not sensibly. I've got to take time out and try to make myself understand that it's real, and it's happened. After I've sat here quietly for a while, and pulled myself together, I want to see you and really talk with you. Will you be at the club, or where?"

For all that Humphrey looked baffled and confused, Asey thought, the man's eyes were brighter and he seemed more genuinely interested in the forthcoming answer than he had been in all the rest of the preceding conversation.

"Why, yes," Asey said slowly. "Yes, I guess I'll go to the club now, an' most likely I'll be there this evenin' an' far into the night."

"Right," Humphrey said. "I'll see you there, then."

Asey strolled back to his roadster, got in, turned around and headed for the village in a terrific burst of speed.

But at the first road fork he encountered, he braked, backed the car up the road to the right, and waited.

In all his experience with murders, he thought, and with people's reaction to the news of murder, he couldn't remember anyone, offhand, who had reacted quite as Humphrey Bunting had.

Others, to be sure, had also looked baffled and dazed and confused, and had admitted to a natural and understandable inability to think clearly.

But Asey couldn't think of anyone else who had neglected to ask, practically at once, who did it?

Humphrey hadn't even asked the alternative questions. He hadn't demanded to know what Asey thought, or who Asey thought was responsible.

Instead, Humphrey had asked first of all about Ben. Where, Humphrey had asked, was Ben.

"Now I wonder," Asey said aloud, "if maybe perhaps you won't go an' try to find him, now that you've found out for certain that I'm goin' to the club!"

He hardly finished speaking before the green sedan,

with Humphrey at the wheel, flashed along the shore road.

"Uh-huh," Asey murmured, as he started after it. "Just sittin' quiet, an' pullin' yourself together! Huh! I kind of thought so."

Humphrey Bunting, Asey thought, had better take care. Humphrey had a foolproof alibi from noon on, but the fact still remained that Mrs. Newell had been given that drink around eleven-thirty, presumably before Humphrey had left the Yacht Club.

He followed along at a safe distance behind the green sedan, which swung off at last onto the East Sketicket road.

About a quarter of a mile from the Thackaberry house, Humphrey parked his sedan by the side of the road, and set off on foot in the direction of the house.

"Huh!" Asey murmured. "I can do that, too! I can do it better!"

Swinging his roadster off the road so that it was hidden from sight, Asey cautiously proceeded to trail along after Humphrey.

It was a little foolish, he decided as he continued to stalk the man, but no more foolish than Humphrey was in circling the house and conducting a preliminary survey that would have done credit to a prospective burglar.

Before the stealthy survey was over, however, Asey began to feel that maybe all that caution had been worth while.

For the one remaining car parked in the Thacka-berry driveway belonged to Picklepuss Belcher, and even as Humphrey watched the car and the back door, and as Asey watched Humphrey, Picklepuss herself came out of the house.

She carried a big market basket, and her green hat bobbled back and forth as she talked energetically with her sister Sadie Thackaberry. Her words were not audible either to Asey or to Humphrey, but that she felt very strongly about the topic under discussion was apparent even at a distance.

The green hat continued to bobble as Picklepuss stowed the basket away in her car and helped her sister into the front seat.

Then she got in herself, and drove off.

At once, Humphrey Bunting emerged from the shadow of the maple trees and strode swiftly to the nearest ground floor window.

Without hesitating or looking around, he unhooked the screen, tossed it inside the house, and eased himself in after it.

Then he placed the screen back in the window and disappeared from sight.

For a man who claimed to have a confused and furry mind, Asey thought, Humphrey was certainly doing all right. Humphrey was doing very well indeed. As far as any casual observer could tell, the Thackaberry house was just as it had been a minute and a half before. Even if Sadie Thackaberry returned unexpectedly, Asey doubted if she would ever guess that her home had been entered in her absence.

Asey found himself looking forward to what Humphrey would do next.

Just as he started to leave his vantage point under the apple tree, he saw a man's head appear around the corner of the kitchen ell.

It was Ben Bunting.

And because the boy didn't cast as much as one suspicious glance in any direction, Asey guessed that Ben was blandly unaware that anyone else might be lurking around.

Asey grinned.

If the boy had stayed where he was by the beach-wagon on the opposite road, he couldn't have missed seeing his father's stealthy tour of reconnaissance, with Asey himself in stealthy attendance.

Probably, Asey decided, as the number of cars in the Thackaberry driveway dwindled down, Ben had impatiently started for the house by way of the meadow. That would have put him far beyond the limits of his father's circuit.

Asey leaned back against the trunk of the apple tree and watched Ben as he continued to creep around the kitchen ell.

After waiting all afternoon for those women to depart, Ben was probably in a pretty savage frame of mind. And after topping his day at the dentist's with his actions of the last twenty minutes, Humphrey was probably in a pretty perturbed frame of mind, too.

All in all, Asey thought, the meeting of the Bunting family ought to prove to be enlightening and of considerable interest.

Ben's approach to housebreaking was even simpler than his father's.

He lifted up the back-door mat, peered under it, and then turned to the shelf of potted plants by the door.

From under the second geranium, he removed a door key, unlocked the door, and went inside.

Following the shadows of the maple trees in the yard, Asey circled around to the ell and walked in through the door Ben had left open.

He couldn't, he thought, ever recall following two more considerate people. Humphrey's survey had kept him from an encounter with Picklepuss, and now Ben left doors open for him.

Asey stood in the middle of the kitchen and listened.

Obviously the Buntings had discovered each other.

Voices were already being loudly raised somewhere in the front of the house.

The loud voices suddenly turned into angry bellows, accompanied by the very definite sounds of a scuffle.

By the time Asey found his way through a side hall to the room where the Buntings were, the two were engaged in a good, hearty, old-fashioned rough-and-tumble fight.

Two chairs and a mirror had already been smashed, and as Asey watched, a glass-topped dressing table with dozens of bottles and vials and jars on it went crashing over on the floor.

From the doorway, Asey suggested sharply that they call it a day.

"Come on, break it up! I said, break it up!"

But if either of the Buntings heard him, they gave no indication of heeding.

Humphrey's fist smacked against Ben's nose, and Ben, with a grunt, butted his father off his feet with such force that the two of them thudded down on the floor together.

"Hey, that's enough!" Asey said. "Come on, you two!"

But Ben and Humphrey continued to roll over and over on the floor, pummeling each other among the overturned powder boxes and cold cream jars and broken bottles.

"That'll do!" Asey summoned up his quarter-deck voice. "That'll do!"

Just the volume of that voice usually compelled people to stop and listen, but it had no effect on the Buntings.

Humphrey's fist went right on pounding at Ben's bleeding nose, and Ben kept right on pounding back at his father's right eye.

"All right!" Asey said. "Keep on, then! Mess yourselves up all you want to! Have fun. Tear yourselves apart. Do all the damage you—oho!"

It occurred to him suddenly that the Buntings were not just trying to mark each other up.

They had some motive for all this savage clawing and pounding.

They were fighting for the possession of something on the floor, and finally Asey managed to make out just what object it was in all the litter that both men made grabs at in the intervals when their hands were sufficiently free.

It was a thin, pencillike bottle of amber-colored glass.

Watching his chance, Asey leaned over and grabbed it himself as Ben knocked it out of his father's reach.

With narrowed eyes, Asey looked at the little red letters on its white label.

The little red letters spelled Atropine.

NINE.

ASEY looked from the bottle to the two men, and then he half turned around as he heard someone coming along the hall behind him.

Ross Ward limped up to the doorway.

"Hullo, who's being killed now? Am I too late?" He stared inside the room. "My God! Why are they killing each other, Asey?"

"I was just considerin' askin' 'em that," Asey said, "considerin' I got what they're fightin' for. What you doin' here? Did you find Clare?"

Ward shook his head.

"I had to give up my projected scouring of the woods—Asey, stop those fools! This is virtually mayhem! Aren't you going to stop 'em? Why don't you?"

"Like how?" Asey inquired.

Ward watched for a moment.

"Hm. I see your point. Well, after they've worked some of it out of their systems, I suppose we can throw water on 'em. Like cats. As I was saying, I gave up my trip to the woods. That sedan was simply an infernal machine. Suicidal. Steered like a boat—Mayo, we really ought to stop that noise. What'll the neighbors think?"

"Wa-el," Asey said, "I'll try."

He took two steps into the room, and retreated when the bottle Ben Bunting picked off the floor and hurled at him missed his head by a sixteenth of an inch.

"My God!" Ward said as the bottle crashed against the wall. "What's that foul purple liquid trickling down the paper? Whew, what a stink! What—"

He ducked as another bottle narrowly missed his own head.

"They're berserk!" he said. "Come on, Mayo, move out of their way! They're simply berserk! Smell your coat where that stuff splattered. You'll have to bury it in a hole for twenty-one days—get out of that doorway, Mayo, before you get hurt!"

"I think this's goin' a mite too far," Asey said. "I think I'll stop—"

Ward pulled him back.

"You'll only get hurt! I tell you, they're berserk!"

"But they been goin' at this for some time, Ward!"

"Let 'em finish, then! Let 'em exhaust themselves. They'll only feel thwarted if you stop 'em now. Let 'em get over this fit of temporary insanity in their own fashion!"

Asey moved out into the hall.

"Wa-el," he said, "we'll give 'em a few more minutes. How come you landed here, Ward?"

"I knew I never could drive that vehicle in those woods, so I steered it gently over to the Yacht Club," Ward said, "and prevailed on that state copper Hanson to put out more alarums and excursions for Clare. Then I chatted with your friend Cummings. He said he had something to tell you, but he didn't know where you were, and I said I'd undertake to find you if he'd get me a car. So he did, and I did."

"If he lent you that rattletrap of his," Asey said, "you weren't a lot better off."

"No, he didn't lend me his. He pointed out to Lucia's Austin," Ward said, "and remarked that he didn't think Mrs. Newell would be using it. I like Cummings. He's a realist. He thought you might be here, or at the Buntings' place, so I came here first. Mayo, they're quieting down in there. Think they're finally done?"

"If they ain't, they ought to be," Asey said. "Done, an' done up, too. What did the doc have to say?"

"Oh, he'd heard from Boston, and it was atropine."

Asey nodded.

"I never had much doubt about it," he said. "An' when I found this just now, I felt what you might call convinced."

He held out the thin, amber-colored bottle for Ward's inspection.

"Atropine!" Ward said.

"Uh-huh. That's what the Bunting family started their scuffle over."

"Atropine!" Ward said. "I thought I was going to be the bearer of startling tidings. Like a king's messenger. And you not only knew it all the time, you even found the stuff! I suppose if it'd turned out she'd been given arsenic, you'd just have discovered a couple of barrels of arsenic. Man, how you land on things! How you *land* on things!"

"Uh-huh," Asey said, "but what I want to know now is how both the Buntings landed on it. Let's go see if they're normal yet."

Walking back to the doorway, they stood and surveyed the wreckage of the room.

Humphrey was sitting on the glass-strewn floor with his head resting against a bureau. Both his eyes were closed, and the right one looked as if it might stay that way for some time to come.

Ben was leaning against the wall, mopping at his nose.

He glared sullenly at Asey and Ward.

"Ah," Ward said. "Armageddon! All you lack is a bomb crater to make it authentic. What a nice Golgotha you've created, you two, practically with your bare hands. Asey, d'you suppose they're going to offer any explanations?"

"You go to hell!" Ben said.

"Come, come, young Dr. Kildare!" Ward said. "Snap out of your baleful sulk and stop seething. How are you and popsie talking yourselves out of this?"

"It's none of your damn business!" Ben said angrily. "It's nobody's damn business! You—"

Asey took a step forward and reached out.

A second later, Ben found himself dumped into an armchair, with Asey standing over him.

"It's none of my business, Baby Snooks," he said, "but you can tell me things in a hurry, right now, or you can tell 'em to the judge tomorrow mornin' after a nice restful night in jail. Make up your mind."

"You can't put me in jail! I don't have to tell you anything! It's none of your business!"

"You can begin," Asey said, "with explainin' why you rendered a verdict of sunstroke when you knew it was atropine poisonin', or you can begin with the interment of Mrs. Newell's knittin' bag up by the pond. But you begin before I count three."

"You—you know about the bag?" Ben's truculence began to fade.

"Yogi Mayo," Ward said. "Sees all, knows all, figgers the rest. Better tell him, Dr. Kildare."

"He couldn't have seen me! I mean, I—"

"I did," Asey said. "An' if Hanson gets the chance to combine that knittin' bag episode with your sunstroke verdict an' the bottle of atropine that was rollin' around the floor here, he'll make hash of your future career in just about two shakes of a lamb's tail."

"Tell him, Ben," Humphrey said without opening his eyes.

"But, dad—"

"Tell him!" Humphrey repeated. "Tell him before you make matters any worse!"

Ben drew a long breath.

"You're not going to like it, dad."

"I'm sure I shan't. Tell him."

"Well," Ben said, "well—when Lucia first came here, I fell for her. Hell, I don't know how to tell you this!"

"You fell for her," Asey said, "an' wrote her letters. Right?"

"That's it. Say, how did you know?"

"I told you," Ward said. "Yogi Mayo. Sees all, knows all, figgers the rest. I can do some figuring from here myself, Bunting. I once wrote Lucia some letters. She dangled yours right over your head, didn't she?"

Ben nodded.

"It wasn't exactly blackmail. But if I didn't stop opposing her—well, her going around with dad, and all that—then she threatened to do this and that and the other, and—oh, you know! You know what I mean. I don't know how to say it."

"What you mean," Ward said, "is that she gently blackmailed you. Or said she would. I know. I know Lucia. But she probably wouldn't have done a thing if you'd called for a showdown. Lucia just played at being a *femme fatale*. What she really probably wanted from you was a new bracelet. It should teach you a great lesson, young Dr. Kildare. Never write letters to the Lucias of this world. I know from the depths of my own bitter experience that Lucia never threw away a letter. She kept 'em in packets, all neatly labeled. My crop cost me a pair of earrings and a platinum pin, even after she jilted me."

Ben nodded.

"I caught on to that angle. I found out when a pal of mine crashed through with a diamond wrist watch. I went to work then and found out about a lot of little gifts Lucia'd picked up. But there wasn't any sense in trying to tell dad, don't you see? Lucia had him under her thumb! And I wouldn't pay blackmail! I wouldn't do it!"

"So," Asey said, "this noontime, you thought you had a chance to get your letters back, huh?"

"Well," Ben said, "mostly it was a letter. Not letters. You see, I was ass enough to write her another letter a couple of days ago. I get so mad, sometimes, I didn't dare talk with her. So I wrote her and said that sooner or later dad would find out about her, and when he did, she better look out. Because when dad does manage to work himself up to getting sore, he gets good and sore."

"Uh-huh," Asey said. "So I notice."

"And so," Ben said, "when I saw her there under the umbrella today, that was all I could think of at first. My letters. Particularly that last one. And dad. And what I said he'd do to her."

"You mean," Asey said, "you jumped to the conclusion that your father'd found out she wasn't all he thought, an' so he killed her?"

"No! My God, no! But I knew it wasn't sunstroke. And—well, dad hasn't been quite as keen on her these last two weeks. And—uh—"

"Go on," Humphrey said wearily. "Go on! Don't mind me, at this point!"

"Well," Ben said, "I don't know if he'd got sick of her pursuing him, or whether it was Dudley French. Both of 'em have been after dad all summer. French keeps yapping for things to be built or repaired, and Lucia was always wanting something redecorated or prettied up. Anyway, dad didn't seem so keen about Lucia. And twice, lately, someone's poked around in my professional bag, and the hypo case was disturbed, and I thought maybe someone—oh, I didn't know what to think about Lucia, and so I said sunstroke! I had to say something!"

"I can explain about the atropine." Humphrey opened his left eye, winced, and closed it. "I think I begin to understand, Asey. Ben thought he was shielding me. Ben, you idiot child, you told me you needed some new medical stuff, and I was getting it for you as a surprise present before you left!"

"No! Were you?" Ben said. "Why didn't you tell me?"

"Because it was supposed to be a surprise! I had a catalogue from Grady's, but I had to poke around in your bag to see what you'd already bought from that list you'd marked. That's what I was poking around for! I wasn't seeking out poison! I don't know one poison from another! And I bought this new kit for you, and Lucia was keeping it with some other junk so you wouldn't blunder into it before the proper time! And now," Humphrey added bitterly, "you've gone and trampled on everything! I'd just taken that new kit out of the closet when you came barging in here! That's where that atropine bottle came from, that new case!"

"But when I came in here and found you with a bottle of atropine!" Ben said, "what could I think? Why didn't you tell me? Why didn't you explain about the surprise and all?"

Humphrey sighed.

"You gave me a lot of opportunity, didn't you? Jumping on me before I could open my mouth! And what d'you think *I* was thinking, after Mayo'd just told me that Lucia was poisoned with atropine, but you claimed it was sunstroke! I almost broke my neck getting here to grab that kit before Mayo or the police found it and started suspecting you!"

"Gee, dad," Ben said, "I'm sorry! It's all my fault, all of this mess!"

"Not all," Humphrey said. "Some of it's mine. Like your nose."

"No, it's my fault entirely, dad! I—"

"Save that," Asey said, "till I straighten out some

more. What made you think your letters was in that bag?"

"Because Lucia told me once that there wasn't any need of my trying to steal the letters," Ben said. "She told me she had 'em in a safe place I'd never think of looking. And I knew she carried a lot of junk in that bag, and she nearly always had it with her. I figured maybe she kept the letters in it. But she didn't. Then I thought she probably kept 'em here in her desk, and I rushed here to see. But the place was being mobbed by the Ladies' Aid or something, all afternoon, and I never got the chance to get in here till just now. I thought those women would never go!"

Asey picked his way across the floor and looked thoughtfully at the desk in the corner.

"Does it look as if the letters were there?" Ben asked. "What with dad, and all, I never did get to hunt for 'em—say, that's funny, the pigeonholes are all empty! Look in the drawers!"

Except for some old theater programs and a brand new box of unopened stationery, the drawers proved empty.

"Well, well!" Ward said. "Maybe there were two other fellows hunting the letters they'd penned to Lucia, and maybe they got here first! Hm. Mayo, that opens up an entirely new line of thought!"

"Uh-huh," Asey said, and thought of the market basket that Picklepuss Belcher had carried out to her car. "Uh-huh, it does. It sure does. I wonder if that was why that hat bobbled. Huh!"

"Ben," Humphrey said, "I want to tell you something. You too, Asey. I never had any serious intentions about Lucia, no matter what she may have thought. I've just been trying to run the club, and keep peace, and pay the bills, and balance the budget. And once in a while, Lucia had a good idea. Lucia was shrewd."

Ward nodded. "Not awfully bright, but very shrewd and very amusing, in her way. I always enjoyed her. Mayo, what are you brooding about? You look like Barlo Spratt, about to pounce on a shred of oakum."

"I was wonderin'," Asey said, "what Ben said to Mrs. Newell when he gave her your drink that had the atropine in it. An' what she—"

"What *he* said? What Ben said? He? *Him?* He gave her my drink?" For once, Ward lost some of his aplomb. "Ben gave her my drink?"

"What do you mean, your drink?" Ben retorted. "What did you have to do with it?"

"So you gave it to her!" Ward said. "Just as I was beginning to convince myself I'd wronged you! Just as I was putting you and popsie over into the innocent bystander class! Mayo, you don't mean to say that Ben was the one who took that drink out to her!"

"Uh-huh," Asey said. "An' I keep wonderin' what he said to her, an' what she said to him, an' if she knew it was your drink, an'—"

"Now, wait!" Humphrey said plaintively. "Wait! Let a man catch up! Let me get this clear. When you told me she'd been poisoned by atropine, Mayo, you didn't mention anything about a drink! What's this drink? Why did Ben give it to her? What's Ward got to do with it?"

"I ordered a drink sent out to her!" Ward said. "But young Dr. Kil—"

"Oh, you did! It seems to me," Humphrey said, "that Lucia told me you were an old, old friend of hers, and you said something about writing her letters. Now, I wonder—"

"Don't bother," Ward interrupted. "Asey knows I ordered a drink sent out to her. He knows all about my life with Lucia, and how I feel about her. I told him. He found out about the drink, and I recounted the whole situation to him in the woods while he was pretending to be unconscious! I ordered her a drink for Auld Lang Syne, and all that, and there's nothing more to it! Bunting, how did it happen that you took that drink out to her? Leo was supposed to!"

"For the love of God," Humphrey tried to get up, and then limply sat back on the floor again, "Ben, did you take her out a drink? Did you? Isn't there anything you can't stick your foot into?"

"Look, dad, I met Leo just after I left your office this morning!" Ben said. "He was out in the hall. And—"

"Why did you rush away like that, anyway?" Humphrey demanded. "What did you go tearing off for?"

"Oh, after all my efforts to talk turkey to you about Lucia and Dudley, and I thought I was getting somewhere at last, you walked over to the window to wait for her to pass by so you could wave at her!" Ben said. "That was the last straw. It made me so damned mad that I left before I got any madder!"

"You know, young Dr. Kildare," Ward said, "what you probably like to think of as your self-control is a strange and wonderful thing. How did you get into this drink business?"

"I'm trying to tell you, if you'll all stop interrupting and give me a chance!" Ben said. "Out in the hall after I left dad's office, I met Leo, and he was carrying a tray with a drink on it. And I asked him to get my bag from the locker room when he was free and had the chance. And he said he'd get it right away if I'd take that drink out to Mrs. Newell."

"What?" Asey said. "Say that again!"

"He said, he'd be glad to get the bag right away if I'd take that drink out to Mrs. Newell, and he stuck the tray in my hand, and rushed off. I called out to him to carry the damned drink out himself, but he'd gone, so I took it out."

"Huh!" Asey said. "That's very interestin'. Leo told me that you bullied him into gettin' your bag, an' grabbed the tray out of his hand."

"I never did!" Ben said indignantly. "Leo's a weaselly little liar, anyway! So I took the drink out to the beach, and stuck the tray down in the sand beside Lucia, and said there was her drink. Then I left. That was all I said to her, and she didn't say anything to me."

"Who'd you meet on your way to the beach?" Ward asked. "Did anyone stop you, or pass by close to you? Did you stop, or leave the drink, or anything?"

"I didn't stop, and nobody stopped me. I wouldn't know who might have passed by. Lucia was under the umbrella, and I left the drink and went on to the boat. And I stayed there working on it till Charles rowed out and said that Mayo wanted to see me by Mrs. Newell's umbrella."

"If you'd only be consistent," Ward said, "I'd like you better, I think. But one minute you call for bags, implying that you're going somewhere, and the next minute you say you spent an hour or so fixing your boat! Just what was your underlying thought?"

"I was going away on the boat!" Ben said. "As soon as I got things ready, I was going ashore and get my stuff—see here, I didn't put any atropine into your old drink! I didn't know you ordered it. I didn't know anything about it! If atropine was put in that drink, it was put there before I carried it out. Or afterwards. I didn't have anything to do with it!"

"What makes you think that atropine was put into the drink before you got it?" Ward demanded. "It was a spur of the moment gesture, my ordering that drink sent out to her then. No one knew anything about it except Leo, and for all he may be a weasel, you certainly can't accuse that nitwit of having any motives for killing Lucia! I doubt if he was one of her intimate friends! I doubt if *he* wrote her any letters!"

While Humphrey and Ward and Ben debated the point, Asey walked over to the window and looked thoughtfully out over the Thackaberry orchard.

"I wonder, Ward," he said at last, "if maybe you ain't perhaps possibly approachin' this from the wrong angle. Perhaps it's not so much a question of someone's bargin' into your plans, as that maybe your plan of sendin' her out a drink just fitted in awful neat with someone else's plan to kill her."

"A more intricate, complicated and thoroughly involved statement I never heard!" Ward said. "What are you talking about!"

"Wa-el, nobody could of banked on your droppin' into the club an' orderin' a drink sent out to Mrs. Newell, could they? Nobody knew you was goin' to order a drink sent out to her at eleven-thirty, or any other time. But if someone was aimin' to poison Mrs. Newell anyway, you sure provided 'em with one elegant opportunity, Ward."

Ward snorted.

"But that takes you right back to Leo! Leo made the drink. Leo wouldn't know atropine from sodium chloride or the man in the moon! He hasn't any reason to poison Lucia! He's just a nitwit. You know he's a nitwit!"

"I sure thought so when I talked with him," Asey said. "I put him down as a stupid sort of feller with an itch for easy money. He fell like a ton of bricks when I led him into thinkin' that his hundred dollar bill was a fake. 'Course, he might have been puttin' on an act, but I didn't think so. I just thought he was dumb."

"So he is," Ward said. "And that—"

"I don't think so," Ben said. "That flat forehead makes him look stupid, but he isn't. He's bright in a weasely way. On the other hand, I agree with Ward that he isn't bright enough to know how to poison Lucia with atropine, and I don't think he would have if he had known how."

"Well," Ward said, "suppose I did provide someone with an opportunity, and suppose Leo was the tool. Who's behind Leo?"

Asey pointed out that the only person he found behind Leo was Ward himself.

"You an' your hundred dollar bill," he added. "An' I meant to ask you. Did you ever find him an' send him on that South American cruise?"

"Oh, why bring that up!" Ward said. "I thought you and I settled all that by mutual thought waves. I knew you were faking there in the woods, and you knew I knew! I didn't even see Leo back at the club. They said he'd gone—what're you murmuring about?"

Asey grinned.

"I just said, so you asked for him, did you? But I

knew you probably wouldn't find him. He told me it was his afternoon off."

"You know, Mayo," Humphrey said, "there's been trouble with Leo's accounts, and I don't intend to keep him beyond the end of the season, but he doesn't know that. What I'm driving at is that he hasn't any motive for revenge toward me or Ben, and as far as I know, he had no reason to dislike Lucia. She always tipped him well. But he did make that drink, you say? He admitted it? Well, why don't we find him and look into it?"

"You've got a fat chance of finding Leo on his day off," Ben said. "He'll be off on his weekly drunk."

"I know where he lives," Humphrey said. "Suppose we go there and see if we can't locate him. If I have the strength to get up and get into the car, that is."

"Do your eyes hurt badly?" Ben said. "I'll fix you up. Which eye feels worse?"

"It isn't my eyes," Humphrey told him rather pettishly. "It's my tooth. The novocaine's worn off— what're you laughing at, Ward?"

"If you could see your eyes," Ward said, "you'd be laughing too! Your tooth! Man, from where I'm standing, no one would ever suspect you of having teeth. Your face is just a big bulge. Mayo, why don't we divide up and tackle some of these loose ends and ramifications? Cummings said he wished you'd wander back to the club. So why don't you? The Buntings know where Leo lives, so why don't they go there and see if they can get a lead on where he is—who knows, he may be curled up on the sofa with a good book. And if I hurry, I ought to be able to take a look around for Clare before it gets too dark."

"Where'd she go?" Ben asked. "I wondered."

"Why, young Dr. Kildare!" Ward said. "That's the first cordial note I've heard in your voice today!"

"Well," Ben mopped at his nose, "I was awfully rude to her. She came over and talked with me after Cummings came, and I was so worked up about everything, I guess I sort of ignored her. I want to apologize. Where'd she go?"

"Clare's temporarily mislaid," Ward said. "Lost or strayed or stolen or something, we think."

"What?" Ben demanded. "Has something happened to her? What do you mean, sitting there doing nothing if something's happened to her!"

"Ah," Ward said. "Young Dr. Kildare Crashes Through. I'd forgotten, during the last year, what it took to arouse young American manhood. Still—"

"Stop talking!" Ben said. "Stop talking so many words! Words, words, words! If something's happened to her, why don't you *do* something? What happened?"

"She vanished from Asey's roadster up in the woods beyond the village, and I assure you," Ward said, "that we've done what we could. The cops are looking for her, and her description's gone out on the teletype, and all that. Asey and I hunted her, and I'm going to hunt some more while you and your father get hold of Leo."

Humphrey moaned as he got to his feet.

"Mayo, what'll I do about this foul mess?"

"Wa-el," Asey said, "I've heard beefsteak spoken of quite highly."

"I don't mean my eyes! I tell you, they don't bother me half as much as my tooth does! I mean this foul mess here in this room! Ben, I wish you were the sort who thought first! I wish you didn't leap into things so! Why did you ever start anything like this?"

"Why did I start it? I never did!" Ben said. "I only tried to take that atropine bottle from you, and you wouldn't let me!"

"You distinctly said, five minutes ago, that it was all your fault!"

"Well, in a way it was my fault, and I'm sorry about your eyes, but I didn't start it! You shoved me away, and then—"

"You jumped me," Humphrey said, "before I could utter a word!"

"Dad, you pushed me, and then—"

"If you ask me," Asey said, "it was six of one an' half a dozen of the other, an' I don't see how either of you's got the strength to bicker! If you'll take my advice, you'll throw yourselves on the mercy of Sadie Thackaberry, an' split the damages."

Humphrey shuddered.

"That woman! She's more adamant than Belcher,

and deaf as a post to boot! She'll hold us up. Oh, well, I suppose I can get around her. She makes quilts, and I suppose I can always buy some of the damned things! Come on, Ben. The sedan's up the road."

"I've got the beachwagon," Ben said.

"Have you? Well, then we'll go separately and meet at Leo's. Maybe you better see what you can do with my eyes, too," Humphrey added casually, as if the topic had never before been mentioned.

Ward lingered behind after the Buntings finally departed.

"Mayo," he said as he followed Asey into the kitchen of the Thackaberry house, "who cleaned out Lucia's desk? Who took those letters?"

"I don't think it was the Buntings, either of 'em," Asey said. "Get along an' hunt, Ward. I'm beginnin' to be a little worried about Clare."

"So am I. Mayo," Ward said tentatively.

"Uh-huh."

"Don't you think it was strange that Ben should jump on his father that way?"

"Like you said yourself," Asey said, "Ben's self-control's a strange an' wonderful thing. He's had quite a day, what with findin' Lucia, an' worryin' about his father, an' rushin' off with that bag, an' then waitin' an' waitin' for a chance to get here."

"But why didn't he just ask his father to explain, when he found him with the atropine and the hypo case? Why'd he leap at him?"

"Why," Asey returned, "didn't you ask those women that chased you in the woods what they was up to? Why'd Clare go away without a sound? I don't know! I don't know why people do things like they do. But from what I seen of Ben, he's just a kid that acts first an' thinks later. Get along an' hunt Clare."

"I'm going to. Mayo, I'm a little worried about you."

"Why?"

"Your score today is two shots that nearly got you, and one biff that wasn't so good. I'm not an esoteric thinker like you and Barlo Spratt, but those three misses prove two things to me. They prove that whoever's after you is a tenacious sort, and has missed you three times."

"So what?"

"So I'd be very careful, if I were you," Ward said. Asey grinned.

"For all the shootin' an' the biffin'," he said, "the only real damage I sustained up to now is a few ant bites."

"To hear you and Barlo Spratt brag," Ward said, "anyone would think you'd been washed in a magic stream that rendered you bulletproof! Look here, Emperor Jones, if I were the lad who's after you, I think I'd make sure of you next time. I'd make sure by luring you into my little parlor, and then I'd give you the works."

"Meanin'," Asey said, "that you'd place Clare in the parlor window as a kind of lure? I been broodin' over that angle, myself."

"Oh, my God, Yogi!" Ward said. "How do you do it?"

"Wa-el, it's a sort of logical conclusion to come to," Asey said. "Clare don't know anyone hereabouts, an' nobody knows her. But if she's seen in my car with me, somebody might conclude that I'd make an effort to locate her if she disappeared. It's a notion worth toyin' with. After all, for all we know, the man in the car with her was holdin' a gun at her ribs when Dudley French seen her in the woods."

"If that fat fool had only noticed more!" Ward said. "Well, I'll get along. Be careful."

"I will," Asey assured him. "If I get any calls to come quick to Clare, I'll proceed with caution. Get along. I want to look around here before I go to the club—oho! Look who's comin' up the driveway!"

"Clare?" Ward asked excitedly.

"Your pal, Dudley." Asey pointed. "See him stompin' along?"

"Ga! That white-bellied anteater!" Ward said. "I'd immortalize you in headlines if you could only ring that lad in as a suspect! Could I do a job on him! I do not like that big hulk!"

"Tell me, just what *did* take place this mornin' between you an' him? You must have irritated him somethin' awful."

"I did. He caught me in a bad mood, and I cut loose," Ward said. "I was so nasty that Clare chided me for it. I don't recall just what I said, but it was mostly about his waistline. That's his weakest point. Trouble with lads like him is that they can dish it, but they can't take it. And lads like that," he added with relish, "are my meat! I murder 'em. What the hell does he want, I wonder?"

Asey went over to the screen door as Dudley started to pound with his fist against the door frame.

"So you're here!" Dudley said. "Where's Ward? I want Ward! After I get through with him, I'll have a few words with you, Mayo!"

"With me?" Asey asked. "What've I done?"

"What have you done! You stand there and ask me what have you done! Mayo, who in hell do you think you are? My cousin is killed, murdered before your very eyes, murdered practically in your very presence, and—"

"Now, wait!" Asey said sharply. "Hold on, French. I wouldn't go that far. Don't make it sound like I was a party to it all!"

"I'm not sure you're not!" Dudley said. "Why didn't you tell me what had happened? Why wasn't I told at once? As far as I can find out, you didn't even tell the authorities at once! You made no effort to summon the police! I have actual eyewitness proof that long after Lucia's body was found, you sat on the beach and twiddled your thumbs, wasting valuable time!"

"I called the doctor," Asey said. "Matter of fact, I called two doctors."

"Bah! You called young Bunting, but you can't refer to that nincompoop as a doctor! Let me tell you, Mayo, that of all the wanton interference I ever heard about, you're guilty of the worst! But you can keep. I'll settle you later. Right now I want Ward. Where's Ward?"

"Here." Ward stepped to the doorway beside Asey. "Why, it's Big Chief Heap Much Waist! How! How's scalping?"

"I want you!" Dudley said. "I want you!"

"Whatever for, dear?" Ward asked tenderly. "Have you finally learned to care?"

"You'll find out!" Dudley said. "You'll be laughing out of the other side of your face soon enough! I was at the club when you came there a while ago! I saw you. I noticed! *I* noticed!"

"Was my slip showing again?" Ward said. "Mayo, remind me to take a reef in those straps. I simply can't do a thing with 'em!"

"I noticed," Dudley said, "that you were *not* limping!"

He paused dramatically.

"Hear that, Mayo? He was *not* limping! That was all I needed. So I sat down at the telephone—"

"Can you really fit into a phone booth?" Ward interrupted. "Honest?"

"And I called your paper," Dudley was breathing hard and his face was purple, "and I called some people I know in New York, and I found out all I needed to know about you, Mr. Ross Ward! Hear that?"

"Why, man, you've frightened me into goose-pimples!" Ward said. "What fell villainy did you manage to uncover?"

"I found out enough! You got back from France the week before last, all right, but your wound was only a scratch, and it was healed and well ten days ago! Your limp is a fake! Your cane is a fake! And what have you got to wisecrack about that?"

Ward smiled.

"I still think," he said tranquilly, "that a limp becomes me, Fatty. It's picturesque."

"People told me you practically went on your knees and begged to write those articles about the Cape!" Dudley went on. "I thought those articles were fishy! I told Humphrey Bunting as much this morning! I spotted you then for a fake! A man with your reputation doing that stuff! Why, they told me you weren't paid enough to cover postage. Those articles have just been a blind!"

"What for? Tell me quick! I'm as excited," Ward said, "as a child. What are they blinding?"

"They're a blind so you could track down Lucia!

You used to know her! She jilted you! And you ordered a drink sent out to her. Hanson found that out. Someone overheard you giving the order. And Dr. Cummings says—"

"That atropine was put in that drink," Ward finished up. "We know. Now you've got it all off your panting chest, run along. Mayo and I have work to do."

"You knew that?" Dudley waggled his forefinger at Asey. "You knew that, and yet you're letting this murderer run around loose with you? You're protecting him, that's what! Protecting and harboring a murderer!"

"Come, come!" Asey said. "Don't go off half-cocked on this! You don't—"

"Half-cocked, am I? You're the half-cocked one!" Dudley spluttered. "Thinking you can get away with a thing like this! Well, you can't, Mayo! Hanson's going to arrest Ward!"

"If Hanson attempts anything of the sort," Ward said, "I shall see to it that he gets a lousy press. Why, in God's name, should I suddenly want to kill Lucia for jilting me in my youth? I haven't seen Lucia for years. I haven't thought of her in years!"

"Aha! But Lucia was in France!" Dudley said with triumph. "So were you!"

"So," Ward said, "were fifty million Frenchmen and several other people. Go find me a nice motive, Captain Bligh, and if you'll come back in six or eight weeks, we'll see if we have anything for you then."

"Hanson will find a motive!" Dudley said. "He'll find one!"

"If you force Hanson into finding a motive for me—ee," Ward said in a childish treble, "I'll make Hanson find a motive for you—oo! Yah, yah! I'll draw a picture of you in words that'll burn you up, and I'll put it in the paper. So there!"

"You won't laugh when Hanson comes!" Dudley said furiously. "And he'll be here any minute! Because when I saw the Austin outside, I phoned him from Snow's, down the road. I saw you leave the club in the Austin. That's how I tracked you down. Hanson knows you're here, and he's on his way to arrest you!"

"The smack of the informer's lips," Ward said, "could be heard resounding throughout the length and breadth of West Gusset, and was reported audible to several listeners on the quaint outskirts of South Clambake township. I feel that—hey, look!"

Ward broke off suddenly and pointed.

"Look, Mayo! See that? That was Blue Blouse!"

"Who?" Dudley turned around. "I didn't see anyone."

"He started up the drive," Ward pushed past Asey and shoved the screen door open, "and then he saw us and ran! Come on, Mayo, let's get him this time!"

"Where'd he go?" Asey demanded. "You sure you saw him, Ward?"

"Oh, don't ask silly questions! Come on, head him off by the barn! French, quit being mad and help us! Don't just stand there!"

"Who is this person and what do you want him for?" Dudley demanded as Ward hurried past him and across the driveway. "I didn't see anyone."

"Ward did," Asey said, "an' maybe we—French, circle around by the orchard. I'll go this side of the barn. Fellow in a blue blouse an' red pants. Come on an' help!"

Ten minutes later, when Dudley and Asey returned together to the kitchen steps, Ward was nowhere to be seen, and the little red Austin had disappeared.

"It was a ruse!" Dudley said angrily. "A ruse! You knew all the time it was a ruse for him to escape, Mayo!"

"I did not!" Asey said. "There is a fellow in a blue blouse an' red pants that's been sighted around today, an' if Ward was doin' any rusin', he fooled me as much as he fooled you."

"Bah! It was a ruse! Just something else for you to try and explain away!" Dudley said.

"I believed Ward, I tell you!"

"You didn't. And I'll tell you, Mayo, that for your disgraceful, interfering behavior today, I'm going to see you get yours! If this case of Lucia isn't settled to my satisfaction by midnight tonight, I am going to take steps. Hear that?"

"Uh-huh," Asey said, "an' it sounds to me uncommonly like a threat."

"You find Ward!" Dudley said. "I know him for what he is. So do you! Hear that? Get him! Hear that? Get him, and get full proof of his guilt!"

"Or else," Asey said, "what?"

"I'll break you! I'll break you so hard that no one can find the pieces! I'll turn on so much heat that you'll never dare show your face around here again! And it won't make any difference if your friends the Porters come to your rescue. I know just as many important people as they do, and I can match them dollar for dollar. Hear that?"

"Know what I think?" Asey said. "I think someone ought to have spanked you a lot more when you was young, French."

"You dolt! You fool! Is that all you can think of to say?"

"Why, no," Asey said gently. "I can think of lots more, but it'd only be a waste of good breath. You can forgive a spoiled kid for makin' a fool of himself, but there ain't a lot you can say to a spoiled man."

Asey thought for a moment that Dudley was going to strike him.

But Dudley turned and stamped off down the driveway.

Asey grinned, and went back into the Thackaberry kitchen.

He'd heard the little Austin when it drove away,

and only then had he tumbled to the fact that Ward was putting on an act. Ward was prompted, Asey felt sure, not by any fear of being confronted by Hanson, but by the desire to have another hunt for Clare before darkness finally fell. And it certainly was the simplest way to elude Dudley without fuss. In Ward's place, Asey rather thought he might have made a similar gesture.

Retracing his steps through the hall, Asey returned to the shambles of Lucia Newell's bedroom, and then walked beyond to the dressing room and the sitting room which apparently made up her apartment in the Thackaberry house.

After a thoughtful survey, he went back to the bedroom and snapped on the lights.

The damage done by the Buntings had caused them to be a little sheepish before they left, and they certainly had every reason to feel sheepish. The room was a mess.

Asey grinned as he recalled Humphrey's parting statement, some amiable philosophy about things working out all right in the end, and enough having been settled about Ben and himself to have been worth the battered room and his battered eyes. Probably, in time, Humphrey would get around to thinking that it was a good thing and all for the best, and Asey had no doubt that he would wangle Sadie Thackaberry into agreeing with him.

He picked his way through the litter to the desk.

Picklepuss and her cohorts must have cleaned out Mrs. Newell's letters and papers, for there was no evidence of any careless, frenzied haste. It had been a ruthlessly neat and cold-blooded removal. Probably Picklepuss was over at his home waiting for him this minute, with the basket of letters sitting beside her and four million questions on the tip of her tongue.

Asey sighed.

He could have made more progress, he thought, if the Minutewomen had stalled their armed mobilization for a few days.

Sitting down on the edge of the bed, he took out his pipe.

It seemed to him that the earlier part of this affair had been nothing but speculation. Now, since he had left the Yacht Club, it had been nothing but choppy little snitches of action. Just a lot of moving from one place to another place, and being thwarted by someone or something at practically every step of the way. And, when you came right down to rock bottom, nothing very much had emerged either from the speculation or the action.

Or had it?

Asey chewed on his pipe stem and tried to do some mental sorting.

Mrs. Newell obviously hadn't been killed for her diamond bracelets. Or for her possessions, if the contents of these rooms was any guide to their value. Or for her income, if what she herself had told him about her finances was true.

That cleared up the money end.

To judge from what Ward and Humphrey and Ben said, none of them felt so deeply about her as to kill her for love or revenge or any of their ramifications. The consensus seemed to be that Mrs. Newell was all right, but no one you got too serious about for too long.

That settled that.

And it left you, Asey thought, with one of those backhanded motives. Mrs. Newell had been killed before she could disclose something.

Both Ben and Ward claimed that she went in for ladylike blackmail. If that was the case, and someone thought she knew something, why hadn't they bought her off?

"Why," Asey murmured, "did they bother to kill her? Why'd they go to all that work?"

Because anyone who knew her would have known of her weakness for diamond bracelets and platinum pins. Anyone who saw her once, in fact, might well have guessed.

Why, then, hadn't someone tried to buy her off instead of involving themselves in a murder?

Was it too big a thing to bribe her about, or what?

At any rate, it had been big enough for her to call him about, and she had made a fatal error in not making clear just how important it was. Mrs. Newell was shrewd. Everyone agreed on that. She was shrewd enough to understand that she was on to something, but had she understood its importance, herself?

She must have understood it to a certain extent, or she wouldn't have told Jennie when she called his house that it was nothing she could discuss over the phone. That insinuated that she didn't wish to be overheard.

Why, Asey wondered, hadn't she got into her car and driven over to Wellfleet to see him in person? Had she been afraid to leave? And with all those phone booths, couldn't she have found one where she felt safe to talk?

Had she been overheard, anyway, and had someone decided that Mrs. Newell better be stopped right there and then?

"Mayo," Asey said to himself, "you're a dumb-head!"

With all the speculations and distractions and the running around, he'd never stopped to consider just what was implied in the fact of his being shot at, down by his garage, at the same time Mrs. Newell phoned his house.

It was just chance timing, that the phone call and the shot had been more or less simultaneous.

If it hadn't been for the button that had to be sewed on his coat, if Picklepuss hadn't barged in, if there hadn't been all that talk about arming the Minute-women, he would have gone to the garage half an hour earlier than he did. And he would have been shot at then, before Mrs. Newell called.

Her phoning for him hadn't been so important, after all. Whether she'd been overheard or not, someone had already planned to kill her, and to shoot him, too!

Of course, Asey thought quickly! Of course! Mrs. Newell's drawing Ward to one side and suggesting that she had some exciting story to tell didn't mean that she might not already have told the Buntings, or hinted about it to half the people she knew. She might have mentioned it the day before, or days before.

The point was not her telephoning him, or the possibility of her being overheard. The point was rather why she had been killed today, and why he had been shot at today? Why had she waited until today to call him? Why had things come to a head today while Ward was around? Was it possible that Ward might be snooping around on the track of the same thing that Mrs. Newell had stumbled on?

Asey shook his head.

Whoever shot at him from the dune might have been waiting there since daybreak, before Ward ever came to the club or before his prospective visit became generally known.

Why had things all happened today?

Asey wished he knew.

He wished he knew, too, if the person who biffed him in the woods was there by accident, or if the person had followed him on another road in the same fashion that he himself had trailed Ben?

Persons, he mentally amended. There was the biffer, and there must have been someone else. The biffer and his friend.

Was it possible that they might have been following Ben, anyway, and not Asey himself?

That almost made more sense, Asey decided. That would explain why no trusty rifle had been unlimbered and let loose on him. No one had been gunning for Ben, so the rifle wasn't at hand. And so, out of necessity, the biffer had to biff. And the appearance of Clare and Ward had gummed that up.

But could people have followed Ben and not known that Asey was following Ben, too?

And *why* follow Ben?

"Yah!" Asey said suddenly. "I think I got it!"

Before leaving, Ben had told him that he used a pass key to slip into that west wing room and get Lucia's knitting bag. Ben said no one saw him, but Ben might well have been mistaken. Suppose someone had seen him, and had watched him hide that knitting bag in the wooden tub on the terrace?

No one was going to park beside it any more than Asey had. No one was going to lurk around suspiciously. No one had. The only cars parked around the club were the doctor's, Ward's, the Austin, and his own roadster.

After seeing Ben plant the bag, Asey decided, someone had taken himself to a convenient dune and watched through binoculars from a safe distance.

Then, the minute that Ben was seen to grab the bag and leave in such a rush, someone—probably the biffer and his pal—had rushed to their own car and taken up the chase on the shore road, somewhere beyond the potholes.

Even so, Asey thought, they ought to have spotted the chromium of his roadster!

On the other hand, it was possible that they were too preoccupied to notice, just as he himself had been too preoccupied to realize that Ward and Clare were trailing him.

Then, too, he had been watching only Ben's beachwagon with the flapping curtains.

He hadn't noticed or paid any attention to any intervening cars. When Ben swung off the main road, he had swung off on a parellel road. It was perfectly possible that one of the several cars he remembered between his roadster and Ben's beachwagon might have driven along the tarred road some fifty yards and then switched off on still another parallel road. There were at least four lanes that branched off there in addition to the old coach road.

Why should they be so interested to find out what Ben did with the bag?

What did they think Ben was after? Not letters, certainly.

They must have thought that Ben had a clew. That Ben had caught on to something.

And, when you came right down to it, if a woman was as shrewd as Mrs. Newell was supposed to be, wouldn't she have left some sort of clew around, anyhow?

By killing her, people had prevented her from making any startling disclosures. But people still had to face the possibility that she might have done considerable hinting around before she was killed.

"Which," Asey muttered, "is why they went gunnin' for me! They couldn't even take the chance that she might of given me any hints! Huh!"

People were even willing to race around after Ben Bunting to see if he might have caught on to something!

There must be something that someone feared would come to light. It—

A voice from the hall put an abrupt end to Asey's mental sorting.

"Stick 'em up, you!"

TEN.

"STICK 'em up! Put up your hands!"

It was a woman's voice.

"Oh, it's one of you!" Asey said wearily as he peered out into the darkness of hall. "Okay, Moll Pitcher. It's only me. Honest to goodness, can't you let a man alone for ten minutes? Can't you let a body think?"

"Put up your hands, or I'll shoot!"

"Come on in here," Asey said firmly, "an' if you got a gun, give it to me an' stop this tomfoolery nonsense!"

"You put up your hands, or I'll shoot!"

Asey arose and started across the room.

At once a revolver barked and a bullet whined past his shoulder and thudded into the wall beyond.

"That'll do!" Asey said. "That—"

A second bullet practically scraped his ear.

"Next time," the woman in the hall said, "I'll part your hair. Stick up your hands!"

Asey stuck up his hands.

The gray-haired, midde-aged woman who strode into the bedroom was no one Asey had ever seen be-

fore, although as far as dimensions went, she bore
more than a sneaking resemblance to his Cousin
Jennie. She wasn't a whit perturbed about having shot
at him, and from the easy, businesslike way she carried her forty-five Colt, Asey gathered that she was
quite ready and willing to shoot at him a third or even
a fourth time if the necessity arose.

"Who," Asey said in a restrained voice, "are you?"

"Who," the woman returned, "are you? Hey, Mrs.
Thackaberry!" She raised her voice. "Hey, you! Hey,
Sadie! Hear me? It's all right now. You can come
in."

Sadie Thackaberry appeared in the doorway.

"What say, Minnie?"

"I said it's all right, you can come in now."

"You shoot him?"

"Yes!" the woman yelled.

"I thought I heard you," Sadie said. "My, my, what
a mess this room's in! Why, it's awful! It's worse
than when we peeked in the window! That poor woman's things! Who is he, Minnie?"

"I don't know," Minnie said. "Hey, you! Who are
you?"

"Asey Mayo," Asey informed her tartly. "You know.
The one you ladies was goin' to protect an' cherish
an' keep from harm, come what might includin' rattle-
snakes. Remember, huh?"

"Who?" Sadie said. "Who?"

"Asey Mayo! Sadie," Asey said impatiently, "come

in here an' stop gapin' an' tell this woman who I am!"

The woman yelled his message to Mrs. Thackaberry, who edged a little farther into the room.

"Land's sakes, this mess! That poor woman's things! He deserves to be shot! Ask him what he did!"

"What did you do to make this mess?" Minnie inquired.

"*I* didn't make it! I didn't have a thing to do with it! This was done by two other people!"

"Was, was it?" Minnie said. "Humpf!"

"Yes, it was!" Asey said. "I'm just an innocent bystander! I'm just here! This ain't any of my doin's! Look, I'm Asey Mayo! I'm the one that you an' Picklepuss Belcher an' the rest of you Minutewomen was supposed to protect from sabotage! Now, put down that Colt, an'—"

"Keep your hands up! If you move," Minnie told him, "you'll get drilled."

"Say, who in time are you?" Asey demanded.

"Never you mind who I am, mister! But for twenty-eight years I was billed as the Queen of Sharpshooters. So," her hand fondled the Colt, "don't you try any tricks!"

"Listen, Annie Oakley," Asey said, "I don't intend to try any tricks. I'm just tryin' to tell you that I'm Asey Mayo! Yell at Sadie to stop lookin' at the floor an' come over here an' look at me! She knows who I am!"

"What's he keep sayin', Minnie?" Sadie inquired.

"He says," Minnie yelled, "he's Asey Mayo. Is he?"

"Well, he is *not!*" Sadie said. "I never seen Asey Mayo wearin' white pants an' a blue coat in this world! I know Asey. I seen him around for years. He wears ole dungarees, most usually, or corduroy pants, an' a duck coat, an' a yachtin' cap. That's not Asey Mayo!"

"For Pete's sakes, Sadie," Asey raised his voice. "Sadie, look at me. Listen to me! Say—there's a copy of *Newsorgan* over there on the floor. It's a got a picture of me in it. In the auto section. Me an' Bill Porter. Pick it up an' look at it, you an' Annie Oakley, an' then take a look at me! An' hustle up. I got things to do!"

After a lengthy discussion, during which the barrel of the forty-five was trained unwaveringly at Asey's heart, Minnie tossed the magazine aside and shook her head.

"I guess you can't fool me an' Sadie, mister," she announced. "You do look kind of like him in a way, but the face isn't a bit the same."

With a touch of bitterness, Asey suggested that she and Sadie might make some allowance for a news picture.

"Also for some ant bites I picked up today," he said. "I can't help it if my left cheekbone don't look just like it does now! Come on, you two, can't you be reasonable?"

"You ain't Asey!" Sadie said. "You're a fake!"

"You're an impostor." Minnie nodded knowingly. "That's what. An impostor."

"Besides," Sadie said, "where's your car?"

"It's parked down the road a piece!" Asey jerked his head in the direction of the village. "Come along an' I'll show it to you. An' my license, an'—"

"We just come from town," Minnie said. "We just walked up that road, and we didn't see any silver-plated car, like this magazine says you always have with you."

"It's parked off the road, in the bushes! Come on," Asey said, "stick your gun in my ribs an' march me out if you want to, but let me show it to you! If you'll only just let me take my hands down, I'll show you my wallet, an' some letters."

Minnie laughed.

"You sure think we're dumb, don't you? Men always think a woman with a gun's a fool. You think if you can get your hands down, or get outside, you can get away. Not from me, mister! I guess you better lie down on the floor and stay there till Mrs. Belcher comes."

"Now, see here! You ain't goin'—"

"Lie down, and roll over!"

"You want," Asey inquired, "a few barks thrown in, too? Listen, I've had just about enough—"

"Mister," the Colt was ominously steady in Minnie's hand, "lie down!"

"Okay," Asey said. "Okay, Annie Oakley. I'll lie

down in the nice glass. You know what? You've taught me somethin'."

"That's good."

"I used to think," Asey kicked a broken perfume bottle out of his way and cautiously eased himself down on the floor, "I used to think that just about the greatest menace a body could meet up with was a woman armed with a gun she didn't know how to use. I take it back, Minnie. You know how, an' that's worse!"

"Roll over on your face," Minnie said unfeelingly, "and keep your arms stretched out. If you move, it'll be just too bad!"

"Come on, have a heart!" Asey said. "It's all perfumery an' cold cream an' goo down here!"

"Roll over!"

Asey looked at the barrel of the Colt, and rolled over.

"I s'pose," he said, "that a whiff of perfume won't matter much when Hanson turns up. My, ain't Hanson goin' to enjoy this!"

The sight of him spread-eagled out on the floor was going to give Hanson more pleasure than the man had had in years.

And if Dudley French turned up!

Asey chuckled at the thought.

There was always the consolation of knowing that no matter how silly a position Hanson found him in, Hanson's arrival should be a matter of seconds, and would put an end to the menace of this large female sharpshooter with the itching trigger finger.

At the end of ten minutes, Asey began to wonder uneasily if possibly Dudley French hadn't intercepted Hanson en route.

"Look, Minnie," he said at last, "be a good girl an' phone someone to identify me, will you? Phone anyone. Call my Cousin Jennie. Or Doc Cummings. Or—or anybody. Only just call, an' let me get up an' get out of here. I got things to do, woman, an' this's gone far enough!"

"The only person I know hereabouts," Minnie returned, "is my Cousin Mabelle I've come to visit—"

"Call her, then! I know Mabelle. She knows me," Asey said. "I met up with her an' her girl friend Effie in the woods only this afternoon. Call her. Call her quick!"

"She hasn't any phone. And I should think," Minnie told him, "if you knew her so intimately by her first name, you'd know she didn't have any phone!"

"Well, call someone else, then! Call—"

"There's no need your going through all those names again," Minnie said. "I don't know any of 'em. I don't know if they're good or bad. I'm not going to take the word of somebody I don't know about you. For all I know, they might be some of your burglar gang. Stop wriggling. You want me to shoot?"

"Well, then, talk with Sadie!" Asey begged. "Make

her look at me! She ain't hardly bothered to give me a passin' glance!"

"Sadie's upset," Minnie said, "and I'm not going to scream myself hoarse at her and upset her any more. She's real worked up, what with you, and the state of this room, and that poor woman and all. Just you stay put till Mrs. Belcher comes."

And she clung to her stand in the face of every argument Asey could think to muster.

"See here, you," she said at last, "I know Sadie. I used to know her when we both lived in Medford. She says you're not Asey Mayo! I know Mrs. Belcher. If she says you are, well and good. But until she comes and says you are or you aren't, you stay right where you are!"

"If you'll call—"

"I'm not going to leave you to make any phone calls! I wasn't born yesterday," Minnie said. "Where'd you be, before I got to the phone? And Sadie's no earthly good on the phone. She can't hear a thing. Keep still, and stop fussing!"

"Well," Asey said resignedly, "will you break down enough to have Sadie get me somethin' to eat? Toss me a snippet of dog biscuit, or somethin'. I'm starvin' hungry. Hear that, Sadie? I'm starvin'! I think the least you can do is feed me."

The two women consulted, and Sadie finally brought him in two slices of unbuttered bread. After further consultation, Minnie permitted him to move his left hand enough to eat with it.

And, while he ate, the Colt remained inexorably trained on him.

"Don't your hand," Asey inquired, "ever get tired?"

Minnie advised him to start some trickery and find out how tired her hand was.

"Keep remembering," she added crisply, "I made my living with this gun for twenty-eight years. And I still keep in trim. My husband says it's foolish but I always claim you can't tell when a good shot'll come in handy."

"Uh-huh," Asey said. "I'm not goin' to force you into any demonstration. Hey, Sadie, think you could see your way clear to followin' up with a cup of coffee? Or somethin' that'd wash down the crumbs?"

"She didn't hear you," Minnie said, "and I think you've had enough. I think we been pretty good to you, for a man that's caused all the damage you caused here."

"I never did! I told you I never had a thing to do with this mess!" Asey protested.

Minnie smiled.

"All right!" Asey said. "If you're so sure I did, then you telephone the police to come here an' arrest me for it!"

"I guess that proves you're a fake," Minnie said. "Because the police are all busy with a murder. And if you really was Asey Mayo, you'd know about it! There was a murder over at the Yacht Club."

"Is that so!" Asey said with irony.

"Yes, and if you want to know, it's the woman who rents these rooms that was killed, and that's why I'm here with Sadie. Because she was so nervous and upset when she heard the news, she wanted to come straight home. So I said I'd come home and stay with her while Mabelle and Mrs. Belcher was busy. I hadn't hardly got off the bus or got unpacked, but I'm always willing to oblige. Now, you keep quiet and stop talking. Sadie can't hear what we say, and that makes her uneasy, and I'm tired screaming at her."

Mrs. Thackaberry kept wandering in and out of the room at intervals, clucking her tongue, and deploring the awful state things were in.

"I wish Pussy'd come!" she said during one trip. "She'd know what to *do* with this man! It don't seem right for him to stay here this way, but I'm sure *I* wouldn't know what we ought to do with him! Minnie, I've got some of those quilt patterns."

"Now, that's fine! Let me see 'em!" Minnie said with enthusiasm.

Asey moaned.

"Keep still, you! Show 'em to me, Sadie," Minnie yelled. "Mabelle wrote me I'd find some lovely patterns here. She said yours were just fine. Always winning prizes."

Mrs. Thackaberry said modestly that she most usually won with her patterns, if she did say so herself, and summer folks thought they were fine, too.

"Show me the Grange one," Minnie yelled. "The one Mabelle said you're saving for the Grange Fair!"

"I'll get it," Sadie said, and trotted off.

"See here!" Asey said. "Isn't it enough for me to lie here in all this glass an' face cream an' goo without havin' to hear about quilts? Don't you think I suffered enough, Annie Oakley? Ain't you got even a teaspoonful of milk of human kindness? Be charitable! Let me get—"

"You stay right where you are!" Minnie ordered. "Quilts are my hobby, and that's mostly what I came to visit Mabelle for, to see quilts here on Cape Cod and add the patterns to my collection. When I get through looking at 'em, I'll twist 'em around so you can have a look, too, if you're getting restless!"

Asey mentally catalogued the ensuing minutes as some of the most trying he ever remembered living through.

Sadie Thackaberry kept trotting in with quilt after quilt, and pattern after pattern, and design after design. By moving his head and peering out of the corner of his eye, Asey could see the pile of quilts and the heap of patterns growing beside Minnie.

But that individual never let herself get carried away beyond the point of rhapsodizing over the quilts and the patterns.

The hand that held the Colt never wavered one iota.

While Asey tried to concentrate on what Mrs. Newell had stumbled into, and why she had been killed today, and why he had been shot at today, Minnie and Sadie Thackaberry discussed quilts. While he tried to figure what had happened to Clare, Minnie yelled tidbits of quilt lore into Sadie's ear. While he wondered where Hanson was, and where Ward was, and where Dudley was, and where the Buntings were, and if they'd found Leo, Minnie and Sadie continued to discuss quilts. They discussed patterns. They compared designs. They argued about stitches. They considered materials.

Asey began to understand how Ben Bunting must have felt that afternoon as he waited and waited for the Minutewomen to leave.

But at least, he thought, Ben didn't have to listen! He didn't have to lie on a glass-strewn floor while two women screamed about quilts!

"The Grange one's best," Minnie said. "It's far and away the best. That's good!"

"I copied that pattern, but I think I made it better," Sadie said complacently. "I'll try and hunt up the original so you can see. I expect to win the Grange Fair with that."

"It's that variation that does it," Minnie said.

"That's like the one I copied. Mine's different in the colors. Now—"

It was nearly nine o'clock before relief arrived in the form of Picklepuss Belcher.

Asey blessed her loudly and devoutly, but he knew better than to move at once.

"Tell Minnie who I am!" he said. "Tell her quick!"

"For mercy's sakes, Asey Mayo, what're you doing on the floor in all that mess!" Picklepuss said. "For mercy's sakes!"

"Is he?" Minnie demanded. "Is he really Asey Mayo? He *is*? Humpf! You just can't believe a thing you read, can you? It said in that magazine he was real clever. 'Alert, brainy Mayo,' they called him, or something like that."

"I can't understand, Asey," Picklepuss said plaintively, "what you're doing lying there on the floor! Jennie claims you do some awful queer things, but I can't imagine what'd make you want to lie down on floors! Particularly a messed-up floor like this!"

"Don't you think for one minute," Asey said as he stood up, "that I was lyin' there from choice! The only reason for me bein' prone among this—this cosmetic chaos here is the Colt your girl friend's got in her hand! Minnie," he added, "knows how to handle a gun."

"She's promised to show us girls how to shoot," Picklepuss said. "I was so glad when Mabelle said she'd changed her mind and decided to come for two weeks, after all. What's the matter, Minnie, what are you shaking your head for?"

"Just thinking," Minnie said, "that he wasn't so alert and brainy. You see, I held him up." She went into the matter in some detail. "And so," she concluded, "you see, he *let* me! Why, my husband—my first husband, that is—why, he'd have had that gun out of my hand before I could pull the trigger! He was an acrobat."

"I don't know," Asey said thoughtfully, "whether I ought to wish I'd been an acrobat, or thank my lucky stars I wasn't your first husband."

Minnie favored him with a broad grin.

"Say," she said, "you don't seem to be very mad with me. You don't seem so sore."

"I stopped bein' both," Asey said, "about a quarter to nine. At this point, I've give up feelin'. Pussy, the Buntings made all this mess in a fight they had. Explain it to your sister Sadie before she goes crazy tryin' to figure out what we're sayin'. The Buntings'll settle with her for the damages. Now, I'll be gettin' on to the club, to—"

"Wait!" Picklepuss said. "I've got a lot of things you've got to see." She drew a sheaf of papers out of her handbag. "Here's the report of what she did yesterday."

"You mean," Asey eyed the sheaf, "*all* that's just about what Mrs. Newell did yesterday?"

"What she did, and where she went, and who she saw. And you wouldn't believe it!"

"Believe what?" Asey asked.

"Who she saw," Picklepuss said. "You'd never guess."

"Who was it?"

"Men."

"What d'you mean, men?" Asey demanded.

"Just men," Picklepuss said succinctly. "Nothing but men. Just one man after another."

"Like who?"

"Humphrey Bunting, and John Coppinger, and Admiral Carey—"

"The old fellow in the wheel chair?"

"He was frisky enough when he talked to her, I was told," Picklepuss said with a sniff. "And Fred Parsons, and Bobby Ott—"

She went on and on through a list of names, most of them familiar to Asey.

"See?" she said as she concluded. "All men!"

"But no strangers, or nobody you didn't know or recognize?"

"Only one. That Georgeopolis one. But he just turned out to be the fruit man's nephew that was helping him for the day. And then of course I suppose that Eric's a stranger to most people. Eric Martin. He's the artist that comes down twice a year and draws pictures for my advertising. Lucia Newell went out with him last night. She—wait, Asey, wait! I want you to see the letters that was in her desk. You wait, now. I've got the basket right here!"

"You don't expect me to read all those letters!"

Asey protested as she dragged the basket toward him.

"We did," Picklepuss said. "We went through every one. And they prove two things!"

"I wish I could prove two things," Asey said with a sigh. "Ward can, an' you can, but all I can do is sort of speculate. What do they prove?"

"They prove that Lucia Newell was no better than she should be," Picklepuss said darkly, "and was a Fifth Column!"

"You mean, you surmise she was," Asey inquired, "or did you find some proof?"

"All those letters," Picklepuss pointed dramatically at the basket, "was from men! Only men! From France and Spain and Portugal and the Argentine and Cuba and Italy and Rumania. And two from Berlin. They were just about salmon fishing in Norway, those two were, but I haven't a doubt it's all code. I tell you, she was a Fifth Column! Don't you think she was?"

"Wa-el, no," Asey said, "I don't. After hearin' her tell me about her place in France that got bombed, and about all the people she knew that was killed, I don't think you'd ever call her any Fifth Column. On the contrariwise."

"Then," Picklepuss said tartly, "why'd she only get letters from *men*? And all of 'em from all those foreign places?"

"Probably," Asey said, "because she happened to know a lot of men that happened to live in those foreign places. That's about the best reason I can think of to give you."

Picklepuss sniffed.

"Well," she said, "I think she was a Fifth Column. I think that's why she was killed. And after reading some of those letters, I'm not surprised a bit that she was. I think it's a wonder that someone didn't kill her before. Why, you wouldn't believe the things in—"

"Say," Minnie interrupted, "a car just came in the driveway. And there's another. Want me to go see who it is?"

"It'll be Hanson," Asey said. "Or Ward. Or someone for me. I'll go."

"It'll be Mabelle or some of the girls," Picklepuss said. "I'll go!"

Picklepuss, they found when they got to the kitchen, was right.

It was Mabelle and Effie, and sandwiched between them was a man in a blue blouse and red pants.

"We got him," Mabelle said with pride. "We finally got him, Pussy! Here he is!"

Picklepuss clucked her tongue.

"Why, Eric!" she said. "I didn't know they meant you! I never dreamed it might be you!"

"Mrs. B.," the man in the blue blouse said unhappily, "are these women all right? I mean, are they sane?"

"Why, Eric! Well, well," Picklepuss said, "now what do you know about that! And you told me yourself you were going to walk out to the dune this morning! But I never thought of you. You never entered my head. And I never thought of you with a blue blouse and red pants. You usually wear green or gray!"

The man said rather coldly that he had several suits.

"Isn't he a sabotager?" Mabelle demanded. "Isn't he the one that shot at Asey from the dune?"

"My dear good woman, I'm an artist, and I'm doing local sketches to dress up Mrs. B.'s pickle advertising for the coming year!" the man said. "Mrs. B. knows me. She knows my father, my sister, and two uncles! I kept telling you that! Mrs. B., what's this all about, anyway?"

"Well, it certainly is too bad, this little misunderstanding!" Picklepuss said hurriedly. "Asey, this is Eric Martin. And just think, Mabelle and Effie have been chasing him all day!"

"Haven't they," Erie said with feeling, "haven't they just! Mrs. B., I want some explanations, if you please!"

"She'll give 'em to you," Asey said. "You will, won't you, Pussy? Only before she starts in, tell me somethin'. Did you notice anyone wanderin' around that dune this mornin' with a gun?"

"Only these two women." Eric pointed to Mabelle and Effie.

"See anyone with a gun later, after you left the dune?"

"I met a man who said he was a plainclothes cop who asked me that," Eric said. "But as I told him,

I hadn't seen anyone except these women on the dune. Of course, there might have been someone, some man with a gun around. But I wasn't paying much attention to things."

"How about still later, in the woods?"

"Only these two again. Practically everywhere I've looked," Eric said, "I've seen these two. They just yanked me away from my dinner in a restaurant up in the village. Mrs. B., what's the idea?"

"Tell him, Pussy," Asey said. "I'm runnin' along now. Good-by, Minnie. Good-by, girls. I'm through. Yell good-by at Sadie for me an' thank her for my stale loaf. Say, Minnie, would you do me a favor an' lend me your gun?"

"Why?"

"Because," Asey said, "I been intendin' all day to go home an' get my own Colt, only I never managed to get around to it."

"I don't know as I'd like to let you take this particular one," Minnie said, "but you can have the one I carry in my pocketbook, if that'll do you any good. It's just a little thirty-eight."

"Just a wee mite of a spare, huh? I think I'd like to borrow it," Asey said. "An'—er—good as you are, don't go cuttin' loose on anyone in a reckless fashion, will you?"

Minnie smiled and shook her head as she gave him the spare from her bag, and Asey tucked it in his belt and departed for his car up the road.

Before he backed the roadster out of the bushes, he saw a small convertible coupé drive past. It was one of the two that had been parked in Sadie's driveway, and Eric was driving.

A half minute later, Mabelle's car followed.

Asey chuckled and wondered if the girls were calling it a day and going home, or if maybe they might still be keeping Eric under surveillance anyway. He had a feeling that Picklepuss's identification of the man had not entirely pleased Mabelle and Effie.

He drove directly to the Yacht Club, but at the turn by the potholes on the beach road, a state cop stopped him.

"Hi, Charley," Asey said. "On guard?"

"Just trying to keep out the riffraff," the cop said. "All God's children been around here today, and the club members got so sore that Hanson posted me to shoo 'em away."

"Am I raffish," Asey inquired, "or can I go on?"

"Sure you can go on! What'd you think, I didn't know you when you streaked along that road? I only just stopped you to tip you off that Hanson's peeved with you, Asey."

"With me? Why?"

"I guess you know, all right!"

Asey shook his head.

"Well, he'll get over it," Charley said. "But I thought I'd be a pal and tip you off."

"What's he peeved about? Ward? Has French been gettin' him worked up?"

"Is French the fat guy? He's the guy got sore at everybody being around," Charley said. "But he didn't get Hanson peeved with you. He didn't even know about it."

"About *what?*" Asey said. "I don't know what you're drivin' at."

"Can't even guess, I suppose!"

"No, I can't!" Asey said. "Come on out with it! What's Hanson peeved with me for?"

"Just take it a little slower, old-timer. That's all! I'll be seeing you."

Asey shrugged as he drove along to the club.

He still couldn't guess what Hanson was peeved about, but if Hanson was around, he would probably find out soon enough.

As he got out of the roadster, Dr. Cummings bustled down the terrace steps towards him.

"My God, where have you *been*, Asey? Can't you just manage, just once in a while, to get in touch with me? Can't you even leave a phone number?"

"Most of the places I been this afternoon," Asey told him, "didn't have phone numbers. What you so het up about?"

"Who wouldn't be het up? You don't know the afternoon I've put in! I phoned here for you, I phoned there for you, I sent people after you, and they just disappear into a void, too! For the last two hours, I've even had my wife driving around trying to find your car! Why can't you stay *put!*"

"For the last hour or so, I been more put," Asey said, "than you'd imagine. I—"

"I don't believe it. You couldn't have been! Asey, Hanson's earnest and he's honest, but you know as well as I do, Hanson mustn't be tried too far! He—"

"Look here, I don't know why he's peeved with me! I haven't any idea why—"

"Hanson," the doctor ignored Asey's interruption, "is capable of coping with one corpse, after a fashion, but you shouldn't expose the poor man to a wholesale massacre! He simply can't cope with it!"

"Doc," Asey said, "are you tryin' to break it to me gentle that we got another corpse?"

"Why, yes," Cummings said. "Leo."

"Leo?"

"Exactly. And a very messy bit of business, if you should ask me. Very messy indeed."

ELEVEN.

WHEN did this happen?" Asey demanded. "The Buntings left to get him—did you see 'em?"

"As far as I know, the Buntings have disappeared into the void with Ward—did you ever meet up with him? He went off in Mrs. Newell's Austin, hell-bent on finding you, and I haven't laid eyes on him since! If people would only let me know—"

"Yes, yes! What happened? When? Here, let's go inside where we can talk!"

"Well, I don't know where you can go," Cummings said. "The place is full of cops, and where there aren't cops, there are red-faced men talking about sea power. The bar's closed, out of deference or something, and so's the dining room. Here, come sit in the car. No, not yours. Somebody'll just spot you in it and whisk you off somewhere else. Come sit in mine."

"Okay." Asey got into the doctor's sedan. "Now, what happened?"

"Well, Hanson went to get Leo after he found out about the drink situation, and then he sent for me. I tell you, Asey, the state of that cabin where he lived is one of those sights I'm going to remember along with the shambles when old man Drown ran amok and chopped up his wife with an ax. Remember that? I always thought that was a nasty sight, but Leo's cabin was worse."

"What'd happened?"

"Well," Cummings lighted a cigar, "as far as Hanson can find out, he left the club a little after three in his jalopy, and he told people he was going straight home to change his clothes, and then he was going to Provincetown to see his girl. Well, he got to his cabin —it's a shack on that godforsaken stretch near the Weesit line. By the marshes. And he started to change his clothes. And then he had, or was given, a drink with some atropine in it."

Asey whistled softly.

"Like Mrs. Newell, huh?"

Cummings nodded.

"Huh!" Asey said. "He left here before you heard from Boston. Presumably he didn't know about Mrs. Newell bein' poisoned or even that she was dead. At any rate, I'd swear he didn't know when he left the bar. Huh. Doc, you think he might know what atropine was?"

"I doubt it," Cummings said. "And even if he did know, I'm sure he wouldn't have put it into his own drink."

"So," Asey said, "you can figure that somebody come to the cabin while he was changin', an' in the course of events, slipped a tablet into his drink. That what Hanson decided?"

"He decided it," Cummings said, "and I proved it. There were just two things intact in that cabin, Asey. One of 'em was the glass, miraculously enough. There was a drop or two in the bottom. Enough for me to work with—by the way, Asey, did you speak with that fellow that brought back Mrs. Newell's glass?"

Asey shook his head.

"Well, I did," Cummings said. "He told me she was sound asleep, and looked hot and red, which proves my thought that she was in a coma and had a high fever. And d'you remember I said she could have had another kind of reaction?"

"Somethin' about she might have gone mad?"

"That's it. Well, Leo did. That's why the place was such an ungodly mess. He went stark, raving mad, and tore the place apart. Literally pulled it apart with his bare hands. I never saw anything so hideous."

"No outside chance that someone might have come to rob him, an' got into a fight?" Asey asked, thinking of the hundred dollar bill.

"No," Cummings said positively. "Of course you can't tell who might have been there. Fingerprints and footprints are out, in all that bloody mess. But besides the glass, the other thing that was intact was his money box. Little tin box that one of Hanson's boys found under a loose floor board. Had about thirty dollars in small bills, and then a hundred dollar bill. Know what Hanson decided at first?"

"What?"

"Decided it was suicide!" Cummings said with disgust. "I said to him, 'Here's a fellow on his day off getting ready to see his girl, with a hundred and thirty odd dollars in his hand, as you might say—think *he's* going to commit suicide?' Then Hanson said maybe it was an accident! Think of it, an accident! Just as if people kept atropine around the house like aspirin, and the slightest little jiggle of your elbow knocked it off the shelf into your drink. Ever hear such nonsense?"

"In a way, no," Asey said. "But in a way, maybe that's how the atropine landed in the drink, doc."

"With a little jiggle, you mean?" the doctor inquired acidly. "Don't be silly, Asey!"

"No, I mean that maybe someone told Leo that the tablet was like an aspirin, or a soda mint, or somethin' that'd cure his headache or make his stomach feel better, or generally do him good," Asey said. "From my own experience with Leo, I'd say you could inveigle him into takin' a pill without much trouble."

"From my own experience with mankind," Cummings returned, "I'd say you could inveigle almost anybody into taking pills. People *like* pills. I've known my own wife to take a pill because she heard someone say that the stuff cured a friend of hers. But I don't think that angle matters so much. The fact is, he got the pill."

"Now, I wonder," Asey said. "Suppose that Leo put the atropine into Mrs. Newell's drink because he was bribed to, without knowin' what it was—"

"Without knowing what it was? Oh, no! People will always take pills themselves, Asey, I'll grant you that. But I don't think people would put pills into other people's drinks without asking a few questions first!"

"You wouldn't, an' I wouldn't," Asey said. "But consider, doc. This is supposed to come out to look like Mrs. Newell had suffered a sunstroke. Right? There was a chance it might have passed as sunstroke. Right? But that plan gets gummed up. Now, with the chance that it might be taken as sunstroke, there wasn't any need to bother much about Leo. But if it turns out as a murder, an' a poison case, then Leo may up an' say somethin' about the pill he was told to put in the drink. So, before Leo can speak up, he's given a nice pill himself."

"That may be," Cummings said. "But I should think Leo'd have been curious about the whole business!"

"Suppose he is. Suppose he wants to know what the pill was. So someone says, with a hearty laugh, Leo can try one himself an' see it's harmless. Tells Leo to put a pill in his drink, an' the fellow'll put one in his, just to prove it's harmless, and wouldn't hurt a cat."

"Whereupon," Cummings said, "the someone puts an aspirin into his own drink, and some atropine into Leo's. Well, we probably won't ever know what went on, or how he was maneuvered into taking it, but, boy, he sure got it! Say," the doctor leaned forward and turned on the car radio, "did you hear about that Cunarder going down, Asey? That's the one I crossed on in nineteen-twenty-nine."

"Doc," Asey said, "don't! Don't put that thing on! Honest, I mean it! Every time I've moved today, or tried to get started on a train of thought, I've heard about those sinkin' ships. The minute I try to add things together, comes another torpedoed ship! Turn it off!"

"Well, if that's all you care about the destruction of civilization!"

"I do care," Asey said, "but right now I've got something else to think about."

"All right!" Cummings said. "All right, but I wish you'd get started. I wish you'd stop sitting on your tail like a book end, and get going!"

"Do, do you?"

"Come, come, don't be that way! Tell me," Cummings said, "what you make of all this. And be quick. I've got calls to make. Who's strewing atropine all over the place? What about Mrs. Newell and Leo? What's behind this business?"

"Wa-el," Asey said, "somebody decided Mrs. Newell was gettin' to know too much about somethin', so they caused atropine to be slipped into the drink Ward ordered for her. That part I'm sort of sure of."

"And Leo put the atropine in it," Cummings prompted as Asey paused.

"Uh-huh. But I don't think he knew what it was, doc. If he'd even had an inklin', he'd never have got caught himself. An' I don't think that it's bein' Ward's drink mattered so much. I think any drink would have served the same purpose as his."

"How? What d'you mean?"

Asey pointed out that anyone could easily have ordered and sent her out a cocktail before lunch.

"For all we know," he went on, "someone may have planned to do just that. But Ward's drink happened to fit into the picture. An' bein' as how that drink was largely a matter between Leo an' Ward, you can figure that Leo provided someone with the information concernin' it."

"Leo," Cummings said, "doesn't seem to have been an entirely admirable citizen. I gathered that from some cracks I heard the stewards making about him. A little on the unsavory side."

"I think Leo's main idea was easy money," Asey said. "He let Ward bribe him, he let me bribe him, so it stands to reason he let someone else bribe him about the goin's on with that drink. Hey, didn't you say that there was a hundred dollar bill, an' about thirty in small bills in his cabin?"

Cummings nodded.

"Then I bet you," Asey said, "that whoever come to his shack an' give him the atropine was the guy that was going to pay him off! Anyway, whether Leo knew what was goin' on or not, he was in on things, an' before he got a chance to sell or tell what he knew, he got erased."

"What's important enough to poison two people for?" Cummings inquired. "You don't go around poisoning people on this scale just for a whim! What's behind all this? Who's behind it? Bunting? What've you found out since I saw you, anyway? Catch me up on things."

Asey's summing up of his afternoon and evening adventures was a masterpiece of brevity.

"My God!" Cummings said when he concluded. "And I wondered why you couldn't manage to leave a phone number! Asey, what about the Buntings? D'you believe 'em? It seems to me that the commodore's just a bit too naïve in his explanations! And Ben and that knitting bag, now—I think that's suspicious as hell, Asey. Why'd he take the bag way off to the woods? You don't have to rush something four miles away just to take a peek inside of it!"

"Before he left Sadie's just now, I asked him why he picked that spot," Asey said. "He told me he didn't want to be seen opening the bag around the club house, where most anyone would recognize it for Lucia's. He said the road to the woods was the first turn he came to that seemed like a good place to go."

"Bah!" Cummings said. "Do you believe that? Do you believe that Humphrey Bunting doesn't know any better than to ask money for one thing and use it for another? And what about Ward? I thought when he walked out to Mrs. Newell's car that he walked pretty spry for a man who'd been limping so. And what about those fool Minutewomen? And Picklepuss?"

Asey chuckled.

"You make 'em all sound like a vast underground movement, lumpin' 'em together like that, doc."

"Well," Cummings said, "I think that Ben went flying away like that to get you off the track. And I think he got the girl. He circled around and came back and crept up on you and got her. She wouldn't yell out at the sight of him, now, would she? No! And I think French is right. I think Ward's up to something. And I think you certainly ought to bear in mind that Picklepuss's factory is around in those woods. And I don't see why you let this fellow in the blouse and red pants—what's his name. Eric.—I don't see why you let him go without first checking up on him!"

"I never thought of him as anything but an innocent tourist," Asey said. "I told Picklepuss so, first off. And I don't think Ward's after anything but some sort of scoop. I think he's on the trail of somethin' he thinks is big enough to make a lot of elaborate plans for. He's one of those fellows who go all up in the air over crazy ideas—"

"Hey!" Cummings said suddenly, and whistled to someone coming down the terrace steps. "It's a steward," he added parenthetically to Asey. "Got another call for me, I suppose. Hey! Hey, you, I'm here!"

The boy came over to the car.

"Want me?" Cummings asked. "Got another call?"

"There's a phone call for Asey Mayo, and someone said his car was out here—oh, hello, Mr. Mayo. I didn't see you in there. Mr. Ward wants you on the phone. He says it's urgent."

"Wait for me, doc," Asey said. "I'll be right back."

He was grinning when he returned from the club a few minutes later.

"Golly," he said, "that fellow can talk fifty to the dozen!"

"What's he want? He found the girl?"

"No. He's just heard the news about Leo, an' he says he wants to join the Clean Breast Department right away."

"Aha!" Cummings said. "He's scared of Hanson, and he wants to get you on his side!"

"I don't think he's scared of Hanson," Asey said. "I don't think he's scared of anybody. But he says he don't feel like bein' curtailed, an' it seems there's two cops spread out on the porch of the Inn, waitin' ominous for him to return."

"Where's he now?" Cummings asked.

"In his room at the Inn, only the cops don't know it. Seems Mrs. Newell's little car broke down, so he

walked back, an' apparently nobody noticed him go
to his room. The cops took it for granted he wasn't
there because the car wasn't. He thinks it'd be nice if
I dropped over so the two of us could pool our information. He's goin' to sneak out an' meet me in the
lane behind the Inn in half an hour."

"*I* think he's mixed up in this mess, that's what I
think," Cummings said. "And if he isn't, he'd better
have a damn good story. He's going to need one when
Hanson pounces on him."

"What's Hanson pouncin' on him for, anyway?"
Asey wanted to know.

"Oh, you know Hanson! You know how impres-
sionable he is when he's confused!" Cummings said.
"And with that fat French barking at him that Ward's
a villain—what's French got against Ward, anyway?
Did they know each other before? Were they old
friends, or old enemies, or something?"

Asey shrugged.

"Far's I know," he said, "they never met till this
mornin'. But they had a spat out on the dune, an'
Dudley's still smartin' from Ward's wisecracks. He
took it hard."

"Well, he's been roaring around, denouncing Ward
left and right," Cummings said. "Bossing everyone—
I knew he was a touchy sort, but I didn't know he was
so bossy. He got in my hair."

"Offhand, I'd say that gettin' into folks's hair is the
thing Dudley does best," Asey remarked. "He got

tangled up in mine a little while ago. Ordered me to arrest an' convict Ward an' hang him by midnight—"

"Or he'd break you into so many little smithereens that all the king's horses couldn't put you together again," Cummings finished up the sentence. "That's what he's been telling Hanson, and Hanson was falling for it. Hanson's—my, my," he added as a police car sped up to the terrace steps and came to a noisy stop, "speak of the devil!"

A moment later, Hanson stalked over to the car.

"Hullo," Asey said. "How you doin'? How—"

"Now, see here!" Hanson said. "I've had enough! You've just gone too far, Asey!"

"What d'you mean?"

"You know what I mean! You slow down!" Hanson retorted.

"Look," Asey said, "what *is* this?"

"I suppose you didn't force two cars off the Weesit road this afternoon, going around a hundred and ten?"

"I did not!"

"Oh, you didn't! I suppose you didn't just kill Ott's dog, over in Wellfleet?"

"I did not!" Asey said. "Who says so?"

"Ott saw you himself! He saw your car! I tell you, I won't stand for these sort of things, Asey! It's okay by me if you want to kill yourself racing around back roads, but when it comes to ditching cars and killing dogs and racing like a fool around main roads, I'm calling a halt!"

"But—"

"I'm not kidding you!" Hanson gave Asey no chance to speak. "I've had enough, see? As soon as I get this mess cleared up, I'm going to have your license taken away—no, you needn't try to talk me out of it! You needn't bother to say a word. That's that!"

He stalked away toward the club.

"I told you so!" Cummings said. "I told you that some fine day you'd get into trouble, tearing around the way you do! What happened?"

"Nothin'."

Asey watched thoughtfully as Hanson mounted the terrace steps.

"What did you *do?*" Cummings persisted.

"Nothin'," Asey said again. "I already told you what went on this afternoon an' this evening', an' you didn't hear any details about my forcin' cars off the road, or runnin' over dogs, did you?"

"But, Asey, if Ott saw you! He knows your car! He wouldn't make any mistake about your car!"

"I wonder, did it ever occur to you, or Hanson either," Asey said, "that my Porter roadster ain't the only Porter roadster in the world?"

"But isn't yours different? Isn't yours unique? I thought," Cummings said, "that your roadsters were always super-special models built just for you. Aren't they?"

Asey shook his head.

"The one I got now ain't. Oh, the engine's a little

fancier, an' there's a few special gadgets here an' there that's sort of on the de luxe side, but the body's standard, doc. So's the chrome finish. Huh. Now that I think of it, Clare claimed that she saw me yesterday, dawdlin' along the Orleans shore."

"And you weren't?" Cummings asked, and then immediately answered his own question. "No, of course you weren't! You never dawdled along that road in your life! Not when I was ever with you, anyway. Asey, you'd better look into this. If there's someone else racing around in a Porter, doing things you're going to be blamed for, you'd better locate him. Because *I* think that Hanson's going to get tough with you. I think he meant that about taking away your license!"

"I'm sure he did," Asey said. "Huh!"

Cummings leaned back and laughed.

"I don't know why," he said, "but the thought of you trudging along the dusty highway on foot is just too silly! Ha ha! Wonder if people'd recognize you without a car?"

"Judgin' from my experience at Sadie's this evenin'," Asey said, "the answer's ha-ha-no. Doc, it just occurs to me that maybe it might be sort of bright for someone to get a car like mine hereabouts."

"It'd be nice for Porter's business, I'll admit," Cummings said, "and I'd think I was pretty bright if I owned one."

"What I mean is, s'pose someone was aimin' to engage in a lot of underhanded work," Asey said. "They could get away with quite a lot, couldn't they?"

"Asey, what a hell of an idea!" Cummings sat up straight. "Say, why didn't anyone ever think of that before? With a car like yours, people could come and go and rip around—why, anyone could get away with murder before you caught on! Go phone around, Asey. See if you can't find out who it is!"

"I think," Asey said, "that maybe perhaps I will."

"And while you're gone," Cummings snapped on the radio, "I'll hear a little news. It's just time for Burton Grimming Smith, Junior. I like him."

Smith, Junior, was just winding up his recapitulation of the day's bombed areas and sunken ships when Asey returned.

"Find out?" Cummings pushed some sheets of paper into a portfolio. "Here, let me shove this out of the way before you get in. Find out who?"

"By dumb luck, yes. I called Harry's garage, an' Harry found out from some of the boys in the back room. Doc, this is sort of interestin', this is."

"Who?"

"Remember," Asey said, "a fellow named Ramon Barradio?"

"What? That wart? I thought he was safe in Atlanta for life! They never got him for any of the killings, but didn't they salt him away for income taxes along with Alex and the others?"

"Uh-huh. But he's out, he's home, an' he's drivin'

a brand new Porter just like mine. After I go see Ward—I bet he's frothin' at the mouth waitin' for me—after I see Ward, I'll hunt Ramon up," Asey said, "an' have a little chat with him."

"Asey, if he's got a new Porter, Ramon's in the money again!"

"Seems," Asey said, "as if."

"Well, he's not running rum, and he's not mixed up with these problems here. You could bet your last dollar that Ramon'd never bother with poison as long as bullets were being manufactured. Asey, what d'you suppose he's up to?"

"I think it'll be very interestin' to find out," Asey said as he opened the door of the sedan. "An' I'm not goin' to waste much time before I do find out, either. Because Harry said he'd been around town three or four days, an'—"

He broke off and stood with one foot on the running board as Ben Bunting's beachwagon rattled up, and Ben jumped out.

Clare Heath jumped out after him.

Asey yelled at them as the pair started for the terrace steps.

"Asey!" Clare said. "We were just going in to find you! Asey, I've had the most exciting time!"

"Where'd you come from? Where've you been? You all right? What happened?"

"I found her," Ben said. "Over in the woods beyond Belcher's pickle factory. I stumbled over her. Literally,

I mean. Tripped over her and fell headlong. Wasn't that luck? I'd been hunting her since I left you at Sadie's, and I was just on the verge of giving up and going home."

"So you didn't go to Leo's, after all?"

"Oh, I intended to," Ben said, "but then I decided it would be better if I hunted Clare. And it was, wasn't it? You see, we used to have a house on the shore there, and I know those woods like a book. Dad located Leo for you all right, didn't he?"

"I wouldn't know," Asey said. "I haven't seen him. Probably he had a better idea, too. Clare, what happened?"

"Well, I know now I was all wet, if that makes you feel better," Clare said. "But it was one of those things that seemed sheer genius at the time. I heard a noise just after you left the car, Asey, and I started to press down on the horn. Then I had this inspiration. I thought, why scare this person away? If I blow the horn, he'll only run away—don't you think they would have, Asey?"

"Maybe. Go on," Asey said.

"Well, it seemed so utterly ridiculous to scare people off," Clare said. "Because you'd only have to keep on hunting them. Or you wouldn't know who in the world it was. And nobody knew me—"

"So you thought you were safe," Asey said. "Uh-huh. Go on."

"Well, I thought that someone ought to find out

who this person lurking around really was. What he looked like. I thought if I could catch a glimpse of him, I could draw you a sketch. Now, don't you think that was an inspiration, even if it didn't work out? After all, I didn't think that the person who biffed you would biff me, when they didn't even know me!"

"But they did, huh?" Asey said. "Even though you hadn't been introduced."

"Asey, I don't know *what* happened! I walked on towards this rustling noise, and all at once, something went around my mouth, and my arms were grabbed from behind, and my eyes were blindfolded and then I was trussed up—"

"And how!" Ben said. "You should have seen her when I stumbled over her, Asey! She was gagged and bound—she looked like a mummy!"

"Was it tape?" Asey demanded.

"Was it tape?" Cummings asked in the same strained voice.

"Why, yes! Adhesive tape! How'd you ever guess?" Clare said.

"Something within me," Cummings said, "has suddenly got to feeling like a hunk of lead. Did you hear that, Asey? Tape! The good old days! Tape! How many men were there, Clare?"

"How many jumped on me, you mean? I don't know!"

"But you must have some idea!"

Clare shook her head.

"It seemed like thousands at the time, but it might have been only two. After I was all bound up, someone lifted me onto his shoulder and carried me off. And the most incredible thing, Asey, was how little time it took! It happened simply in a flash. One second I was walking toward a rustling noise, and practically the next second, there I was being carted off like a log of wood, apparently by a lot of rustling noises. It was the quickness that stunned me more than anything."

"Did you hear me yellin' for you?" Asey asked.

"Yes. I heard you the first time I was dumped down, and I guessed we were hiding from you. I got dumped down a dozen times or more before they finally dumped me for good. It seemed miles from where we started."

"Were you always carried on the same shoulder?" Cummings inquired professionally. "Could you tell? What I'm driving at, there might just have been one man."

"Frankly," Clare said, "in the position I was in, you don't think much about things like shoulders, and if they're the same. I don't know. Nobody spoke to me, or said a word, or made a sound. All I heard was the rustling as we moved along. It was simply uncanny!"

"D'you remember the sound of their footsteps?" Asey asked. "Did it seem like two men, or a bunch?"

"Sometimes it seemed like lots, and sometimes only one. I can't explain exactly—"

"They kept step, an' then broke it, most likely," Asey said. "Might have been accidental, might have been to keep you from bein' able to tell how many people there was around, when you told your story later. Huh. So they just dumped you an' left you? Didn't they leave a guard?"

"I think someone stood around for a while," Clare said. "I heard the scratch of a match and smelled a whiff of cigarette smoke. And then I think I fell asleep."

"Now there," Cummings said appreciatively, "is a nervous system for you! Most females would have gone mad!"

"Oh, I knew Asey would find me. Or Ward. Or someone. But I really was beginning to get worked up by the time Ben came. And it took us simply years to get that tape off, and I was stiff as a pig. We had to stop at a drugstore and get some cleaner stuff to get the gum off my face and eyebrows, and my hair's still gummy in spots."

"See anyone around in the woods, Ben?" Asey asked.

"Not a soul," Ben said. "And d'you know, when I took the tape off her, she quipped about quaint Cape Cod? She actually quipped! I think that's—"

He broke off as Clare suddenly squealed with pleasure.

"Oh, Dr. Cummings, you've got my easel! Isn't that my easel in the back of your car? And my portfolio and my drawings! Oh, I'm simply delighted! I forgot all about 'em this noon, after I rushed Asey over to the umbrella to meet Ward, and I was sure they'd been washed away with the tide! Did you bring 'em in from the beach?"

"One of the stewards did," Cummings said. "I took 'em. I was going to give 'em to Ward, but I forgot. I looked at your pictures—I hope you don't mind? Because I—"

"Mind? I'm flattered pink! And I can't tell you how glad I am to get my truck back!"

"My wife was here a while ago," Cummings cleared his throat, "and she wondered what they were, and she looked at 'em too. She wanted me to ask you if you—well, do you ever sell your pictures? She wanted to buy one."

"Which one? You can have it," Clare said. "Any of 'em. I'm so glad to get the easel back—which one would you like?"

"The one of the point and beach."

"Not the black and white!" Clare said. "I thought that was awful! That was terrible!"

"Let *me* see," Ben said, as Cummings opened the portfolio. "Turn it around to the spotlight here. Say, those are good!"

"The first black and white I did was simply ghastly," Clare said. "There, see? The crumpled one. Then I did this black and white here, and then I learned that you can't *do* Sketicket Point in black and white. At least, I can't. But those color sketches aren't bad—"

"Mittens!" Asey said suddenly.

"What?"

"Mittens, doc! Mittens! By golly, she *did* leave us a hint!"

"*What* are you talking about?" Cummings demanded.

"Mittens!"

"What mittens? Whose mittens? Mittens where? There aren't any mittens in this sketch! It's a sketch of the Yacht Club and the beach and the umbrellas and the dunes and the gulls and the waves of Sketicket Point! And if you can find one single, solitary mitten in it, I'll eat my hat!"

"Mittens!" Asey said. "An' the quilts! Now I get it. The umbrellas!"

"What's the matter with you? Hey!" Cummings yelled. "Where are you going? Ben, what's that crazed idiot doing?"

"Getting something from his car—why, it's Lucia's knitting bag!"

"Designs!" Asey said a minute later. "See here. Look. Here's the mitten Mrs. Newell was makin'. Here's the pattern for it. Now, look at the design! It's the same as the quilt that Sadie Thackaberry made for the Grange Fair prize!"

"Sit down, Asey," Cummings said soothingly. "Sit down, and take a couple of deep breaths. Where do you feel worst? Is it your head?"

"It's yours," Asey told him. "My head's all right, but you're bein' dumb! Look. Sadie borrowed that quilt design. She told Annie Oakley so. See, doc, she borrowed it from Mrs. Newell! From these mittens! An' don't you see where Mrs. Newell got the design for the mittens in the first place? From the pattern of the beach umbrellas! See, like Clare's sketches! Look at 'em again, doc! See how those umbrellas make a pattern along the beach? Look at the color sketch, now. An' now look at the mittens! See? Got it? Don't you see now how Barradio fits into this?"

"Who?" Clare asked blankly.

"Barradio," Cummings said, as Asey continued to scan Clare's sketches. "He's an ex-rumrunner who's just come home. One of a gang Asey used to help the cops chase in the good old days. I understand what he means by Barradio. When you said adhesive tape, I knew he was the one that spirited you away. But the rest of what Asey's talking about is sheer gibberish. Asey, stop purring like a cat over those sketches, and explain all this nonsense!"

"The mittens," Asey said, "are like Sadie's quilt, an' both come from the umbrellas. An' the umbrellas change, pattern an' color both! Doc, I think we *got* this!"

Clare nudged the doctor.

"Maybe Ward'll know what he's talking about," she said. "Go in the club and get him, Ben. I want him to know I'm back safely."

"Ward's not here," Asey said as he looked up. "I'm just goin' after him. An' now I think I begin to see what he was on to, too. After I talk with him—"

"*After* you talk with him? Isn't Ward here with you?" Clare asked.

"No, I'm goin' for him this minute!"

"But you just *got* him! Truly, Asey, isn't he here?"

Asey shook his head. "What made you think he was?"

"Why, they said so, didn't they, Ben? They said he left in Asey's roadster. Someone saw him drive off with Asey from the Inn."

TWELVE.

"ARE you sure?" Asey demanded.

"Why, of course we're sure!" Ben said. "That's what the maids told us! You see, after we left the drugstore, we went straight to the Inn on the chance of finding Ward to let him know Clare was okay—"

"And there were some cops on the porch," Clare broke in, "and they said they were waiting for Ward, and they asked if we knew where he was. They said he wasn't there and they hadn't seen him. But as we were leaving, our chambermaid and her sister on the next floor took us aside and told us privately that Ward *had* been there, and they'd seen him sneak out the back way and then drive off with you, Asey! That's what they told us!"

"And they knew your roadster," Ben added with finality.

For a fraction of a second, Asey and the doctor surveyed each other.

"Barradio!" Cummings said. "And Ward thought it was you! What in hell is going on, Asey?"

"Ben," Asey said swiftly, "take Clare into the club

house. Stay there, near the cops. Don't either one of you give in to any of your inspirations an' impulses, no matter who calls, or what happens, till I get back! Understand?"

"Yes, Uncle Asey," Clare said. "We'll stay put—but where are you going? What happened to Ward? If you didn't drive him away, who did? Where is he now?"

"That," Asey said, "is what I'm about to look into. Go into the club, an' stay there! Go on! Right now! Git! Doc, you comin' with me?"

Cummings hesitated.

"D'you really think you ought to tackle this alone, Asey? Hadn't you better tell Hanson, and get a bunch of his fellows together, and organize before you—"

"How many times in the old days did the cops get together an' try dragnettin' for Barradio an' his bunch?" Asey demanded.

"Oh, I know they did it a million times and kept bungling it, and the only times any of 'em got picked up, you did it alone! But—"

"Doc, Hanson an' his boys are a new generation. They don't know the woods, or that bunch, or their methods. I can't wait to get 'em collected an' organized an' show 'em the lay of the land! There's no time, if Barradio snaked Ward off right after he phoned me!" Asey got into his roadster and jabbed at the starter button. "Well, you hang around, watch those kids, an' if I ain't back in a reasonable time, have Hanson scour—"

"Wait, you idiot!"

Cummings fumbled around in the back seat of his car, and then, stuffing something into his pocket, he got in beside Asey.

"I'm not going on any madman hunts," he said as he slammed the door, "without precautionary measures—Asey, this is insanity, going off like this! And what's it all about?"

"Wa-el, we're goin' to get Ward," Asey said as the roadster shot away, "if we can."

"I know! I mean, what was that gibberish you were talking before you found out about him? All about mittens and quilts!"

"Oh, I think I got to the root of this," Asey said. "Only I feel like you felt about the atropine. I'm goin' to look an awful sap if I ain't right. An' there's still things I can't quite fathom, sort of."

"Tell me!" Cummings said. "I guess if I'm virtually hurling my life away on a crazy expedition like this, I've got a right to know why!"

"Look, doc," Asey said. "Lucia Newell tans herself out on that beach by the club for the last three months, an' as she sits there, she knits. An' one day she looks around an' thinks what a nice design the pattern of the beach umbrellas would make. So she makes one, an' she knits it into a pair of mittens. See?"

"But what the hell's that got to do with *quilts?*" Cummings demanded. "And all the rest of it!"

"Sadie Thackaberry told Annie Oakley that she started her Grange quilt from this borrowed design about six weeks ago, so Mrs. Newell must have made the design as far back as that. Probably she's been makin' mittens an' scarves an' things in that design all summer. You know, I'd never have caught on to this," Asey drew up for the four corners traffic light, "if I hadn't had to lay on the floor an' look at quilts all that time! The pattern of that Grange quilt got engraved on my mind for eternity. The girls deserve a lot of credit for this—"

"For what!" Cummings almost yelled. "Credit for *what?* For—oh, blow your horn and make that fool get on before the light changes again! And don't try to beat it, because there's a cop watching you! Credit for what, Asey, what are you *getting* to?"

"Clare's sketches, of course," Asey said as the roadster darted forward again. "Because I didn't pay much attention to the mittens when I hunted through that bag for a match. An' I'd never have connected 'em with the quilt design if it hadn't been for Clare's sketches. Now d'you see?"

"No," Cummings said, "I don't. I get your point that the umbrellas on the beach gave Mrs. Newell an inspiration for a design, and she made it into mittens, and Sadie Thackaberry borrowed it for her quilt. But what the hell's that got to do with Ward and Barradio and the *rest?*"

"Did you notice the pattern of the umbrellas in Clare's sketches?"

"They made a line, like any other rows of umbrellas on a beach!"

"Uh-huh. Now, listen, doc. Mrs. Newell sits an' knits, an' as the summer wears on, it occurs to her that the umbrella pattern changes. Maybe there's two rows instead of one. Maybe it's the groupin' of the colors she notices. Say, the red umbrellas are on the left one day, an' the green ones on the left the next day. Maybe she noticed that the two or three striped ones got shifted around peculiar. I don't know how she come to notice it. But she did. Now, in Clare's first black an' white sketch, the umbrellas are set in one row. In the second sketch, the one she made later, there's two rows!"

"In other words," Cummings said impatiently, "more people came to the beach, so more umbrellas were put up! What of it?"

"That's what you might think, doc, but today, this noon, people didn't keep comin' to the club in droves. They kept leavin' in droves to go to Molly Coppinger's bazaar thing."

"Asey, do you feel all right?"

"I feel better," Asey said, "than I felt all day. You want to bet that Leo had charge of the umbrella department? Want to bet he was the one that put out the umbrellas every mornin'?"

"I bet," Cummings said, "there's a truck on the curve ahead, and I bet we never know what hit us. What has all this dither got to do with Barradio and Ward and Mrs. Newell and all the rest?"

"I tell you, Mrs. Newell noticed this change, this shift from one row to two, or two to one. The differences in where the colors were—"

"For heaven's sakes, you'd hardly expect a lot of umbrellas to be put in exactly the same place all the time!"

"That's another thing you'd think, doc. Honest, this was pretty bright! An' they couldn't have been shifted very often or to any great extent durin' the day, what with people sittin' under 'em. After all, you can't march around snatchin' all the red umbrellas from over people's heads an' stickin' green ones in their place without raisin' a few questions!"

"Asey, let's go home!" Cummings sounded worried. "You're obviously not yourself tonight, and besides, I think we're being followed. I feel followed. Matter of fact, I feel haunted. Come on. Let's turn back!"

"We're not bein' followed, an' we're not turnin' back! On the other hand, doc, people was discouraged from movin' the club umbrellas around casual, themselves. All the umbrellas was set in holders. I noticed that. All but Mrs. Newell's. That means she probably lugged hers off some distance an' set it up so she could watch the rest. That's most likely what she was waitin' for, to check on today an' see if they changed. What it boils down to is that the umbrellas got set out a certain way by the management in the mornin', an' then maybe around noontime when folks drifted away for their lunch, then some umbrellas was taken in, or more was put out, or they was somehow shifted. See?"

"No! I can't see why the movement or the shifting of a lot of silly umbrellas should have any connection with Mrs. Newell's being killed, or Ward's being taken away, or any of the rest of it!"

Asey sighed.

"Doc, pay some attention to me. In Clare's first sketch there was one row of umbrellas. Got that? An' there was two rows in the second sketch. In the color sketch there was three green umbrellas, an' then three red, an' then three green, an' so on. Now, listen! S'pose Mrs. Newell begun to realize that they'd be set out like her knittin' design for a few days, an' then they'd change. S'pose on Tuesdays an' Thursdays, say, there was always two short rows with all the red umbrellas on the right. 'N'en s'pose on Mondays an' Fridays, say, there was one long row, an' all green umbrellas on the right. Maybe Mrs. Newell might have begun to wonder if there wasn't some reason for it all, facin' the harbor there."

"For God's sakes!" Cummings said. "If you mean the umbrellas were a signal, why in hell didn't you come out and say they were a signal, without all this insane beating around the bush!"

"Because if I had," Asey said, "you'd just have laughed scornful an' said I was crazy. So would Hanson. You wouldn't believe me. Now, do you begin to get to the root of this?"

"By George, Asey," Cummings said, "you know it *is* damn clever! The average person'd never notice which umbrella was where at any given time. Not unless they had some terribly special interest, like Mrs. Newell and her design. If anyone ever gave it a thought, they'd just take it for granted that the number of rows changed with the size of the crowd, and the color variations were perfectly natural—Asey, is this the old coach road you've swung onto?"

"Uh-huh," Asey said as he switched off the headlights.

"I wish you wouldn't take these damn detours!" Cummings said. "I hate this road! Asey, the umbrella scheme's good! By George, it *is*! The holders are all set out, and on certain days, certain colored umbrellas get stuck in certain patterns. One pattern means one thing. Then if they wanted to get another idea across, they changed—hey, Asey! Across to who? Who are they signaling? Signals for what?"

"That," Asey said, "is where our pal Barradio comes in. Also what Ward's after. Also what they didn't dare let Mrs. Newell hint to me about, after they found out she had an inklin' of somethin' goin' on. Give a guess, doc."

"Guess! Slashing over this damned, benighted road without headlights," Cummings said indignantly, "and you ask me to guess! Look here, it's all I can do to talk! This place always scares me to death! Signals for what?"

"It's been told you dozens of times today," Asey said. "Handed out to you on a silver platter. To me, too, only I was so dumb thick I didn't catch on for a long while."

"Nobody," Cummings said with bitterness as the car hit a series of bumps, "has told me a thing today! Not a damn thing! Asey, what're you keeping on this infernal road for? With all of Cape Cod spread out before you, why pick this hell-awful spot to hunt Ward? You certainly don't think Ramon would be fool enough to go back to his old stamping grounds, do you?"

"They picked up Clare here, didn't they?" Asey returned. "An' I remember thinkin' this afternoon that some of the roads was pretty worn an' used lookin' for just bein' driven over by berrypickers an' parkers, an' such. I never thought of goin' anywheres else, doc. I told you before we set out that Hanson an' his boys didn't know the woods!"

"I thought you meant woods in a broad sense," Cummings said. "If I'd really thought you were coming here, I'd have stayed at the club. Well, for Ward's sake, let's hope they're not as quick on the trigger as they used to be. Let's hope they've aged—Asey, I'm not kidding you. I have this feeling we're being followed."

Asey chuckled.

"You always used to say that, doc. An' I'm not kiddin' you, either, when I say we're not. There wasn't a soul behind us when we turned off the main road. Or even before."

"Maybe so, but I feel someone," Cummings said peevishly. "What're you stopping *here* for? You intend to park in this inky pool of bushes? How in hell'll I ever find my way back here if I get separated from you, I'd like to know!"

"Same way you always did," Asey said. "You got the best bump of direction of anyone I know. You know it, too. Stop your grousin' an' get started. I think we'd better make for the shore, an' follow it along to the old boathouse. What's clankin' so in your pocket?"

"My precautionary measures. I'll fix 'em—Asey, that old boathouse is across the bay from the Yacht Club! I've got it! It's that dope ring they had a lot of stuff about in the Sunday paper!"

"Nope. I thought that too, for a few minutes. Guess again."

"I'm not going to strain my mind with guessing, while I—hell's bells, I've twisted my ankle!"

"Hurt?" Asey inquired. "Like to stay here in the car?"

"Oh, I suppose I can manage to drag along! Wish there was a moon so I could see my hand before my face!"

"It's a lot better for us that there ain't any," Asey said.

"Well, why can't the stars twinkle some more, then? If I'm not obliterated by Ramon's slugs, I'll probably trip and break my neck! Hm! Wonder if my wife remembered the insurance?"

The doctor's grumbling increased as they advanced, but Asey noticed that he cut down on his volume as they neared the boathouse. And his progress, furthermore, was as noiseless as if he were tiptoeing in rubber soles down a hospital corridor.

Both stopped as a flashlight winked and then swept the water's edge beyond them.

"At the boathouse, all right!" Cummings spoke in Asey's ear. "Fools! Still flashing lights! I see two figures. Three—"

They found, on edging nearer, that there were four men.

And Ward.

"He's japing with 'em!" Cummings said in an awed whisper. "Kidding 'em! Oh, he's daft! He's asking for it!"

Asey motioned for him to be quiet as Ward's clear, sardonic voice carried out beyond the group. It carried so well that Asey wondered if Ward wasn't rather deliberately and hopefully trying to make himself heard by anyone, like some straying couple, that might be in the vicinity of the beach.

"Well, Ramon," Ward said, "I'll tell you how Father found out. The size of the roll you were flashing around Dinty's place last week started me thinking about you, because I was told you'd been on the bum only the week before. So I chucked my other plans and came up here in the guise of a limping man to nose about. You fitted in so swell with a tip I got in London! And then of course I wanted to see you, too! You know what a sucker I am for your charm!"

Ramon's reply was inaudible, but it led to a long argument with one of the other men on the advisability of getting rid of Ward then and there before he shot his mouth off any more.

"What you waiting for anyway?" Ward asked interestedly. "Or who? Any chance of meeting the boss? I always wanted to. It's the same brains that kept you going so long, isn't it? Of course, Ramon, it's only fair to point out that the longer you let me live, the better my chances!"

Ward's chances were promptly and grimly summed up by the argumentative man as being somewhat less than zero.

"Comrade," Ward said, "you're not half as ominous as you are ungrammatical. Ever know a lad named Luigi? The one without ears? Well, one classic night,

Luigi threatened to pour me into concrete—or was it concrete into me? Anyway, when it dried, I was going to be forever a part of the East River bottom. But nothing came of it. Nothing'll come of this, if you keep on dallying. I'm expecting Asey Mayo shortly."

Asey shook his head at the doctor's inquiring pressure on his arm. He didn't for a moment think that Ward knew of or even suspected their presence. Ward was merely trying to size up the bunch and his chances.

"Discount Asey, do you?" Ward asked as the quartet laughed. "Well, maybe you're right. Maybe he is a back number. Did you or the boss think up the idea of working from Sketicket Bay? It's a peachy place. By the way, how did Lucia Newell guess about you?"

Ward was strongly advised to shut up.

"Why?" Ward asked. "What's the harm of my asking questions? You might as well let me approach my Maker with a serene mind. Was it you who killed her and Leo, Ramon? Or the boss? It smacks of him. Ah, I get it! You're waiting for him to come now, aren't you? That's why you're dallying with me. Then when he comes, he gives me atropine, and the verdict'll be suicide from remorse, after killing the other two."

The mention of atropine brought forth no comments from the four men. The silence, in fact, was rather strained.

Asey thought he knew why, and Ward echoed his thoughts almost at once.

"Oh, you didn't like the idea of atropine, eh? You lads wanted to take Lucia and Leo for nice rides, and the boss said no, that would brand it with your own mark. The boss is good, boys. Very good. The Porter roadster like Asey's was genius. So was the frenzied phone message from Asey's supposed dear friend, saying Asey'd got track of the girl, and to meet him at once back of the Inn."

Ramon gave it as his opinion that if Ward was so smart, he wouldn't have fallen so hard.

Ward laughed.

"You don't know the funny part! The funny part is that I warned Asey of the same ruse! And then I fell like a bomb, myself! Oh, my! I must say that when your boss's mind shows through, it displays finesse! Wish I could say as much for—there's a light!"

Two of the men jumped to their feet.

"Where?"

"Yah!" Ward said derisively. "Jittery, aren't you? There isn't any light. I just wanted to see if you'd react."

Ward was forthwith gagged.

His last audible words concerned the dullness that would follow the gesture, and he was right. The four men sat and smoked in silence, and the minutes dragged into half an hour.

Asey mentally debated the chances of hiking back to the roadster and returning for Hanson before something happened to Ward. He considered sending the doctor back.

Then he shook his head. He couldn't take the chance of leaving Ward, and the doctor could never pilot the roadster back over those roads without lights. It was better that they just stay and watch for an opportunity to act.

Finally Barradio and another of the group walked up the beach, passing so near where Asey and the doctor crouched in the bushes that either could have extended a hand and touched them.

"He's late!" the man said anxiously. "Suppose he had trouble getting the new charts?"

"Probably stuck with the cops," Barradio said. "They're all over. Don't worry. He'll be here. He'll manage. He always did, didn't he? Nobody knows this harbor like him. Nobody ever did."

"Yeah. Say, what about this guy Ward?"

Cummings shivered at the sound of Barradio's laugh.

"But he knows too much!" the man protested. "He's on! Suppose he told Mayo?"

"If Mayo knew a thing, he'd never let us get this far! He's all tied up with two murders. He's all sewed up."

"I still think we ought to have got *him!*"

"The boss," Barradio said, "said Ward was the guy that was on. Forget Mayo."

"Are the new charts coming from the Yacht Club?"

The doctor's fingers dug into Asey's arm.

"Bunting!"

As Cummings formed the name with his lips, the hum of an approaching motorcar sent both Barradio and his companion racing towards the boathouse.

A car door slammed, and a figure loomed along the path.

Asey grinned at the sharp intake of the doctor's breath on recognizing the outline, and Cummings saw enough of the grin to realize that the man's identity was no shock to Asey.

"Forgotten everything, Barradio?" Dudley French said angrily. "Forgotten about guards?"

"But—"

"Who's guarding the girl?"

"She's all right," Barradio said confidently. "She didn't need any guard!"

"No?"

"Why, say, she was so taped up, she couldn't get away!"

"It will interest you to know," Dudley said, "that she is now at the club. No, don't gurgle. I'll settle with you for that. I'll also say for Alex, he left nothing to chance!"

"But—"

"I said, I'll settle with you! Here are the charts. Take 'em out. Everything's set. They've got two hours after they get to Sketicket Bay. No more, or they'll get in trouble with the tide. If they can't make their

repairs in two hours, they'll have to come back another night. Hurry, and tell them to hurry. And
where," he demanded as Barradio yanked Ward to
his feet, "d'you think you're taking him?"

"Aw, I'm dumping him overboard!"

"Who said so? Bring him back here!"

Cummings watched the barrel of the Colt that had
appeared in Asey's hand.

"He's going into the mud pond, with the other
snoopers," Dudley went on. "Forgotten the pond,
too?"

Cummings nudged Asey.

The mud pond, off the old coach road, probably explained the lack of incriminating corpses that had always annoyed the cops during prohibition days.

"And drive that Porter in," Dudley ordered.

"But that's mine!" Barradio protested. "That's my
car! I paid for—"

"Drive it in! I'm giving orders here! Or do you,"
Dudley inquired, "wish me to settle with you in some
other way?"

Barradio subsided.

"Hanson," Dudley said, "is going to be made to believe that Mayo took Ward away in his own Porter,
and that Ward has skipped. Mayo can try to explain
that. Then I shall have Hanson pin both murders on
Ward. He'll be hunted from coast to coast. Take off
his gag."

"Well, well!" Ward said briskly. "Fatty! Fancy

meeting you here! I had my money on Commodore Humphrey Bunting, if you'd like to know. He's such a damn hearty good fellow, I thought it was all front. I never thought this of you. Honest! You just seemed a genuine nuisance or natural-born boss. All part of the act, Captain Bligh?"

"What do you think?"

"I think you're pretty bright," Ward said. "I've just been telling the boys so. I take back the white-bellied anteater."

"You're a little late," Dudley said, "for that."

"No, I've thought of something better. You're a gloating bloater. You can reverse it, and say you're a bloating gloater. It's good either way. And frankly, Fatty, you have the right to gloat. If I were in your boots, the shores would resound with my last laughs. What an act! What an actor!"

It was clever flattery, Asey thought, just peppered with enough insults to make it sound genuine.

Dudley laughed a self-satisfied laugh.

"And you missed a lot. You should have seen the act Leo and I put on for Mayo, to bring your hundred dollar bill to his attention. That was good. Mayo never gave me another thought."

"You've had a full day," Ward said, "what with Borgiaing, and potting at Asey and all. You must be a good shot, Fat Stuff!"

"I am. He was lucky. Matt, take Ward and—"

"Wait," Ward said. "Tell me how you managed the

atropine jobs. You know, those were good. I said as much to the boys. No hint of gang work about poison! That was bright. Did Leo help?"

"He fixed Lucia, but he didn't know it was atropine, and later," Dudley said, "it didn't seem wise to have him guess. I had other plans for him, but he responded too quickly to cash."

"Exit Leo, left center," Ward said. "No, wait a bit more! How'd Lucia ever catch on to you if I couldn't?"

"She never caught on to *me!* She always thought I inherited my money from Uncle John," Dudley said. "So does everyone else. She thought she was on the trail of a dope ring. She told me all about it. But she found out enough to make her dangerous, and I couldn't buy her off. I knew better than to try. She'd have bled me forever, and probably squealed anyway. I couldn't chance her getting to Mayo today. And you worried me, snooping around this morning. Matt, take him and the car and get rid of 'em. I've got to get back to Molly's dance."

"Watch out for the punch, Borgia!" Ward said. "Watch out for the scrambled eggs!"

Dudley laughed. "There won't be any atropine!"

"I'm thinking of your waistline," Ward returned as Matt took his arm. "If you ever feel a warning pinch on the bloat, that'll be me. I'm going to haunt every mouthful you stuff—"

"Take him along, Matt!" Dudley said. "I've wasted enough time with him!"

"Boss, how do we get back? If we dump the Porter in the pond, Ramon'll need the sedan, and what if—"

"Oh, you fools!" Dudley said. "You incompetent fools! I shall welcome Alex's return! Take him along, Matt! Get things ready. I'll help you with the finishing touches after the others get off. Then I'll drive you back to town! Now—"

"Boss, if anyone comes—"

"Well?"

"Well, if anyone comes, or there's any trouble—"

"Finish Ward yourself, fool! Get on! Ramon, you and Karl get along with those charts. Shove 'em off, Jake!"

Two minutes later, a speedboat set off from the shore by the boathouse.

Dudley watched it, turned and surveyed the departing Porter, and then turned back and watched the boat again.

"The fellows with Ward'll hear if you shoot," Cummings breathed in Asey's ear. "But I've got a can of ether and some adhesive tape in my pocket. Think you can jump him?"

Asey nodded.

Then, as Dudley started back to his car, Asey quietly started after him.

Then he stood like a statue as three figures loomed out of the bushes beyond Dudley.

"That ain't Asey!" It was the voice of his Cousin Jennie. "He's too fat!"

"Well, who is he?" Picklepuss Belcher demanded. "Hey, you! Who are you? What're you doing here? What's going on? Cars rushing around and boats going out the harbor! I want to know the meaning of this!"

Dudley found his voice.

"Who are you?" There was a touch of bewilderment in his fury. "What are you doing here? Get off my property!"

"Mister," Annie Oakley spoke up, "it looks to me like you were reaching for a gun! Mister, put up your hands! Because you're covered with my forty-five, and I wasn't billed for twenty-eight years as the Queen of Sharpshooters for nothing! Put up your hands!"

"You—you—"

While Dudley spluttered, Asey strode forward.

Before Dudley realized what was happening, Asey's left hand was clapped over his mouth, and Asey's right hand had his wrists in a grip of iron.

"Thanks, girls," he said. "Quick, doc, the tape! Do his mouth an' wrists first! Hustle!"

"Watch out for his feet," Annie Oakley said as Cummings's fingers worked like lightning. "He's trying to trip you!"

"Uh-huh. I know. Okay, doc? Now," Asey said, "I'll just lay him down, an' you girls can sit on him while the doc finishes up. Come on, all of you. If he gets fresh, give him a spot of ether, doc, or let Annie Oakley wham him with the butt of her trusty Colt. I'm goin' to get Ward—"

"Asey!" Cummings said as he turned away. "Asey, what the hell *is* this all about!"

"Submarine, doc. 'Member the torpedoed ships on the radio?"

"A sub? Asey, get Ward quick! We'll rush for the Coast Guard!"

"No need—"

"Why not? Hurry, man!"

"They got the new harbor charts," Asey said with a chuckle, "an' we'll be waitin' for 'em, right in Sketicket Bay!"

At six that morning, Ward followed Asey up the path to the latter's house.

"What a night!" Ward said for the hundredth time. "What a scoop! What a—"

"Even after that phonin', ain't you hoarse," Asey asked, "yet?"

"What a finale! Pure Rollo Boys. The Coast Guard, the Navy, the planes, the Boy Scouts, the Minutewomen! Oh, Asey, how did those three ever happen to land there by the boathouse? I never got a chance to find out!"

"They was too excited to tell a coherent story," Asey said, "but I managed to piece it together. Seems Annie Oakley talked with Picklepuss after I left

Sadie's, an' they decided if I wanted a gun, maybe there was somethin' big afoot, an' maybe they better guard me after all. They phoned the club to see if I was there, an' folks told 'em I wasn't—matter of fact, I was out front with the doc. Then they come here to see if Jennie knew where I was, an' she joined up with 'em to track me down. An' while they was cruisin' around, Picklepuss decided to drop off at the factory to see if some cooker thermostat was okay. An' on the way, they spotted my roadster where I parked it. An' somehow, heaven knows how, they made their way to the shore. The doc kept sayin' he thought we was followed, an' he claims he heard 'em, but I don't think he did."

Ward laughed.

"Well, their pictures'll fill the papers tomorrow! Asey, the nerve of that bunch, bringing that sub smack into the harbor for quiet repairs—look, must you *yawn?* Didn't any of this impress you?"

"Uh-huh. I was glad Dudley hadn't bothered to take the bottle of atropine tablets out of his pocket. I thought," Asey said, "that was co-operative of him."

"Oh, *that!* I meant about the sub walking right into things! Say, Humphrey Bunting thinks this is why Dudley was after him all the time about the channel, and dredging the harbor—d'you realize he's been running small supplies out to that sub for nearly a month? Asey, I think he'd have been wiser to have stuck to just those three fellows, instead of importing

more, like Barradio. D'you suppose, after the big outfit he used to have, he kept itching for more men to
boss?"

"More men and more money," Asey said. "Dudley
was greedy for dough, greedy in the old days when he
was rumrunning and now greedy enough again for
dough to utilize his old rumrunning technique and to
be willing to take Nazi money for running supplies out
to the sub. I kind of think myself that most likely he
had some notion of keepin' a few more subs."

"What? I never thought of that!"

"Wa-el, don't worry about 'em. This one's bein'
interned'll scare off others for a while. An' the Coast
Guard cap'n thought they could probably pick up the
tanker that's been fuelin' this one, because he found
a schedule sayin' it was due day after tomorrow—
whatever become of Clare?"

"She and Ben," Ward said, "are still sitting on the
club porch, as far as I know. Cooing. Like doves. My
God, in the face of two murders, two kidnapings,
any number of near-murders and a captured submarine, she takes time out to fall for an impecunious
youth! Ah, well! Asey, how'd you know it was
Dudley?"

"He fooled me at first," Asey said honestly. "I just
thought he was a fat nuisance, like you did. 'N'en it
begun to dawn on me that he was either on your tail
or tryin' to distract me, right from the start. You
really started me wonderin' about him when you said—

'member?—why hadn't the fat fool noticed more about Clare an' the man he claimed she was drivin' in a car with, in the woods. After the way he'd barged around, fussin' at everyone, an' askin' questions, an' wantin' to know why people was trespassin', I thought it was sort of funny he never said a word to 'em. Made me wonder if he wasn't lyin'."

"Yogi Mayo!"

" 'N'en, I remembered he knew the woods so well that he turned the way he wanted to go without stoppin' to get his bearin's, that time he left us with Mabelle an' Effie. I think his mistake was in lettin' Ramon loose in the Porter, an' in biffin' me. He didn't expect me there in the woods, an' when Dudley don't have a plan all thought out beforehand, an' plenty of people around to carry out each little detail, he kind of falls short. Like when the girls confronted him by the boathouse. He was awful confused there, for a minute."

"But what a setup he had!" Ward said. "He gives orders to Leo, Leo makes signals with the umbrellas, the men work from them. They can sit there at the shore with their boat, waiting. No apparent connection with Dudley. No incriminating rushing around. No phoning. No need for radios someone'll ferret out. What a corking setup! And using ex-bootleggers who knew the ropes! Asey, did I ever thank you properly for rescuing me from that mud pond?"

"Twice. Ward, why'n time didn't you tell me what you were after?"

"In the first place, you wouldn't have believed me, and in the second place, if you had believed me, you'd have started rushing around and tipped the crowd off. I just had this hazy tip from a London pal that a sub might be laying for ships on their way to join convoys out of Halifax. In New York, they laughed at the idea that a sub could be around and not found out—I wonder how they'll feel when they read there was one off the Cape for nearly a month, and it actually got into harbor to make repairs on itself! Oh, my, what a night! I don't think West Gusset ever had such excitement!"

"Oh, I don't know," Asey said. "We had a sub off Orleans in nineteen-eighteen, an' it shelled us—"

Ward was too busy talking to hear him.

"I'm going to fly back to New York. I want to see my headlines! 'Deadly Sunshade Leads to Foreign Sub!' Of course, only the bright ones'll get that pun on deadly sunshade and deadly nightshade and atropine, but that doesn't matter. My photographers are coming in a plane, and you and I'll fly back with 'em. Then we can really do a job on you, Mayo! Newsreels, and banquets, and the keys to the city—"

Ward was so engrossed in his plans that he didn't notice Asey's departure for fifteen minutes, and it took him another ten minutes to locate Asey in the kitchen, where he was eating breakfast.

"Asey, what's the idea?"

"Wa-el," Asey said, "two dry crusts aren't sustainin'. I was most famished with hunger, an'—"

"I mean your clothes!" Ward pointed to Asey's corduroys and blue flannel shirt. "What're you dressed like that for? You're coming back to New York with me!"

"Sorry," Asey said, "I got a big date."

"But the newsreels! The photographers! The—oh, I don't believe you! What kind of a date have you got?"

"I'm meetin' the Minutewomen at nine," Asey said, "to teach 'em how to shoot. I thought they deserved it."

"But you've got to come to New York with me!"

"Run along," Asey said. "Eat the banquets yourself! As far as I'm concerned, the deadly sunshade's furled!"

Other Books from the Foul Play Press

Margot Arnold

The mysterious adventures of British archaeologist Sir Toby Glendower, and American anthropologist Penelope Spring, will take you to the near and far corners of the globe.

> *The Cape Cod Caper*. 192 pages $4.95
> *Death of A Voodoo Doll*. 220 pages $4.95
> *Exit Actors, Dying*. 176 pages $4.95
> *Zadok's Treasure*. 192 pages $4.95
>
> ... and more to come.

Phoebe Atwood Taylor

Enjoy the adventures of the Cape Cod Sherlock, Asey Mayo, and his north-of-Boston counterpart, Shakespeare look-alike Leonidas Witherall. Written in the 1930s and 1940s, they are as popular today as when they first appeared.

Asey Mayo Cape Cod Mysteries

> *The Annulet of Gilt*. 288 pages $5.95
> *Banbury Bog*. 176 pages $4.95
> *The Cape Cod Mystery*. 192 pages $4.95
> *The Criminal C.O.D.*. 288 pages $5.95
> *The Crimson Patch*. 240 pages $4.95
> *The Deadly Sunshade*. 297 pages $5.95
> *The Mystery of the Cape Cod Players*. 272 pages $5.95
> *The Mystery of the Cape Cod Tavern*. 283 pages $5.95
> *Out of Order*. 280 pages $5.95
> *The Perennial Boarder*. 288 pages $5.95
> *Sandbar Sinister*. 296 pages $5.95
> *Spring Harrowing*. 288 pages $5.95

Leonidas Witherall Mysteries

> *Beginning with a Bash*. 284 pages $5.95
> *File For Record*. 287 pages $5.95
> *Hollow Chest*. 284 pages $5.95
> *The Left Leg*. 275 pages $5.95
>
> ... and more to come!

Available from booksellers in the United States and Canada or by mail from the publisher, The Countryman Press, PO Box 175, Woodstock Vermont 05091-0175. If ordering by mail, please add $2.50/order for shipping and handling. Thank you.

Prices and availability subject to change. 4/1989.

A Phoebe Atwood Taylor Rediscovery

Murder
at the
New York World's Fair

By Phoebe Atwood Taylor,
writing as Freeman Dana

Few of Phoebe Atwood Taylor's many fans are aware that, as "Freeman Dana," she was also the author of this delightful period mystery. First published in 1938, Murder at the New York World's Fair offered a preview of the gala 1939 event while introducing a heroine, Mrs. Daisy Tower, that could hold her own against even the likes of Asey Mayo and Leonidas Witherall.

" It is a merry melange of mirth, murder and mystification." — *New York Herald Tribune*

Also includes an introduction and an afterword presenting a behind-the-scenes look at the book and its author.

256 pages; 5-1/4" x 7-1/4"
ISBN 0-88150-095-X
Trade Paper: **$8.95**

Available from booksellers in the United States and Canada. You may also order by mail from The Countryman Press, PO Box 175, Woodstock VT 05091-0175. Please add $2.50/order for shipping and handling. Thank you.